Tempted BY EDEN

INTERNATIONAL BESTSELLING AUTHOR

JADE MAY

TEMPTED BY

EDEN

MEMBERS ONLY

ISBN: 978-1-7635917-1-4

Formatting and Chapter Art: Katelyn at Design by Kage
Cover Art: Katelyn at Design by Kage
Editing: Penny Carroll
Proofreading: Stacey's Bookcorner Editing

To all my escapists:
Let's escape to somewhere we only know.

Author's Note

Dear reader,

Thank you so much for choosing my book to read. I hope you enjoy it.

Tempted by Eden is the first book in the Eden series, a collection of interconnected standalones. This re-release is a complete rewrite of the original with an expanded storyline.

Please be aware that it contains mature and graphic scenes, along with language that is suitable for those who are 18+. It also contains scenes that may be triggering to some readers, including; single mom in an attempted custody battle, parent with cancer, light domination/submission, and degradation kink.

Much love,
Jade xx

Chapter One

Cora

The espresso martini slides down my throat, leaving a trail of warmth as it settles in the pit of my stomach. The sharp bite of alcohol competes with the rich bitterness of coffee, making my nose wrinkle. It could really use a hint of sweetness—a dash of sugar syrup, maybe. Honestly though, I'm surprised the bartender managed to pull off a cocktail in a place like this. Tucked away in a quiet backstreet in the capital of Malta, it's a far cry from the city's swanky nightlife scene—no hip bartenders in suspenders mixing up artisanal cocktails, no carefully curated playlists or Instagrammable décor.

"What's the difference between a G-spot and a golf ball?"

"A guy will actually search for a golf ball."

Laughter erupts behind me, loud and infectious, from a group of guys propping up the bar. I giggle into my drink. The drunker they get, the cruder their jokes become, and despite myself, I'm drawn in.

"What's the difference between a hooker and a drug dealer?"

"A hooker can wash her crack and resell it."

I snort, glancing over my shoulder at the four gorgeous men huddled together, whiskey glasses in hand. For the past twenty minutes I've been shamelessly eavesdropping on their contest to see who can recall the most outrageous joke. Their banter fills the bar, cutting through the low drone of the soccer game playing on the TV.

I lick my lips, savoring the bitter coffee as my gaze sweeps over the sagging soccer memorabilia on the walls and the grime-coated tables. The bartender coughs without bothering to cover his mouth, then takes a long drag of his cigarette. Despite the bar's questionable hygiene standards and décor, the night is turning out better than expected. At least it's a step up from doing laundry at my hostel.

A distant "Val-let-ta" chant from the city drifts through the humid air, bringing a smile to my face. There's always a bittersweetness to the end of a trip. After six incredible weeks backpacking across Europe, the memories are etched into me for life. It's been one hell of a journey.

Thoughts of home creep in and I find myself wondering how Dad is holding up without me. Part of me is eager to get back to him, but the idea of leaving all this behind for the monotony of everyday life... I let out a long sigh.

I'd always envisioned traveling after earning my communications degree, but as the saying goes, "Life happens while you're busy making other plans." Graduation came three years later than expected; Mom's passing was the hardest detour life could throw at me. Now, at twenty-four, my long-awaited solo adventure has finally happened—thanks in no small part to Dad's gentle push.

A familiar ache tightens in my chest at the thought of Mom. I inhale deeply, trying to chase away the dark clouds threatening to roll in.

Another sip of my drink sends a rush of dizziness through me.

Shit, the bartender's heavy-handed tonight.

The men's roar of laughter pulls me from my thoughts.

Damn, I missed that one.

Their conversation grows louder the more they drink. Not only are they hilarious, but they stand out—they're unmistakably American and impossibly good-looking. In a bar this quiet, with only a few loners sipping their drinks in the shadows, they're hard to miss.

I finish off my martini; it's time to call it a night. Even on vacation, it's well past my bedtime. With an early flight back to Sydney tomorrow, I know better than to tempt a hangover on a twenty-one-hour journey in cattle class, so I head to the bar to settle my tab.

"Okay, okay, okay, I've got it." The man closest to me raises his voice to signal another joke. "What did the leper say to the sex worker?"

Knowing this one, I can't resist butting in. "Keep the tip."

There's a brief pause before they all erupt with laughter.

"Nice one," slurs the blond and tallest of the group. "What's a place like you doing in a girl like this?" The others groan at his botched pickup cliché.

"Ignore him, he's wasted." Gorgeous dark eyes lock onto mine. They're so strikingly beautiful that for a moment I lose track of everything around me. His deep brown gaze, framed by tousled black hair that falls just over his forehead, pulls me in. A strong, square jawline balances his full, irresistible lips, and I realize, too late, that I'm biting my own bottom lip.

Jesus Christ.

He catches me eyeing him, and a slow, knowing smirk tugs at his lips. "Enjoying the view?"

Heat rises from my chest to my cheeks, and I know I'm burning bright red. "Absolutely." I bite the inside of my cheek to suppress a grin. Boldness isn't usually my style, but with liquid courage pulsing through my veins, it's seemingly effortless.

"Jonathon." He takes my hand in a firm grip without waiting for me to offer it. His long fingers are slightly calloused, and his touch makes my skin prickle.

"Cora," I breathe out.

"Nice to meet you, Cora. That's an Aussie accent, right? Take a seat." Jonathon gestures to the stool behind me and my eyebrows shoot up at the order.

"You know what? I think I'll stand. Didn't your mother ever teach you to ask a lady nicely?" I squint at him.

"She did. She also taught me that eavesdropping was rude." His eyes sparkle with amusement.

Shit.

My cheeks flush with embarrassment at being caught out again. I hate blushing—there's no hiding it. Thanks to my mother's northern Italian genes, my skin can't mask anything. When I'm embarrassed, angry, or aroused, it's right there for the world to see. If I could change one thing about myself, it would be to hide my emotions better.

"How much have you had to drink?" Jonathon's voice cuts through my thoughts. He inspects me from head to toe, as if he can assess my sobriety with a single look. At five foot two, I'm no model, but I know how to work with what I've got. He towers over me, and I curse myself for choosing flats instead of heels tonight. At least my hair is on point—smooth brown waves cascading down my back—and my jeans are doing their job, highlighting my curves, making my ass look fantastic. Small wins.

"Excuse me?"

Ignoring my biting tone, Jonathon signals to the bartender and orders a water.

"It's a simple question, Cora. How much have you had to drink?"

"Why do you care?" I snap back.

The bartender sets down a bottle of water and a questionably clean glass with ice. In the background, his friends have shifted from crude jokes to quoting terrible pickup lines.

I eye the water, my resolve weakening. Hydration wins out over pride, and I grab the bottle, taking a long sip.

"Because I consider myself a gentleman, and I don't fuck drunk chicks," he deadpans.

I choke on the water, spraying it everywhere.

What the fuck?

"I want my woman to feel every inch of me," he says, lowering his voice, "sliding in and out, without her senses numbed." He picks up a napkin and leans in, wiping the water from my chin. "Let's hope you swallow better than that," he adds with a wink.

Heat floods my cheeks as the pull of arousal in my abdomen drifts lower.

"Jesus, arrogant much? It's a shame you'll never find out." My voice holds steady, but my mind is racing.

Damn it, I do love a challenge.

He leans in closer, and I catch an intoxicating mix of cologne, whiskey, and mint. His eyes scan my face, lingering on my flushed cheeks.

"Your blush is gorgeous, Cora," he says, tone softening. "How about we make a deal? If I can make you blush again in the next minute, I'm coming back to your hotel room."

"And if I don't, what do I get?" I ask, pitching an eyebrow.

"My tongue in all three of your holes," he murmurs, "as I tongue-fuck you until you can't remember your name."

Well... that's a win–win situation if I've ever heard one.

The flames licking at my cheeks give me away, and we both know it. I've already lost this game—and I'm not sure I even want to win.

But I'm never one to back down from a challenge. I meet his stare with a playful grin. "Let's make this more interesting." My eyes flick to the pool table behind him. "How about a game of pool? If you win, I'll come back to your hotel, and nothing is off-limits. I'll be at your complete mercy—"

"Nothing?" he interrupts, eyebrows shooting up.

I roll my lips over my teeth to fight the grin from spreading. "Nothing," I confirm, feeling a surge of adrenaline at the audacity of my offer. "But if I win..." I pause, thinking on my feet. The last thing I want is him coming back to my hostel. It's not exactly the vibe I'm going for. "Same rules, but you're under my control. Anything I say goes. You game?"

My sultry smile seals the deal.

"Let's go." The mischievous glint in his eyes spells trouble for me. But he doesn't know what he's up against.

I gulp down the rest of my water and follow him to the pool table, my eyes roaming over his muscular back, tight ass, and lean frame. A white T-shirt clings to his shoulders, and his dark blue jeans and sneakers give him a casual, relaxed look. He's effortlessly handsome, and I can't think of a better way to end my vacation.

The pool table has clearly seen better days, its green felt worn down to patches of bare wood. He rubs his jaw, eyeing the dilapidated surface.

"Are you sure about this? I'm pretty good at pool."

I tilt my head. "So, it's an easy win for you," I taunt, shrugging my shoulder.

"Okay. Your loss." Jonathon hands me a cue and then proceeds to chalk his own, his eyes flicking to me every few seconds, assessing the competition. I smirk, setting up the balls in the rack, confident that I'm about to give him a run for his money.

"Wanna flip to see who breaks?" I offer.

"Ladies first. I'm a gentleman, after all."

I chalk my cue, pursing my lips as I blow off the excess. Our eyes lock and the attraction between us is thick in the air. There's an undeniable tension, a magnetic pull that makes it hard to focus on anything else.

As I position the cue for the break, I glance at him, half-tempted to act coy and ask him to show me how it's done, just to feel his body close to mine. I can already imagine the warmth of him, the way his muscles would press against my back, his breath hot on my neck. But I'm not the type to play helpless, and I'm definitely not one to lose. I could beat him with my eyes closed. But I won't. He's too fucking cute.

With a swift, practiced motion, I take the shot, smoothly breaking the balls and sending them scattering across the table. A striped ball sinks into the corner pocket, and I grin, lining up my next shot. His eyes are on me, watching, hungry, as I pocket ball after ball. One shot. Then another. And another. The balls disappear in quick succession.

"Why do I get the feeling I've just been hustled?" he grumbles, amusement flickering in his eyes.

I twist my lips, satisfied, and with only two striped balls left on the table, I make my move. Walking over to him, I place a hand on his chest. His heartbeat is strong and rapid under my palm. My other hand snakes up his neck, fingers playing with the soft ends of his hair. He groans, low and deep, and the sound sends a shiver through me.

"You shouldn't have been such a gentleman and let me break," I whisper, rising up on my toes to meet his mouth as his head drops towards mine. I bite his lower lip, tugging it gently between my teeth before releasing it. His eyes darken, the desire in them unmistakable.

"Wanna get out of here?" he rumbles.

I nod, the game already forgotten. He tosses our cues onto the table and grabs my hand, threading his fingers through mine. Without another word, he throws some cash onto the bar and leads me out to the cobbled street.

He mentions that his hotel is only a couple blocks away, but the short walk stretches into a drawn-out journey. We stop every few steps, too caught up in each other to care about getting there quickly. Pressed against buildings, our kisses are frantic, hands roaming wildly. A few people glance our way—some amused, some annoyed—but I don't give a fuck and I don't think Jonathon does either. Tonight is about pure, unfiltered pleasure, two bodies colliding in the pursuit of nothing but feeling good. Just one night of no-strings-attached fun before reality catches up with me.

By the time we reach his hotel, we're breathless, laughing as he fumbles with the key card. When we stumble into the room, I glance around—it's sleek, modern, and spacious. Worlds apart from the cramped, dingy hostel I've been staying in. The bed is huge and inviting, and I'm relieved we're here. This place is the perfect escape for a night like this.

Jonathon grabs me and tosses me onto the bed. Then he's quickly on me, lips crashing into mine and stealing my breath. His hands are everywhere, possessive, hungry, and I can't get enough. We tear at each other's clothes, desperate to be skin-to-skin. It's frantic, raw, and every touch is electric.

When he finally pulls back, we're both panting, eyes locked in a haze of shared lust. Then he slowly makes his way down my body, trailing kisses across my skin, lower and lower.

I catch my breath, trying to steady the pounding of my heart. "What are you doing?"

His gaze lifts to mine, a wicked smile spreading across his lips. "What I promised."

A flush creeps up my neck as the memory of his earlier words floods back. I flop onto the bed, more than ready for him to make good on that promise—to keep going until I forget my own name, until nothing exists but the pleasure of his wicked tongue.

CHAPTER TWO

Cora

Five years later

"Leo, sweetheart, please put your shoes on!" I call, hoping this morning's routine will go more smoothly than yesterday's.

"Nooo! I don't wanna go!" His voice rings out from the bedroom, muffled.

I let out a sigh, quickly scanning the living room as I finish packing his backpack. Lunchbox, water bottle, hat—check. I add an extra banana, just in case. "Leo, we do this every morning," I plead, trying to inject some patience into my tone.

"Kindy sucks!" his small voice huffs.

"Language, Leo!" I scold, shaking my head.

Where does he pick this stuff up from? And why are we always yelling in this house?

A loud retching echoes from the bathroom, and I wince, my own stomach turning in sympathy. Dad had another round of chemo yesterday, and it always leaves him like this—weak, nauseous, and spending too much time with his head in the toilet.

"Are you okay, Dad?" I knock softly on the bathroom door, hating how helpless I feel.

"Yeah, I'm fine. Just the usual." His words come out with a raspy edge.

"Can I get you anything?" I offer, even though I already know the answer.

"I'm okay. Just need a moment."

I rest my hand on the doorframe, staring at the chipped paint. "Try to rest in bed, Dad. I'll put a bucket and some towels in your room when you're ready to come out."

"Thanks, love. I'll be out in a minute." There's a pause, then, "You need to leave soon, or you'll be late again. Say goodbye to pumpkin head for me."

I close my eyes for a second, willing myself to keep it together. "Will do. Love you," I reply, hoping he hears me as another wave of nausea overtakes him.

I head to Leo's bedroom, pausing in the doorway. The sight of him hiding under his quilt makes me smile, despite everything. Even at four, he still believes that if he can't see me, I can't see him. I crawl into the bed and pull the covers over my head, joining him in his hiding spot. "What are you doing in here, baby?"

"Hiding, Momma," he giggles.

"Hmm, I can see that."

"Can I stay home with Grandpa?" His hopeful voice makes my heart ache.

"Sorry, baby, Grandpa's not feeling well today."

Leo's face falls, and guilt hits, sharp and deep. I don't want to disappoint him, but I don't have any other options. "How about we stop for a milkshake after kindy?" I offer. A little bribery can go a long way.

His eyes light up. "Strawberry?"

"Sure, any flavor you like."

"Okay, Momma, let's go. Don't wanna be late." He flings off the covers and dashes to the front door to put on his shoes, his earlier defiance forgotten in a heartbeat.

Cheeky monkey.

As I follow him, I hear my phone ring from the living room. I lunge for my purse, fingers scrambling through the clutter until I finally grab hold of it. Missing a call—and a potential job offer—isn't an option. Not anymore.

"Hello, Cora speaking," I answer, trying not to sound as out of breath as I feel.

Fuck's sake, when did I get so out of shape?

"Hi, Cora, my name is Hailee, and I'm calling from Eden. You recently applied for a cocktail waitress position. We're pleased to inform you that you've passed the background check, and we'd like you to come in for an interview tomorrow evening at eight if you're available?"

"Ah, sure… I mean, yes, I'd love to! Thank you so much, Hailee!" I reply, excited but a bit surprised. After providing the address, she hangs up, leaving me with a glimmer of hope I haven't felt in a long time. I don't recall agreeing to a background check, but whatever… I'll take anything at this point.

A job. Finally. I can almost feel the weight lifting off my shoulders.

But then, of course, his smug face flashes in my mind, and that weight comes crashing back down.

Fucking prick.

How is it fair that my married ex-boss had an affair with *his* assistant, and *I'm* the one who got fired? Ten months on, my savings are stretched thinner than my panties. He gets to keep his cushy job while I'm tossed aside for not being able to bury the story. As if that wasn't enough, the asshole blacklisted me, making sure I couldn't find work in my field. He screws up, and I pay the price. The corporate world is brutal, and I've learned that the hard way.

I've applied for countless jobs, sat through dozens of interviews, but every door slams shut because of him. It doesn't matter how good my résumé is—his influence overshadows everything. I eventually turned to a recruiter for help, hoping she could open some doors for me, but so far, nothing.

I quickly type "Eden club" into Google on my phone. It instantly pops up as an "exclusive gentlemen's club" in Double

Bay. I blow out a deep breath. I don't remember applying to such a place, but with all the wine-fueled late-night job hunts, it's not impossible. At this point, beggars can't be choosers.

Scrubbing a hand down my face, I slip my phone back into my purse. With Leo's backpack over my shoulder and my purse slung across my body, I make a quick stop at the bathroom door.

"Hey, Dad?" I ask, hesitant. "Can you watch Leo tomorrow night? I have a job interview."

There's a pause, then a weak but determined voice. "Of course, darling."

"Thank you. I appreciate it." Guilt claws at me, but I push it aside. "I hope you feel better."

"Momma, you coming?" Leo's voice rings out from the hallway.

"Coming, pumpkin!" I sing, rushing to catch up.

With a quick glance at my reflection in the hallway mirror, I gather myself and head out the door with Leo in tow.

Balancing motherhood, caring for Dad, and being the sole financial provider for our family is a juggling act that I can't afford to drop. For Leo's sake, and Dad's, I have to keep going, even if it feels like I'm barely holding it all together.

This interview is important. I can feel it.

Maybe this is the first sign of things finally falling into place.

Chapter Three

Standing outside a mega-mansion in Double Bay, I pull out the scrap of paper with the address Hailee provided, double-checking it against the towering gates in front of me.

Surely this can't be right.

The mansion is enormous, like something straight out of an architecture magazine—modern with sleek lines. The windows are tinted dark and there are no signs outside, so the place looks uninhabited. My heart races as I stare at the long, paved driveway leading to the front door. The whole place screams exclusivity, and a prickle of unease winds its way through me.

I take a deep breath and make my way through the gates and up the driveway. Pressing the doorbell, nerves crash over me like waves against a cliff-face. As I wait, I smooth down my fitted, high-waisted black pencil skirt and adjust my cream-colored blouse, trying to look more confident than I feel.

It was a rush to get ready after tucking Leo into bed and ensuring Dad was well enough to watch him. I only just managed to curl my hair and paint my lips a soft pink. When my rideshare arrived, I slid on my black stilettos, gave Dad a quick kiss on the forehead, and dashed out the door. But now, standing here, I wish I'd taken more time to prepare.

I glance at my phone. Eight o'clock, right on time. At least they'll know I'm punctual, even if it does feel weird to have a job interview on a Saturday night. Sucking in another deep breath, I plaster a big, fake smile on my face just as the door opens, revealing a stunning blonde woman dressed in a simple black satin gown that skims the floor.

"Hey," she says with a warm smile. "You must be Cora. Welcome to Eden."

She's not at all what I expected. She looks my age, maybe a bit younger, with straight blonde hair that falls to the small of her back, flawless tanned skin and big green eyes.

She's gorgeous. The kind of woman who belongs at Paris Fashion Week. She's hardly wearing any makeup and a thin black ribbon tied around her neck is her only accessory.

"I'm Hailee," she says. "Come on in, don't be shy! Madame Sophia's expecting you."

"Thank you, Hailee," I manage, her kindness reassuring me a little. I give her a genuine smile in return, relaxing slightly.

As she turns to lead the way, I notice she's barefoot. I'm about to ask if I should remove my heels, but all thoughts vanish as I take in the interior of the mansion.

Everything is glass and black marble. High ceilings, sleek floors, and massive windows give the space a minimalist, almost exposed feel. It's oddly sensual, though—soft lighting casts warm shadows, and erotic black-and-white boudoir photography lines the walls.

The loud click-clack of my heels on the marble echoes through the foyer as we walk down the corridor, passing multiple closed doors. The ambiance is both intimating and captivating, and I'm grateful that Hailee doesn't expect conversation. I'm too busy trying to make sense of the place, my mind racing with questions I'm not sure I'm ready to ask.

We stop at a door, and Hailee gives me an encouraging smile before she knocks. As we wait, my gaze drifts to one of the photos on the wall—a striking image of a naked woman on her knees, her hands tied behind her back. She's staring directly into the camera, her expression euphoric, her mouth open, with what looks like cum dripping from her lips. The raw intensity of the image makes my stomach flip, and I swallow hard.

What kind of club is this?

Before I can ask, the door opens.

A beautiful woman in her late fifties, dressed in a black cocktail dress that hugs her figure with precision, greets me. Her bright red hair is pulled into a high ponytail, and her crimson lipstick matches her nails perfectly. She's wearing at least eight-inch heels, and she towers over me.

Shit. Definitely should have made more of an effort.

For a moment I hesitate, feeling underdressed and out of place, but I force myself to hold my head high. This might be way out of my comfort zone, but I'm here now. And I'm not going to blow it.

CHAPTER FOUR

Cora

"Is this a brothel?" The question bursts from my lips, unable to be contained a second longer.

Madame Sophia gestures for me to sit in the luxurious armchair opposite her desk. Her office is as elegant and intimidating as she is, tastefully decorated with a blend of modern and classic elements. The dark timber desk dominates the space, flanked by bookshelves and art pieces, and a large frosted-glass windowpane stretches across the opposite wall.

Her lips curl into a slight smile as she takes her place behind the desk. If my outburst surprises her, she hides it well. "Eden is a unique establishment, Cora. We pride ourselves on providing an exclusive and sophisticated experience for our clientele. It requires a certain level of discretion, professionalism, and uniqueness. We cater to the discerning gentleman..." she pauses. "Who possess particular desires."

"What kind of desires?" I ask, tilting my head. Anxiety grips me in a tight fist. I desperately need this job; Dad and Leo are counting on me. I can't let them down. A cocktail waitress?

Sure, I can do that. But *hooker?* That's a huge step I'm not ready to take.

Her sharp blue eyes appraise me, and I get the sense that she's the type of woman who doesn't miss a thing. "The majority of our clients come from wealthy backgrounds and hold positions of power. They consider Eden their playground for pleasure and debauchery. This place allows them to live out their fantasies in a safe, consensual way with our goddesses—but more importantly, in a private way." She smiles with a practiced smoothness. "Privacy and integrity are everything at Eden—that's why we have more than two hundred men on our waitlist."

She still hasn't answered my question.

"What does a goddess do, exactly?" I ask, sensing she's avoiding a direct answer.

"There are two main roles," she says carefully. "Goddesses serve drinks to the gentlemen in the bar and, if requested, may spend time with them privately, ensuring their needs are met in... various ways."

I shift uncomfortably in my seat. "You didn't answer me before... What kind of desires are we talking about here?" I do my best to keep the frustration out of my voice.

Her lips twist into a half-smile. "Let me show you instead." She retrieves a remote from her desk drawer and walks to the window, motioning for me to join her. She clicks a button on the remote and the frosted glass clears, revealing the room beyond.

I gasp, my jaw dropping.

On the other side is a large, opulent room, with a bar and plush couches and cushions in black, gold, and deep red. It's a striking contrast to the minimalist glass and marble of the foyer—exactly what I'd imagined for a gentlemen's club called Eden.

The room is filled with well-dressed men in suits. Some sip from expensive glass tumblers filled with amber liquid, while others remain perfectly still, their eyes locked on the front of the room.

What captures my attention isn't the decadence of the interior or the men, but the ten naked women kneeling on a raised platform. Their heads are bowed, and their faces are hidden by a curtain of hair. Each woman wears a delicate black ribbon collar around her neck. With their backs straight and knees slightly parted, the audience can see their glistening lower lips and the obvious arousal shimmering on their inner thighs.

Heat pools in my abdomen, settling in my core. I resist the urge to rub my thighs together. A groan almost slips out when my nipples push against my bra.

What the fuck is happening?

I turn to find Madame Sophia watching me intently. A knowing smile plays on her lips.

"What *is* this?" I whisper, careful not to disturb the tension on the other side even though I'm sure they can neither see nor hear us.

"Our clientele consists of dominant men who seek the company of submissive women. Our establishment operates as a bar each evening, providing a secure and private space where guests can unwind, free from the intrusion of paparazzi or indiscreet members of the public. Our goddesses are on hand to serve drinks and offer companionship, allowing guests to become acquainted with them. This is solely about social interaction and does not involve any sexual activity."

My eyes sweep across the bar, and I let out a startled sound when I recognize a few familiar faces: two high-ranking politicians, a Hollywood A-lister, a rugby player turned commentator, and—

"Is that...?" I murmur, squinting as I spot a famous musician.

Madame Sophia chuckles. "Our members come from a variety of professions," she says.

It's only then that I notice women seated at the men's feet, arranged on various cushions. Barefoot and dressed in the same black satin gown as Hailee, they seem content, chatting with their clients and nuzzling their cheeks against their legs. Some of the men are gently stroking their goddess's hair while watching the stage proceedings. However, a few of the men are unattended, their gazes trained on the women kneeling on the platform as if waiting for something to happen.

Madame Sophia pulls me from my thoughts. "Every Saturday night, we host Le Jardin. A select group of gentlemen may choose one of ten goddesses to enjoy for the evening, but spots are highly coveted and book up months in advance. At the start of the night, each gentleman draws a random number to determine the order of their selection. The goddesses are presented on stage, naked and posed in a traditional submissive stance." She gestures to the women on stage. "This allows clients to select their goddess for the evening. The selection process itself is a form of foreplay, a precursor to the night's activities. It caters to our clients' dominant side through the presentation and appraisal of the female body, tapping into their voyeuristic tendencies. At the same time, it engages the exhibitionist and submissive attributes of our goddesses. It's a potent combination, as you can see."

Even from behind the glass, the room pulses with power, heat crackling in the air like static before a storm. My breath stutters as Hailee moves toward the stage.

"Ah, we're about to begin," Madame Sophia says.

Hailee joins the women on stage. "Welcome to Le Jardin, gentlemen. If you're participating this evening, you have already received your number. We've kept you waiting long enough; it's time to commence your selection." The bar's energy shifts, the tension intensifying as the men prepare for the ritual that's about to unfold.

One by one, each man approaches the stage to make his selection. He attaches a black leash to the wrist of his chosen goddess and leads her out of the bar to their assigned rooms for the evening. Some of the goddesses follow on their hands and knees, guided by the gentle tugs of the leash, while others walk confidently beside their partners.

What the actual fuck?

Madame Sophia, as if reading my mind, offers an explanation. "The client instructs the goddess to either walk or crawl to their room," she says. "Some men enjoy the theatrics of it." She shrugs, her nonchalance only adding to the surreal nature of what I'm witnessing.

My eyebrows shoot up, and I find myself wondering why I'm not more repulsed by the idea. Instead, a curious heat gathers in my core, a swirl of wonder and want that I can't quite unravel.

Why is that so hot?

Once the ten goddesses are escorted out, the room buzzes with animated chatter. Soft music begins to play in the background. It's as if a switch has been flipped, transforming the space from one of intense anticipation to a laidback lounge where powerful men can unwind.

I take a moment to process everything I've witnessed, chewing on my bottom lip as I contemplate my next move. Turning to Madame Sophia, I confess, "I'm not sure I can do this—I mean, if this is the job?" She nods curtly. "This is all... new to me. What if the client wants something I can't do?"

She smiles understandingly, as if she's heard this exact concern countless times before.

"It's a lot to take in, I know. That's why we ask new recruits to come back and serve for one night before deciding to participate in Le Jardin. The only training you need to know for your trial is to avoid eye contact with clients until given permission and kneel when serving their drinks. It's not much more than that."

Her tone is reassuring. I'm still not sure about Le Jardin, but I could certainly give serving a try.

"This isn't a hardcore BDSM club, Cora," she continues softly. "Occasionally, a client may want to explore a particular fetish that involves costumes or equipment. But this will always be discussed and agreed upon beforehand. Only experienced clients with formal training are allowed to engage in riskier kinks. Plus, there will always be security present during your session to ensure safe play."

She walks over to her desk and picks up a folder. "Here," she hands it over with a patient smile. "This is your paperwork. Even though we're not a BDSM club, you still need to fill out your limits list, indicating what you're comfortable with and what's a hard pass. We also use the standard safe word, 'red,' which can be used anywhere in the building. The safety and privacy of my goddesses are of utmost importance. You will also need to sign an NDA and hand over your phone to security upon arrival. This is expected of our clients as well."

I exhale loudly and nod, trying to keep up with everything she's saying. My mind is racing, but I can't deny the temptation of it all—the allure of a world so far from my everyday life, and the excitement of doing something completely out of my comfort zone.

"Come back tomorrow night before making any decisions," she says. "Just remember to give your completed paperwork to Hailee so we can pay you for the trial, even if you decide it's not for you. You have nothing to lose and a thousand dollars to gain." She sits down at her desk with a secretive smile on her lips.

"What?!" I splutter, my eyes widening in disbelief.

"Our rates are five thousand per night for Le Jardin. For bar work, it's one thousand for a six-hour shift. Hair and makeup are done on-site by professional stylists, and the black gowns worn by all the goddesses are provided."

Shit. This is too good to be true.

I can handle the bar work, but Le Jardin…? What if I'm chosen by someone I find repulsive? Could I actually go through with it?

I turn away from Madame Sophia and study the bar once more. The lush surroundings, the well-dressed men, and the beautiful women should make this an easy decision. The money alone is enough to solve a few of my problems. But my dignity…

Dignity isn't going to pay my bills.

And yet, it's more than that. My body's reaction to everything I've seen and heard tonight is undeniable. My panties are drenched, and I'm horny as hell right now.

I shake my head, trying to push the thoughts aside, but they keep creeping back in. Since having Leo, my sex life has been non-existent, so maybe... maybe this is what I need to kick-start my libido. Get back on the horse, so to speak. And getting paid for it? That's just the cherry on top. Five grand for one night of kinky sex is hard to pass up. It's a lot of money.

But is it worth it?

I've got to do something. Dad's medical bills aren't going to pay themselves, and Leo needs more than just a roof over his head. One night of work could make a world of difference.

"Hope to see you tomorrow night, Cora," Madame Sophia says, interrupting my thoughts. Her eyes are fixed on me with that same perceptive smile.

I give a small nod, trying to appear professional. "Thank you, Madame Sophia. I'll... I'll think about it."

She offers her hand and I shake it. "Take your time," she says, the calmness in her tone reassuring. "We'll be here when you're ready."

I leave her office, my mind racing. The echo of my heels on the marble floor seems louder than before as I make my way back down the corridor, past the closed doors, and through the foyer.

With one last glance at the mansion, I walk away. But even as I step into the humid night air, I know I'll be back.

Chapter Five

Cora

"**L**eo, I need to put you in the shopping cart, okay?" I reach to lift him up.

"Why can't I just walk?" He backs away, turning his shoulder to me. His little pout makes it clear he's not thrilled with the idea.

"Next time, alright? We've got a lot of stuff to get, and we need to be quick today."

"Oh, pleeease," he whines, already angling for a delay. He *loves* spending time at the supermarket. "Fiiine," he concedes with a dramatic sigh.

I quickly lift him up and settle him in the child seat of the grocery cart. I love my kid to death, but at his pace, a simple shopping trip can turn into an ultramarathon. When Leo walks beside me, every aisle becomes an expedition filled with detours and distractions.

"Okay, pumpkin," I say, giving him a playful nudge. "Let's make this quick and then we'll have time for a treat afterward. Sound good?"

Leo perks up at that. "Okay!"

"Great. Let's do this." I pull up the grocery list on my phone and guide the cart down aisle one. The bright fluorescent lights buzz overhead as I grab items off the shelves. My hands move on autopilot while my thoughts drift to tonight. The paperwork is done, everything's in place. Anxiety pulses under my skin, my fingers twitching with pent-up energy.

Despite my nerves being shot, I know I'd be foolish to let this opportunity slip away. While I toss a box of cereal into the cart, I remind myself that it's not like I've got a lot of options right now. Making money quickly is the number one priority.

I glance at Leo, who's happily watching the flurry of activity around him. The innocent kicking of his legs reminds me why I need to make this work. Every decision I make is for him. Providing for us and Dad.

As I scroll through the grocery list, an incoming call flashes on my screen.

When I see it's Emily, the recruiter, I quickly hit Accept.

"Hey, Emily! Do you have good news for me?"

"Actually, I do." She chuckles.

"Really?" After months of asking the same question and always hearing "not yet," it's become a running joke between us.

"There are whispers going around," Emily says, her voice dropping to a conspiratorial tone. "Two women are about to come forward with allegations of sexual misconduct against

Sinclair. If this is true, then"—she makes an explosion sound—"this is a game-changer for you."

"Holy—" I catch myself just in time, glancing at Leo. I wink at him and he giggles at my near slip-up.

The news slams into me with the force of a sledgehammer. For months, my former boss Simon Sinclair has been the insurmountable wall standing between me and my job prospects. If these allegations get out, everything could change overnight.

A CEO having an affair isn't usually newsworthy. People have affairs all the time, and it doesn't make national headlines. But when the man in question is a high-profile CEO of the biggest tech company in the world, who also happens to be married to a famous heiress who loves the spotlight, it's a different story. That sort of scandal is guaranteed to make headlines. Especially when he's caught in a compromising position with his barely legal assistant. It was a PR nightmare—and I was head of PR.

I did everything I could to prevent the story from spreading, but I'm no miracle worker. I was up against the formidable machinery of the global media, and it was only a matter of time before the story broke. Expecting me to control the most powerful media outlets in the world was ridiculous.

Once the story gained traction, it was like trying to stop a wildfire with a garden hose. I could only watch as the media frenzy took hold. The tabloids were relentless, and every new detail was scrutinized and sensationalized. It became clear that this wasn't just a personal scandal; it was a spectacle that captivated the public's attention and sent the company's share price plummeting. Despite my efforts to manage the fallout, the damage was done. The CEO's actions had set off a chain reaction that couldn't be contained. Only, I paid the price.

"His ass is about to get Me Too-ed," Emily gloats.

"Thank goodness." I release a long sigh, feeling the tight band around my chest begin to ease.

"I wouldn't be surprised if he steps down by the end of the next week," she adds.

"Really? That quick?"

"It's not looking good for him. As soon as the allegations hit the news, things will move fast. And the second it does, I'll be on the phone making calls on your behalf."

"You're the best, Emily." Thank God I've got this woman in my corner.

"I know," she snickers. Then, more softly, she adds, "Hang in there. It won't be long now."

"Thank you. I'll speak to you soon." I'm a little choked up so I end the call before she can hear it in my voice.

For the past ten months, that fucker has been wreaking havoc on my career and my life. He deserves every bit of what's coming to him.

"I'm booored, Momma," Leo whines, tugging on my sleeve. I run my hand gently over his soft hair and plant a kiss on his forehead.

"I know, baby, I'm nearly done." I continue pushing the cart through the aisles, thoughts racing with the possibility of finally moving forward, free from the shadow of his influence.

Thank fuck.

Chapter Six

Cora

"I'm super pumped for tonight! I'm so glad you decided to come back. I just know we're going to be BFFs." Hailee loops her arm through mine, practically vibrating with energy as she pulls me into the marble foyer of Eden.

Unlike last night, she's a whirlwind of chatter, ready to talk my ear off. There's a warmth about her, a friendliness that instantly puts me at ease. As an introvert and single mom, I've found making new friends as an adult tough, but I like Hailee's vibe. She's easy to be around, and I can see us getting close.

"I can guarantee, one night and you'll be hooked!" she declares with a grin.

That's what I'm afraid of.

I hand her my paperwork, and we make a quick stop at the front desk, where I'm introduced to Rob, the head of security. He's tall, with a no-nonsense demeanor, but the flash of his smile tells me he's not as hard-ass as he appears. I hand over my phone, feeling a strange sense of surrender as it leaves my hand, and follow Hailee into the heart of Eden.

She leads me through an imposing door into a large room buzzing with chaos and excitement. The air smells faintly of hairspray and expensive perfume, accompanied by the soft, constant hum of hairdryers. Some women are in various stages of undress, while others sit in front of brightly lit mirrors, makeup artists hovering around them. It's what I imagine being backstage at a Victoria's Secret fashion show would be like, minus the feathers, wings, and glitter. The women here are incredibly beautiful in their own unique ways. They're all different shapes, sizes, and backgrounds, but they all have one thing in common: a kind of effortless glamour.

"Welcome to the dressing room!" Hailee exclaims, with jazz hands. "Not that we end up wearing much," she adds with a laugh.

At the back of the room is the wardrobe department, where racks of the same black gown Hailee wore last night stand beside a basket of black ribbon collars, and rows of costumes and fetish gear. I linger for a moment, eyes drawn to the more elaborate costumes, but Hailee is quick to reassure me.

"Don't worry. It's actually fun dressing up, and Edward, our resident stylist, will make you feel like a queen no matter what you're wearing."

Somehow, I doubt that.

She points to the back wall near the wardrobe. "The lockers are over there. You can leave your clothes and belongings inside."

Hailee leads me to the hair and makeup station, and we settle into the remaining empty chairs. Two brunettes, one with long, perfectly styled hair and the other with a sharp bob, are deeply engrossed in conversation.

"... he will never leave his wife for you, Sarah," the woman with the bob is saying, shaking her head.

Hailee interrupts, "Ladies, this is Cora. She's one of our new goddesses, and tonight is her first night, so please make her feel welcome. Cora, this is Sarah, who's in love with one of the clients. Let's just hope he doesn't notice you tonight. She's like a bear with a sore paw whenever he turns his attention to a new goddess." Hailee gives an exaggerated eye roll.

"Bullshit! He only does that when I'm shitty at him. He knows it makes me crazy jealous," Sarah protests. She turns to me with a smile that doesn't reach her eyes. "Just stay away from him and we'll be fine."

Great, staying away from this bitch, then.

"God, give it a rest, Sarah," groans the woman with the short bob.

"And this is Jess," Hailee says, introducing her to me.

Jess leans over to offer her hand, which I promptly shake. "Nice to meet you, Cora. Don't mind Sarah; she's just a bitch. Every workplace has one."

"Fuck off, Jess." Sarah sticks her tongue out.

"Nice to meet you both," I reply with a smile, doing my best to look sincere.

The stylists finish with Sarah and Jess, and as they walk away, Jess glances over her shoulder.

"Good luck tonight, Cora. I really hope Sarah's man picks you to serve him." She bursts into laughter, dodging an elbow from Sarah as they exit the room.

I shake my head at their antics and settle back in my chair, letting the hairstylist and makeup artist work their magic. While they transform my look, I work up the courage to ask Hailee a few questions, curious to know more about this world I'm stepping into.

"So... how long have you worked for Madame Sophia?" I ask, glancing at Hailee in the mirror.

"Hmm, about three years now, I think?" she replies, her expression thoughtful. "It was just supposed to be a temporary gig while I finished my accounting degree. But once I started, the money was too good to pass up, and I got hooked on the lifestyle." She shrugs. "After I graduated, I started working here full-time. I handle admin during the day and serve drinks most nights. I only do Le Jardin every now and then."

"Do you like working for Madame Sophia? You think you'll ever go back to accounting?" I ask.

"I love it. She's wonderful to work for." Her lips curve into a smile. "To be honest... I'm not sure if I'll go back. The money is just too good."

Before I have a chance to ask another question, the stylists proclaim they're done. The woman staring back at me in the mirror is nearly unrecognizable. I look sexy as hell. My hair falls around my face in big Hollywood curls, and my makeup is flawless—eyeliner sharp enough to cut glass and lashes that could bat someone to death. Soft pink lips and rosy cheeks perfectly complement my pale skin.

Butterflies flutter in my stomach as I turn to Hailee. "So, what happens now?"

"It's showtime!" she says with a beaming smile.

Eight hours later, I slide my key into the front door and give it a hard shove. The wood groans against the frame before finally giving way with a loud creak, and I stumble. The porch dips awkwardly, forcing me to take a large step over the threshold. You'd think I'd be used to it by now, considering I've lived here all my life. There are so many things wrong with this house, it's practically falling apart. Unfortunately, repairs aren't exactly high on the priority list right now.

I exhale loudly as the door closes behind me. Tonight, I made a thousand dollars. That should feel like a relief, but it won't last two seconds in my account. It's just enough to cover the back log of electricity bills. I've been lucky that Leo's kindergarten hasn't pressed for the voluntary contribution payments—one small relief.

My body sags, overwhelmed by sheer exhaustion. My feet are killing me, my muscles are sore, and my eyes burn from the combination of thick makeup and lack of sleep. I'm definitely more of a sit-behind-a-desk kind of girl than one for manual labor. But honestly, what a rush. What a night.

It was exhilarating to watch the power dynamics play out in that room. I could've easily sat at the bar for hours, just watching the night unfold. The men were all respectful to the goddesses, and it was essentially simple waitressing, just as Madame Sophia had promised—but kinky. And I loved every minute of it.

The entire club reeked of sex, and it was impossible not to be affected by it. The way the air seemed to crackle with lust left me on a high I haven't felt in a long time. Even now with my muscles aching, the excitement remains. I'm more alive than I have been in years. Deep down, I know I'm already hooked.

The flickering light from the TV casts a glow down the hallway. When I step into the living room, I find Dad reclined in his armchair, watching a rerun of a game show.

"You're still up? It's two in the morning," I say, surprised to find him awake.

"Couldn't sleep." He lets out a long yawn, stretching his jaw wide.

"You in any pain?" I frown.

"I'm fine," he reassures me with a small smile. "Woke up about an hour ago and couldn't get back to sleep. How'd it go tonight?"

"It went well. I'm going to take the job." I stifle a yawn of my own. Dad knows I'm doing bar work at a club called Eden, but I've kept the specifics under wraps. That would be an awkward conversation, to say the least. "Leo went to bed okay?"

"Yep, he's fine. He's such a funny little bunny," Dad says with a chuckle.

"Why? What'd he do this time?"

"He was on the toilet and looked down between his legs to watch it drop, but he wasn't ready for the splashback." He laughs quietly. "It got him right between the eyes."

"Oh, geez, Dad, that's gross." I wince, rubbing my tired eyes. Still, I can't help but laugh along with him. I often wonder what these two get up to when I'm not around.

"Well, on that lovely note, I'm heading to bed. You staying up?"

"Yeah, for a little while." His attention drifts back to the TV. "When's your next shift?"

"This Saturday night. Are you okay to watch Leo again?"

"Of course."

"Thank you." I give his shoulder a gentle squeeze as I pass. "Night."

Each step feels like an effort as I haul my aching legs toward my room. Once inside, I close the door behind me and lean against it for a moment, letting the events of the night play through my mind. It feels surreal, like slipping into an alternate reality—a place where power, control, and pleasure exchange hands as effortlessly as currency.

Despite the thrill, a part of me is hesitant. I've agreed to become a goddess, signing up for the next Le Jardin. Honestly, I've got nothing to lose. We're in desperate need of a cash injection, and this is the fastest solution. But doubt lingers at the edges of my mind. What if I can't handle it? What if I'm chosen by someone who makes my skin crawl? What if...?

No. I shake my head, pushing those thoughts aside. I've made up my mind. What's the worst that could happen? If I don't like it, I'll just stick to serving drinks. No big deal—problem solved.

It's not all that different to hooking up with someone from a dating app for a one-night fling, except this time, I'm getting paid.

I slip out of my clothes, change into a comfortable pair of pajamas and climb into bed. Exhaustion catches up with me, but even as I drift off to sleep, one thought remains in the back of my mind.

I've got this. Easy.

Chapter Seven

Cora

I *ain't got shit.*

Pressure builds beneath my ribs, each breath coming out in short, sharp bursts as panic threatens to consume my mind. Desperation threatens to drown me. I force myself to take a slow, deep breath... count to three... then exhale, trying to release the pressure coiled tight around my lungs. The grounding technique my grief counselor taught me after Mom's death comes to the rescue again. If ever there was a moment I needed it, it's now: naked, on my knees, on a stage in front of a room full of powerful men.

My head is bowed, spine straight, knees parted, hands resting on my thighs with palms facing up. A position of complete submission. The cool air of the room brushes over my skin, raising goosebumps along my arms. At least the floor beneath my knees is forgiving—warm, soft carpet that cushions my skin.

As my breathing steadies, the stiffness in my shoulders melts away, and my muscles loosen enough to allow me to settle into this position. With my chin lowered to my chest, I take in my surroundings as best I can.

From the corner of my eye, I glimpse men seated around the club on lounges. Some are engaged in quiet conversation with the goddesses at their feet, while others sip their drinks in silence, waiting for selection to begin. The lightest trace of cologne hangs in the air, blending into the background of low, steady conversation.

As I become more aware of the eyes on me—watching, assessing, wanting—I lose myself in the moment. The feeling of being wanted is a heady aphrodisiac.

One gentleman stands out from the rest. He sits directly in front of me, as still as a statue, yet exuding a commanding presence even in his relaxed pose. His legs are spread wide, and with a flick of his wrist, he checks his Rolex. Not out of boredom, but with a calculated air, as though every second not spent on something worthwhile is a personal affront. A hint of impatience creases his brow, as if he has far more important things to do with this time. From what I can see, he looks to be in his mid-to-late thirties, with dark, tousled hair that falls effortlessly across his forehead. His navy suit and crisp white shirt only add to his charm.

Gorgeous.

There's an aura surrounding him, an understated authority that draws every eye in the room without him having to say a word. It's more than just his looks; it's the way he seems to own the space around him, as though even the air bends to accommodate his presence.

His eyes flick up, locking onto mine with an unwavering focus. A slow smirk tugs at the corner of his lips as he catches me staring. Those dark eyes, so familiar yet so different—harder, colder—catapult my mind back five years.

I gasp, the sound slipping out before I can stop it, and quickly lower my gaze back to the floor, where it's supposed to be. But my thoughts spiral into chaos.

No! It can't be!

I can't believe it's him! What's he doing here?

Does he recognize me?

Oh no! What if he recognizes me... here, of all places?!

After my initial search for Jonathon turned up nothing, I'd given up hope of ever finding him. Now, the possibility that it could be him makes my skin prickle, sending a tremor through my limbs. I'm not certain it's him—I need another look—but I don't dare raise my head to check. His gaze, however, is unmistakable. I can feel it raking over every inch of me on display, burning into my skin like a brand. My body reacts instinctively, as if it remembers that night in Malta all those years ago. Heat spreads in a slow wave, pooling deep and leaving my body taut, braced for what's to come. My skin feels tight, too sensitive under his watch, as if I might come undone at any moment. I start to pant—not from panic this time, but from a deeper primal instinct.

Lost in my own thoughts, the sound of Hailee's commencement announcement fades into the background. The selection process begins. One by one, my fellow goddesses are chosen by a gentleman, moving with a proficient grace that makes the entire process seem natural. Jess and Sarah are among the first to be selected, and if Sarah's small smile is any indication, her man has chosen her again. Everything unfolds so quickly that it almost feels choreographed.

The quiet murmurs of conversation seem to still the moment Jonathon stands up. Even the other gentlemen glance his way, as though silently acknowledging his place among them. He doesn't seem to notice—or care. His focus is entirely on me, as though the rest of the world has ceased to exist.

Jonathon doesn't rush; each step is deliberate, almost predatory, as he approaches me. There's a refinement in the way he moves, every motion calculated, like he's used to making others wait. Even as he crouches in front of me, there's no wasted energy, just pure, controlled power.

My heart pounds loudly in my ears.

Please pick me...

Please don't pick me...

"Look at me," he demands in that smooth American accent. His voice is a low rumble that vibrates through me and settles deep in my bones. His fingers are warm against my skin, firm yet gentle as they lift my chin.

I release a shaky breath and obediently meet his gaze, staring into the dark eyes that mirror my son's so perfectly—except these eyes are cold, devoid of the warmth I remember.

His eyes sweep over my flushed face, taking in every detail, assessing his possession. "Let's go, goddess," he commands, his brow arching with a self-assured smirk.

There's no hint of recognition in his tone or his eyes.

He doesn't recognize me.

Not every one-night stand leaves a lasting impression, but ours certainly did. The way he looked at me that night, the way he touched me as if I were precious. How could that same man look at me now as if I were nothing more than another hole to fill? As I look into his eyes, there's nothing—no spark of familiarity, no trace of recognition, just a blank stare. Maybe I overestimated the significance of our connection. Or maybe he's slept with so many women that none of them embed in his long-term memory.

My heart sinks, and a hollow sensation blooms in my chest, each beat dragging with the painful realization that this moment isn't unfolding as I had imagined over the years. I force myself to breathe, to push down the disappointment threatening to swallow me whole. This isn't the time to wallow—this is the time to stand tall. For Leo. For the future I've clawed my way toward.

My gaze hardens, and I straighten my back, the fire of determination burning away the lingering disappointment.

"Yes, sir," I say softly, with a calculated smile.

He fastens the black leash around my left wrist and commands, "You may walk."

I'm gonna make sure you never forget me again.

Chapter Eight

Cora

We step into one of the bedrooms off the long hallway. The room is bathed in soft light, an intimate warmth that softens every edge. I'm suddenly very grateful for mood lighting. Jonathon drops the leash without a word and strides to the bar on the opposite side. The sound of liquid splashing into a crystal tumbler slices through the air. Unsure of what's expected of me, I remain by the door, my eyes flicking around the lavish space.

The room is luxurious, designed for pleasure. Plush couches in deep red and black fill a cozy sitting area, while a massive bed dominates the center, elevated on a platform that feels almost like a throne. A floor-to-ceiling mirror spans the wall opposite the bed, reflecting every angle of the room. It exudes a sophisticated, almost regal feel—fancier than any five-star hotel I've ever seen.

Jonathon brings the tumbler to his lips, eyes locking onto mine with a gaze that's unhurried, piercing—like a hawk watching its target. Physically he hasn't changed much in the five years since I last saw him. His black hair, tousled yet somehow perfect, only enhances his features—high cheekbones, a straight nose, a strong jaw dusted with light stubble. He's more than handsome—he's captivating.

Standing with his legs spread wide, he shrugs off his jacket, tossing it carelessly over the back of a chair near the bed. He rolls up his sleeves, revealing veined, muscular forearms, and my eyes eagerly trace the lines of his body, snagging on the hard planes of his chest. His hands slide into his pockets with the easy confidence of a man who's always in control, accustomed to having the world yield to his command.

But it's his eyes—dark, fierce—that draw me in. They see everything. Every wave of emotion, every shift in my stance. He catches the shiver that runs through me, the heat that rises to my cheeks, and the way my breath stills in my throat. His smirk says it all. He knows exactly the effect he's having on me.

"Come here," he commands. The deep rasp of his words sends a jolt straight to my core, making my knees wobble.

God, was his voice always this hot?

I lower my eyes, breaking the connection, and pad toward him. Each step is measured, careful, one bare foot in front of the other, as though I'm walking a tightrope. I stop just short of touching him, close enough to share the same breath but not quite close enough to bridge the distance.

He unclasps the leash from my wrist and his fingers glide up my arm. My breath stutters, each inhale shallow and uneven.

He's barely touched me and already I'm coming undone, my composure slipping through my fingers like sand.

He chuckles, a low, rich sound that vibrates in the space between us. Of course he finds this amusing. Heat flushes my cheeks, but any embarrassment is quickly doused by the hypnotic pull of his dominance.

Why can't I fight this?

My body responds to him instinctively, but my mind races. This isn't just lust; it's a deeper need, one I know I shouldn't crave. But I do. God help me, I do.

His hand circles my throat—not squeezing, just resting there—a promise of power held in check. It's a warning, a reminder that control is his to give or take. But even in that grip, I find a strange comfort. His dominance is a weight I can lean into, if only for a moment.

His tilts my chin up with his other hand, forcing me to meet his gaze. Those dark, intense eyes hold me captive, and I'm trapped—caught in the current of his will.

"Kneel," he commands. The thrum of my pulse beats loud in my ears. He releases my throat and I sink to the floor as if I were nothing more than a puppet on his strings. My fingers reach for his belt buckle, but he's quicker.

"No... hands by your side," he snaps.

I obey, letting my hands fall as he undoes his belt. He lowers his suit pants just enough for his cock to spring free, thick and rigid. I never imagined a man's cock could be beautiful, but his is—hard, long, with a perfect mushroom head and a strong vein running along the underside. A bead of pre-cum glistens at the tip, and my mouth waters. I raise my hand to touch him, but he swats it away.

"Ask permission."

Swallowing my pride, I meet his eyes and whisper, "May I?"

He nods, and I wrap my hand around him—velvet over steel. My tongue darts out to taste the salty drop at the tip.

"Mmm, delicious," I murmur, holding his gaze. His groan vibrates through me, spurring me on as I lavish his length with attention, teasing with my tongue and lips.

But my teasing doesn't last long. His patience wears thin.

"Playtime is over, my sweet slut," he says with a smirk.

That word should repulse me, but instead, it lights my body up. I hate that I crave this. The way he reduces me to nothing more than a trembling mess—and yet, I've never felt more alive, more aware of every inch of my skin, every breath I take.

With a rough tug, he fists my hair, pulling me closer, demanding more.

"Hands behind your back, and take a deep breath," he orders.

I obey, placing my hands behind me as he begins thrusting into my mouth. The rhythm is slow at first, giving me time to adjust, but it quickly builds, each movement pushing me closer to the edge of control. Tears prick my eyes and saliva drips down my chin, but I don't care. The pleasure–pain of submission burns through me, and I revel in the power I hold—his pleasure is mine to give, mine to take away. I relax my jaw, opening as wide as I can to take him deeper. His size is too big to slide completely down my throat, but that doesn't stop me from trying.

His breath quickens, and his grip tightens. "Fuck, I'm going to come... make sure you swallow every drop," he rasps.

He thinks he's in control, but the power shifts every time I make him groan, every time I swallow around his length, making him twitch. I'm not just following orders; I'm bending them to my will.

My body shudders, and if my hands weren't behind my back, I'd be reaching between my legs, circling my clit.

When he releases, the force of it hits the back of my throat, and I fight the urge to gag, swallowing him down. He lets go of my hair and I pull back, licking the last of him from my lips. I sit back on my heels, watching him recover, my own breath coming fast—not from exertion, but from the realization that I was on the brink of coming myself.

He looks down at me, a satisfied smile playing on his lips. Tucking himself back into his pants, he offers me a hand. I take it, rising unsteadily to my feet. He leads me over to the mirror opposite the bed, positioning me in front of it with his chest pressed against my back. One arm wraps around my waist, his hand cupping my breast as he whispers in my ear.

"Look," he says.

In the mirror, the power dynamic is stark. He towers over me, still fully dressed except for his unbuckled suit pants, while

I'm completely naked, disheveled, small in his arms. My hair is a tangled mess, my cheeks smudged with mascara, my lips swollen. Yet, the reflection is raw and real, making me catch my breath. The mirror doesn't simply reflect us—it magnifies. In that surface, I'm not just a woman; I'm his possession, his plaything, shaped by his touch. But I also glimpse a flicker of the power I still hold, even in my submission.

"No, really look," he murmurs, wiping a smear of cum from my chin with his thumb. "You've never been more beautiful than in this moment."

When I try to glance away, he stops me. "Keep looking," he insists. "This is what an epic blow job looks like. It's messy, but it's beautiful."

His thumb lingers near my lips, and without hesitation I part them, sucking it into my mouth. He groans softly, his eyes never leaving mine.

"Good girl," he praises, his voice like a caress.

Arousal surges inside me and he motions to our reflection again. "Remember this," he commands, his voice rough and deep. "You hold the power."

The moment his words sink in, he spins me around to face him. His hands cradle my face as he crashes his lips against mine, the kiss fierce and consuming. I gasp into his mouth, trying to match his fervor as his tongue invades, tasting himself on me. His kiss grows more urgent, and I feel him stiffen against me, ready for more.

He pulls back, but only for a breath, just long enough for his lips to brush against my ear. "We're not done yet." I feel those words. God, I feel it everywhere, anticipation winding tighter and tighter, like a spring ready to snap. Then, with a swift motion, he picks me up, and I instinctively wrap my legs around his waist, clinging to him as he carries me to the bed.

He drops me on the mattress, and before I can catch my breath, he's there, pulling me to the edge of the bed. Kneeling between my legs, he locks eyes with me, a smirk playing on his lips as he lets a string of spit fall directly onto my clit. The wet warmth makes me moan, my hips arching involuntarily as he dives in, his tongue flat against my slit. The obscene slurping sounds only heighten my pleasure, my body trembling so close to release.

He teases and tastes, pushing his tongue inside me and pulling back, driving me wild with need. Just as I'm about to come, he rumbles, "Not yet," and flips me onto my hands and knees. He buries his face between my legs again, but this time from behind, his hands gripping my hips, pulling me closer to his mouth.

The sensation is overwhelming, his tongue sliding over my back hole while two fingers plunge into my core, hitting that perfect spot inside me. My body tightens, teetering on the brink of orgasm, the pleasure almost too much to bear.

"Now you can come," he orders, the low rasp of his words betraying his own need. The command pushes me over the line, my body tensing, spine curving as I cry out.

When I finally come back to myself, I'm sprawled on the bed, panting, every muscle trembling. He's beside me, propped up on one elbow, watching me with a self-satisfied grin.

"Welcome back, my sweet slut," he murmurs. "We're just getting started." He rises from the bed, reaching for a condom.

I can't help but laugh, a low, breathless sound.

Bring it on.

CHAPTER NINE

Cora

I wake with a start, disoriented. For a brief moment, I don't know where I am. My entire body feels sore, the kind of deep, satisfying fatigue that follows an intense workout—or a marathon fuck-fest.

Groaning, I roll over and squint at the clock on the nightstand. Almost three in the morning. I sigh and glance at the man beside me, his chest rising and falling peacefully in sleep.

What a night.

A slow smile creeps across my lips as vivid flashes of his hands exploring my body flood my mind; the way we moved through positions—from the wall to the shower, then the couch. No wonder I feel like I've been hit by a bus. It's been five years since I've been fucked like this.

And with that thought, reality crashes back in.

Right before we passed out from exhaustion, he had the audacity to ask my name. *My fucking name.* I was too tired to care then, but now, with the haze of sleep gone, the anger hits like a blow that knocks the wind from my lungs.

He doesn't remember me. All these years, I've clung to the memory of that night—the way he looked at me, the connection we had. I replayed it over and over in my mind, convinced that if we ever met again, he'd remember me the way I remembered him.

Stupid, Cora. So fucking stupid.

This man is wealthy enough to afford a membership at Eden, spending exorbitant amounts of money on sex while I'm struggling to keep my family afloat. The thought makes me sick. My ego isn't bruised—it's crushed. The last thing I want is for him to know about my son.

I can't lie here a second longer. I flick the blanket off and tiptoe to the bathroom, closing the door behind me. The reflection staring back at me in the mirror is a wreck. My hair is a wild mess, dark circles ring my eyes, and my lips are swollen from his kisses. Kisses that feel more like bruises now.

I exhale loudly, trying to gather my thoughts, but panic begins to creep in again, squeezing the air out of my lungs.

I have to get out of here. I quickly use the bathroom, splash some water on my face, and slip back into the room. He hasn't moved an inch.

As I head toward the door, something catches my eye—his suit pants, crumpled on the floor, with his wallet peeking out of the back pocket. I freeze, my fingers twitching.

Should I?

I glance at the bed, my heart pounding so hard it might explode. Without fully processing what I'm doing, I bend down and grab the wallet, the buttery leather soft in my hand. I open it quickly—no ID, no credit cards, no business cards. Just condoms and cash. A lot of cash. Probably around a grand.

Who carries this much cash these days?

Will he even miss it?

I close my eyes and take a breath. Then, before I can stop myself, I snatch the cash, scrunching it in my palm. My stomach twists, but I ignore it. I need this more than he does. I know it's wrong. But survival doesn't care about right and wrong.

I need to get out of here.

I dress in record time at my locker, my hands shaking as I button up my blouse. At security, I grab my phone, trying to act casual, but the tell-tale flush of guilt crawls up my neck.

"Is everything okay, Cora?" Rob asks, his eyes full of concern.

"Yes! Yes, everything's fine," I lie, forcing a smile. "Actually... no, it's not. My son was sick today, so I need to leave early." The words spill out so easily, but I know he sees right through me. He doesn't say a word, just hands me my phone and asks if I need a taxi.

I shake my head. "I'll just order a rideshare. Thanks, though," I mumble, desperate to escape.

I burst through the door and down the driveway as fast as my shaky legs can carry me, which isn't very fast. A sharp, gnawing pain grips my stomach, making me lightheaded. I'm dizzy—the adrenaline that's been building all night finally breaks over me. Thoughts of Jonathon's dark eyes—the same shade as Leo's—rush through my mind, and the stolen cash burns a hole in my purse.

I stumble to the edge of the driveway and throw up in the bushes, the bitter taste of regret clinging to my tongue.

I wipe my mouth with the back of my hand and stay crouched for a moment. My body is heavy, like I'm carrying the burden of every bad decision I've ever made. It's not just about tonight—about the man sleeping in that bed, blissfully unaware that I stole from him. It's everything that led me to this moment: Mom's death, Leo, the tangled mess of my career, Dad's illness. It all comes crashing down around me.

How did I get here? I used to have everything—respect, a career, a reputation. I loved the late nights, the client dinners, the hours spent crafting the perfect media spin. But it all disappeared in an instant, unraveling the moment Sinclair's scandal hit the newsstands. One PR nightmare and suddenly I was the collateral, chewed up and spat out by the industry I'd fought so hard to conquer.

Now, I'm stealing cash from a man who doesn't even remember my name, working at a place where my worth is measured by how well I can submit to the desires of strangers.

This isn't who I wanted to be. This isn't the life I dreamed of.

Keep moving forward, Cora. You have to. There's no going back.

I pull out my phone to order a rideshare and notice a missed call from Emily. My thumb automatically taps the voicemail icon, and I listen as I slowly make my way toward the street.

"Hey Cora, hope you don't mind the late call, but I finally have news! There's a position available for you at Hayes & Hayward Media. Remember you interviewed there a while ago? It's a newly created role in their publicity department, and they're looking for an immediate start on Monday. See, I told you it would all happen quickly. I'll email you the details over the weekend. Let's catch up for coffee once you're settled in. Enjoy the rest of your night."

I close my eyes. A wave of calm rolls over me as relief sinks in, steadying my frayed nerves. For the first time in what feels like forever, I exhale, releasing all the anxiety I've been holding on to.

It's about damn time.

Chapter Ten

Cora

"Momma, you awake?" Leo whispers in my ear. I open one eye to find his tiny face just inches from mine, his breath tickling my cheek.

"I am now," I murmur, trying to stifle a grin while I yawn. I roll onto my back, pulling him into a big bear hug. He squeals, his giggles reverberating through my chest.

The movement sends a dull throb through my muscles, the lingering soreness a reminder of the night before. But it's not the sex or being paid for it that fills me with guilt. It's Jonathon... and the money I stole.

What the hell was I thinking? Taking his cash?

It was reckless, impulsive, beyond stupid. When he reports me to Madame Sophia, I'll have to face the humiliation of explaining myself—and giving the money back. I can't show my face there again. If this new job at Hayes & Hayward Media doesn't pan out, I'll be right back where I started: financially fucked. I've risked everything because of my stupid ego.

Seeing Jonathon again really messed with my head, knocking me off balance in a way not even five-inch stilettos could achieve. I groan out loud, covering my face with my hands.

"What's wrong, Momma?"

"Nothing, baby. Absolutely nothing." I force a smile, pushing the thoughts away. "Alright, time to get up and get cracking. How about we do something fun today?"

"Yes!" Leo leaps off the bed and runs down the hallway shouting, "Grandpa! Grandpa! We're going to the zoo!"

I chuckle. The kid would go there every day if he could. Slowly I peel myself from the bed and stagger toward the bathroom, my core aching from being thoroughly used. A pulse of heat flows through me at the memory of Jonathon deep inside me.

The sex was incredible, his dominance addictive. No denying that. His hands, his tongue, the way he manhandled me—it was everything I remembered and more. But there's an edge to him now, a newfound control that left me breathless. He seemed to have discovered a darker, more commanding side of himself, and damn, did it suit him. His gorgeous body, and that cock. Honestly, it should come with a warning label. The amount of times he made me scream...

I step into the shower, letting the hot water beat down on me. A soft sigh escapes my lips as I trace my hard nipples with my fingers, sensitive after the punishment they received. They're still red and puffy from being pinched, pulled, and sucked. My own touch is a poor substitute for his, but it'll have to do. I pinch them harder, welcoming the sharp, pleasurable burst of pain. My hand drifts lower, circling my needy clit, but just as I begin to lose myself in the sensation—

"Are you coming, Momma?" Leo's muffled voice filters through the bathroom door, shattering the moment.

Sighing, I turn off the shower and reach for a towel. "Another minute and I would've."

"Are you okay?" I ask Dad as we settle onto a park bench at the zoo. He lets out a soft grunt, his face tight with hard lines. We've been here for hours, and he's shattered. There's no way he was well enough to join us, but he'd never say no to Leo. He'd battle the crowds and his own pain just to see our boy smile.

I watch him out of the corner of my eye as he takes a slow breath, trying to mask the discomfort. I want to fuss over him, but I know he hates it when I hover. Instead, I quietly hand him a bottle of water.

The air smells of hay and sunscreen—scents that usually bring me comfort. But today, everything feels distant, disconnected. Leo is at the edge of the giraffe enclosure, his face lit up with fascination as the towering animals stretch their long necks toward a high basket of leaves. But I can't stay present. My thoughts keep drifting back to last night. To Jonathon. To what I did.

"Yeah, I'm okay, darling," Dad finally replies, though the wince in his expression tells a different story. After a pause, he adds, "What's going on with you? You've been lost in your head all day."

"What do you mean?" I turn toward him, my eyebrows pulling together.

He gives me a look—the kind that says "I know you better than that." And he does. We've been close ever since Mom passed away and Leo came along. He's been my rock, the one person I can always count on. But last night? I can't share that with him... not in detail, anyway. The thought of what I did makes my stomach churn. It's not just Dad who's feeling queasy today.

"I saw Jonathon last night," I say, dropping the bombshell with a heavy sigh. His eyes widen.

"What? Where?! What happened?"

I scrub a hand across my forehead, trying to find the right words. "I saw him at the cocktail bar while I was working."

"And?!" He leans forward, urging me to continue.

"And nothing," I say with a shrug, trying to sound casual.

I'm not about to tell him that I was paid to have mind-blowing kinky sex with Leo's father, then stole his money and bolted in the middle of the night.

Exhaling, I opt for the partial truth. "I don't think he's a good person, Dad... from what I saw last night, anyway." Although I'm pretty sure Jonathon could say the same about me. And worse. "He's arrogant, and... I don't know. There's just something about him doesn't sit right. He's not the same man I met in Malta; there's a coldness to him now. And I'm not sure I want him to know about Leo or be involved in his life. Does that make me a bad person?"

The disappointment of Jonathon not being the man I had imagined him to be is like a dead weight I can't shake.

"No, of course not! You do what's best for Leo," Dad says. He takes a deep breath and I know he's going to give me one of his life lessons. "Look, Jonathon might not be the man you once thought he was, but he still deserves to know about his son... eventually. None of us stay the same over time. You're not the same person you were five years ago either, Cora. You've grown. You're a mother now—your entire world has changed." He pats my hand, his thumb brushing over my knuckles.

I nod. It's true. Motherhood has reshaped me in ways I never imagined, shifting my priorities and forcing me to face challenges I never expected.

"You'll know when the time is right," Dad says.

"You're right. Thanks, Dad." I give his hand a gentle squeeze. "But I wouldn't even know how to contact him or find out who he is. Honestly, with this new job, I don't need to go back to the bar anyway." Not that I'd be welcome there after what happened.

Dad's eyes drop to the ground. "I'm sorry to put you under so much financial pressure," he mumbles, his words just above a whisper.

"Dad, stop. Don't even go there," I say, shaking my head. "You didn't ask to get sick. Plus, where would I be without my live-in babysitter?" I nudge him gently with my shoulder.

"Tell me about this new job," he says, his eyes still on Leo, who's absorbed in the giraffes.

I pull out my phone and scroll through my inbox until I find the email Emily sent this morning. "Apparently it's at Hayes & Hayward Media." I quickly scan the message and read out loud, "I'll be their new senior public affairs specialist, working across public relations and human resources to improve company culture and public perception."

We exchange a look, eyebrows raised.

"Well, that sounds interesting. What does Hayes & Hayward Media do?"

"No idea," I reply with a shrug, still reading the email. But I'll find out soon enough.

By the time we get home, Dad and Leo are both exhausted and they retreat to their rooms for naps. But I can't rest—not

with tomorrow looming over me. I need this job at Hayes &
Hayward Media to stick. It has to.

With the quiet time on my hands, I pull out my laptop and
type "Hayes & Hayward Media" into the search bar. Turns
out it's an American media conglomerate with reach in nearly
every corner of the industry: a film company, a major tabloid
magazine, a national news channel, and a telecommunications
giant. The company was founded in the 1940s by two ambitious
young men, David Hayes and Thomas Hayward.

I scroll through a company bio, pausing on an old
black-and-white photo of the founders, back when they started
building their empire. They look sharp, almost defiant, like they
knew they were carving their names into history.

The bio says that a few years back, the founders' sons "boldly
stepped down" as CEOs to give the next generation a chance to
lead the company into a new era.

Instant red flag.

I can spot corporate spin a mile away. I used to be the queen
of it, after all.

I keep scrolling, hoping for some personal tidbits about my
new bosses. Aside from their staggering combined net worth of
nearly one hundred billion, there's nothing but blurry paparazzi
shots and carefully crafted PR. The co-CEOs are blank slates in
the public eye, hidden behind the iron gates of their empire.

The latest news stories on the company are *far* more revealing though. I find dozens of articles on workplace bullying and employee dissatisfaction—at least fifty headlines.

I release a deep breath. Looks like I've got my work cut out for me. Settling into my chair, I click on the first article.

Well, this is going to be fun.

Chapter Eleven

The towering skyscraper looms above me, its glass exterior gleaming in the harsh morning sun. Though it's barely nine, the heat is already oppressive, the kind that clings to your skin and makes the air feel thick and sticky. A bead of sweat trickles down between my shoulder blades.

My power outfit—a sleek black skirt, a cream blouse that feels a little too warm under the sun, and black stilettos that make my legs look longer but are already pinching at my toes—does little to ease the anxiety fluttering in my stomach. The butterflies have turned into a full-on swarm, their wings beating frantically as I stand at the entrance of the glass and steel monolith.

As I step through the revolving doors, the temperature drops and the rush of the city fades away. I'm greeted with crisp, cool air, muffled discussions, and the faint scent of expensive coffee drifting from a café tucked into the corner. This is where I'll start fresh, where I'll leave behind the past ten months and dive back into what I do best.

"Hi! I'm Cora. It's my first day at Hayes & Hayward Media," I tell the receptionist, handing over my ID. She offers a polite smile and checks her computer.

"Welcome, Cora. Here's your security pass to access the lifts. Hayes & Hayward Media is on floors thirty and above. You'll need to check in with Human Resources on level thirty first."

"Thank you," I reply, taking my ID and pass.

Exiting the lift on level thirty, I'm greeted by a man in a gray three-piece suit, complete with a chic pocket square.

Who wears a three-piece suit to work?

Then again, when he looks like that, who cares? Sandy blond hair, just long enough to run fingers through, frames blue eyes that sparkle with a mix of mischief and professionalism.

"Hey, Cora. I'm Nathan," he says, flashing a smile that could charm the skin off a snake. His cheeky wink tells me he caught me checking him out, and a blush creeps up my neck. After Saturday night my libido is wide awake and not going back into hibernation anytime soon. "Tina, our head of HR, was supposed to meet you, but she's out sick today. So, you're stuck with me," he says, framing his face with his hands in a playful gesture that nearly makes me laugh out loud.

"Pleasure to meet you," I manage, doing my best to stifle an unprofessional giggle.

"I work in HR under Tina, so we'll be seeing a lot of each other. Let me show you to your desk."

I follow him through the office, taking in the surroundings. The floor is an open space with about twenty workstations. Light gray walls, charcoal carpet, and bright yellow couches create a surprisingly inviting atmosphere. It's corporate, but it feels... comfortable.

"Everyone has their own desk; no more hot-desking since the pandemic," Nathan says, rolling his eyes. "The open plan thing is supposed to encourage collaboration. Only department heads have offices."

"And the big bosses?"

"James and Dameon? You won't see them often, and that's a good thing," he says, widening his eyes. "The only time you'll have to endure their presence is at the monthly town hall."

"What's that?"

"A company-wide meeting where one of the big bosses updates everyone. It's supposed to foster unity or something, but it's mostly a waste of time," Nathan says. "Oh, and please—since you're here to work on company culture, do us all a favor and change how new employees are introduced. It's brutal."

"That bad, huh?" I raise an eyebrow.

"You'll find out in"—he checks his watch—"half an hour."

We reach my workstation, and Nathan hands me a folder. "The login details and everything else you need are inside. Take your time getting settled in. I'll be back for you before the town hall. My desk is just over there if you need anything." He points to a spot a few desks down from mine.

"Thanks so much, Nathan. I really appreciate it."

"Don't thank me yet—I'm about to lead you to the slaughter in thirty minutes," he quips.

I groan and mutter, "Gee, thanks," under my breath as he walks away.

Nathan must have superhuman hearing because he throws his head back with a laugh and sings out, "You're welcome!"

Sliding into my chair, I store my purse in the drawer then log into the computer. Looking around the office, I see people sipping coffee, typing, or chatting by the couches. Everyone seems relaxed, not stressed out or rushed like you'd expect on a Monday morning. It's a far cry from the hostile work environment I anticipated. But there must be something going on beneath the surface. Especially if they needed to hire someone to improve company culture and perception. I make a mental note to pick Nathan's brain about what's really happening behind the scenes. He seems down-to-earth and genuine. I could use a friend to help navigate office politics.

A ping from my office messenger catches my attention.

Nathan

Ready to go, lamb chop? Town hall awaits. Meet you at the lifts in two mins.

Lamb chop?

Lamb to the slaughter? Not a fan of that kids' show?

Pretty sure I'm not old enough to remember it.

What? Lamb Chop's an icon and so freaking cute!

Umm, okay...

What a weirdo—but I kinda love it. Smiling to myself, I log off and head to the lifts to meet Nathan.

We enter the auditorium on level thirty-six, and Nathan guides me to the side of the stage. The space is huge, with plush red velvet seats arranged in steep, theater-style rows, creating an atmosphere that feels more like a high-end cinema than a corporate meeting room. When the last few stragglers arrive to find their seats, Nathan gives me the rundown.

"Okay, Rossi, when I introduce you, just keep it short and sweet. Don't expect a warm welcome from everyone," he warns.

Nathan strides to the center of the stage, his voice booming as he welcomes the crowd. "Good morning, everyone. Hope you all had a great weekend. Tina is off sick today, so I'll be introducing our new employee, Cora Rossi, before handing over to James for the monthly update. Cora will be working closely with me as our new senior public affairs specialist. Please make her feel welcome."

He motions for me to join him on stage. My heart skips a beat, but I force my legs to move with as much confidence as I can muster. Standing beside Nathan, I project my voice as loud as possible, keeping my message short and sweet like he suggested. "Thank you, Nathan. I'm really looking forward to meeting all of you and working together."

Public speaking doesn't usually faze me, but the sea of blank faces staring back offers no warmth, making the moment feel like an eternity. I can practically feel the walls closing in around me.

Sensing my panic, Nathan steps in to fill the silence. "I'm sure we'll all make her feel welcome and part of the team," he says, glancing off to the side. "Great. James is here now to take us through the monthly update."

We retreat to the side of the stage, and I whisper to Nathan, "Well, that was fucked."

"Yes. Yes, it was," he deadpans.

My relieved chuckle dies on my lips when my eyes lock onto a man staring at me—dark eyes that look so much like my son's.

Oh no.

Please, no.

Oh God, no.

My heart stops. Blood drains from my face and the world around me sharpens and blurs all at once.

Jonathon is glaring at me from the other side of the stage, a storm of emotions raging across his face—confusion, anger, disgust. My knees go weak.

He's the first to break eye contact, striding across the stage and commencing his update in his clipped American accent. But I can't tear my eyes away from him. Here, under the harsh fluorescents of the auditorium, he looks different to how he appeared on Saturday. But his presence is just as commanding, if not more so. The dark fabric of his tailored suit highlights his broad shoulders and lean physique. This time though, his black hair is neatly slicked back, and his sharp jawline is clean-shaven. This man was deep inside me less than forty-eight hours ago, his body intertwined with mine. I can still taste the salty, earthy flavor of his cum on my tongue, feel the roughness of his stubble against my thighs.

The room empties around me, but I'm frozen, the sounds of shuffling feet and low murmurs fading into a dull roar in my ears. I didn't hear a single word of his speech, too lost in the shock of seeing him again.

Nathan's voice slices through my daze like a lifeline. "Cora, are you okay?" he asks. "You're white as a sheet. Do you need to sit down?"

Before I can answer, Jonathon—or James, I suppose—cuts through the crowd like a predator homing in on its prey, his glare locked on me with an intensity that makes my blood run cold. My heart hammers against my ribcage, each beat more frantic than the last as he closes the distance between us. An unreadable look flickers in his eyes, one that sends a chill down my spine and roots me to the spot.

When he stops just inches from me, the air thickens, as if the entire room were holding its breath. "Follow me," he commands. There's no question in his voice—only an ironclad expectation that I'll comply.

Every instinct screams at me to run, but I can't. I can't move, I can't breathe, I can't think beyond the overwhelming presence of him—this man who holds my past and now, somehow, my present in his hands.

Nathan's eyes dart between us. He mouths, *What the fuck?* but I'm already gone, my feet moving of their own accord as I follow James out of the auditorium.

My legs struggle to keep up with his long, purposeful strides. I'm half-jogging, my heels clacking on the polished floor, my breath shallow. The walls of the hallway blur around me.

What the hell is happening?

My mind races, trying to piece together some semblance of reason, but nothing makes sense. Not the way he's acting, not the urgency in his steps, and certainly not the dark look in his eyes.

All I know is I'm following a man who was supposed to stay buried in my past, a man who's now much more than just a memory. As he leads me down the hallway, away from the safety of prying eyes, a cold dread claws at my sanity.

CHAPTER TWELVE

James

When I glance back to ensure Cora is keeping up, I catch her stumbling in her sky-high heels. A slight smirk pulls at my lips but I don't slow down. If she wants to keep up with me, she'll have to work for it. I control the pace—always.

I find the nearest boardroom and push open the door with more force than necessary, the loud bang startling the group inside. Their heads snap up in unison.

"Out. Now," I demand, my voice low and laced with an edge that brooks no argument.

The four employees exchange tense glances, clearly sensing the volatility in the air. Without a word, they gather their laptops and papers, avoiding eye contact as they hurriedly exit the room. One or two of them shoot Cora a curious, almost sympathetic look as she pulls up behind me, slightly out of breath and flushed.

"Inside, Miss Rossi." I hold the door open, nodding my head toward the now-empty room.

She storms past, and her scent—a tantalizing mix of vanilla and citrus—hits me, pulling Saturday night's memories to the surface. I wrestle the urge to react, keeping my composure by a thread.

I follow her inside and close the door with a definitive click. Now that we're alone, I let myself really look at her. Her black skirt clings to her curves in all the right places. Curves my hands know all too well. Her cream blouse offers just a hint of cleavage, enough to make me remember the way her skin felt under my fingertips, and her heels elongate her legs—legs that were wrapped around me, urging me to go deeper, not even two days ago. My cock stirs at the thought, but I grind my teeth, shoving the distraction aside. Now isn't the time.

When I finally meet her gaze, there's anger in her eyes. Her chest rises and falls, her breathing ragged with the strain of holding back. *What the fuck does she have to be angry about?*

I'm about to make her nuclear.

"You're done here," I declare, as I stare her down, daring her to challenge me. "Pack your shit and get out. Now."

"What?" She sucks in a sharp breath.

Did she really think this was going to play out any other way?

"I don't hire thieves and hookers in my company," I snap, my composure starting to fray.

Her mouth falls open, and for a moment, she looks genuinely stunned.

"What kind of shit-show is Madame Sophia running?" I demand, my anger spilling over. "First, you steal from me. Then you find out who I am and waltz in here to do... what, exactly? Blackmail me?"

"What?!" She gasps again, her eyes wide with shock.

Or is it guilt?

"Is that all you've got?" I let the words hang in the air, watching her squirm under the pressure of my silence. When she doesn't answer immediately, I arch an eyebrow. "You'll need a better vocabulary if you want to keep working here, Miss Rossi. I'm beginning to think HR seriously dropped the ball with you."

Her expression hardens, fury sparking in her eyes. Good. She should be furious.

Cora might think she can outsmart me, but I've dealt with women like her before. Whatever she wants, she isn't going to get it. I'm no stranger to manipulation—women have tried before, but they've always been easy to manage. My preference for power dynamics complicates things, but my lawyer handles those situations without breaking a sweat. They typically leave with a settlement and a warning, vanishing just as quickly as they appeared. But nothing like this has ever happened at Eden, which is exactly why I pay their steep membership fees—to ensure a safe, discreet space for play.

When I realized Cora had looked through my wallet and stolen my money, I was livid. I should have reported her to

Madame Sophia, but since she had no way of knowing my identity, losing a grand didn't seem worth the hassle of an investigation. Chump change, really. But now, this is a different ball game. No one plays me.

How she found her way into my company, I don't know. But I will find out. And when I do, she'll learn just how dangerous it is to cross me. I'll crush her little plan before she even knows what hit her.

Cora squares her shoulders and lifts her chin, her stance firm and unyielding as she meets my gaze head-on. The fire in her eyes dares me to try and break her.

"You can't fire me, Mr. Hayes. Or should I call you Jonathon? Or James?" She tilts her head, a silent dare in her eyes.

I freeze, my pulse hammering in my throat.

"What did you just say?" I whisper, my voice nothing more than a low rasp. Now I *know* she's playing me.

She waves a hand dismissively. "Try firing me without cause, Mr. Hayes. Let's see how well that goes over with HR. I'm sure they'll be fascinated to hear why their CEO is so desperate to get rid of a new hire. Care to explain it to them—or shall I?"

She waits a beat, then adds with a smirk, "Exactly. I was hired to improve the public's perception of this company and to enhance the work culture. From what I've seen so far, a fish rots from the head down. And in this case, Mr. Hayes, the stench is unmistakable." Her nose wrinkles in mock disgust as she looks me over, her disdain palpable.

Oh, the feeling is mutual, my sweet slut.

My teeth clench at the way she says "Mr. Hayes" in that condescending tone. Seems Miss Submissive isn't as submissive as she pretended to be.

"Miss Rossi—"

"In the workplace," she interrupts, "the correct title is Ms., not Miss. Or do you struggle with basic etiquette? Don't worry, I'm sure you'll get the hang of it eventually. Let's try again: You can call me Cora."

She gives me a sweet, insincere smile that makes my blood boil.

How about brat? That's a little more fitting.

The urge to bend her over my knee and spank the insolence out of her is almost overwhelming. My hand clenches at my side, and I have to force myself to stay still, to not react the way every instinct is screaming at me to.

I close the distance between us in a single, deliberate step, forcing her to tilt her head back to meet my eyes.

"Alright, Cora. I'm going to ignore the fact you just threatened me and say this only once. Whatever game you're playing, it's not going to work. Resign immediately, and we'll pretend this never happened. But if you stay"—I lean in, my voice dropping to a deadly whisper—"I will make you regret it. You won't win this war."

I stare her down, my eyes boring into hers, making it clear I'm not to be fucked with. Grown men have crumbled under this look, but Cora holds firm, and her defiance only makes me more determined to break her.

She swallows hard, her throat bobbing as she processes my ultimatum. My eyes are drawn to the delicate line of her neck, and the urge to wrap my hand around it is almost too much to bear.

"Bring it on," she snarls. Then, before I can respond, she spins on her heel, yanks the door open and marches out, her fury trailing behind her like a storm cloud.

Alone, I take a deep breath, trying to steady the whirlwind of emotions churning inside me. Her scent lingers in the air, teasing me, and I tilt my head back, staring at the ceiling as if the answers I need might be written there.

"Fuck," I grunt.

Anger still courses through me as I stalk back to my office, bypassing Portia, my executive assistant. She opens her mouth to speak, but one look at my face has her quickly shutting it. I don't have the patience for anything right now.

Throwing open my office door, I find Dameon, my co-CEO and best friend, lounging in one of the chairs opposite my desk.

"How was town—" he begins. "Jesus, what the fuck happened to you?"

Dameon and I have been through everything together. Our grandfathers founded Hayes & Hayward Media, and we were always destined to take over. When my father stepped down earlier than planned a few years ago, Dameon's father did the same, leaving us to steer the ship together. We've faced our share of crises, especially with the Australian arm of the business, but this... this is new territory.

"We have a problem," I say, sinking into my chair.

His eyebrows shoot up. "What kind of problem?"

"Our new senior public affairs specialist."

"Yeah?"

"She's also the new goddess at Eden."

Dameon's eyes widen. "Please tell me you haven't fucked her yet."

"Balls deep on Saturday night," I respond with a wince.

"You're fucking with me."

"I wish I were," I grind out. "Her name's Cora Rossi. She was working Le Jardin on Saturday, and now she's here, trying to play me. My guess is money. It's always about money."

Since she's already stolen from me, a quick payoff should do the trick. But the idea of paying her off grates on me. Still, I'm not about to risk my company over some pussy.

Dameon leans back, rubbing a hand over his face. "This is a fucking nightmare—not just for the company, but for you personally. We need to be smart about this. If she's playing us, it's not just money we should be worried about. We can't let this spiral—"

I cut him off. "I know. We can't afford another PR disaster right now."

"We need to contain this," Dameon says, the strain in his voice stoking my worry. "Quickly."

I grab my phone, dial my lawyer and put him on speaker. Sam is a grumpy old bastard, but he's the best at what he does, and I pay him a small fortune to keep things like this from blowing up.

"Sam, it's James. We have a situation," I say as soon as he picks up.

"What's the problem, sir?" Sam's as direct as ever.

"A woman called Cora Rossi. She started today at Hayes & Hayward Media, and she was at Eden over the weekend. She's here to blackmail me, I'm sure of it. You have my permission to offer up to one million if necessary."

Sam's silence stretches for a moment before he speaks. "I understand your concern, but I don't recommend this course of action. You can't pay off an employee without raising red flags. You'll need to find a legitimate reason to fire her first, then we can talk about a settlement. My advice? Find out what she wants... but tread carefully."

Fuck.

"Understood. Run a credit check on her, will you? I want to know what her financial situation is like," I order, ignoring the questioning look Dameon shoots me.

Sam agrees and I hang up, frustration tightening every muscle in my body.

"Madame Sophia needs to know about this," Dameon muses. "Unless she's in on it too."

"If she is, she'll regret it," I snap, though I quickly dismiss the thought. Madame Sophia wouldn't risk her business like that. She knows we'd destroy her.

Dameon studies me for a moment, a corner of his mouth lifting into a grin. "I assume you've already spoken to Cora?"

I can't help the smirk that crosses my face as I recall our confrontation. Her defiance, her willingness to stand toe-to-toe with me, ignited a powerful possessive urge—a feeling I've never had before. I'm almost glad I can't pay her off. This might be more fun than I anticipated.

"She's feisty, I'll give her that," I admit, reclining in my chair.

"That good, huh?" Dameon chuckles, shaking his head as he gets up to leave. "You lucky bastard."

She was perfect on Saturday night—a natural submissive, pliant under my hands, her body responding to my every command. The way she obeyed, her desperate need to please me... she was mine to control, mine to dominate, and she loved every second of it.

Lucky? I'm not sure that's the word I'd use. But as I sit here, my mind replaying our encounter, a part of me is looking forward to the challenge.

Cora Rossi isn't just another problem to solve; she's a game to be played.

And I always play to win.

Chapter Thirteen

Cora

Back at my desk, I fall into my chair with a huff. *The nerve of that conceited jerk! Who the hell does he think he is?*

I drop my head into my hands, trying to calm myself. The moment I saw him, my stomach twisted into a tight knot, my thoughts scattering, my pulse pounding.

How can this be real? How can he be here?

As my anger cools, embarrassment takes its place, piercing and cold like frost on a windowpane. He wasn't wrong to call me a thief and a hooker... well, not entirely.

Under the circumstances, I can't blame him for jumping to conclusions. He thinks I'm here to blackmail him, and honestly, can I fault him? How am I going to convince him that this is nothing more than a horrible coincidence? Or should I just resign and cut my losses?

I groan, slumping in my chair. This job was supposed to be my lifeline—without it, we could lose everything. Going back to Eden isn't an option. Resigning isn't either. But can I really face Leo's father every day when he clearly hates my guts?

I don't have a choice. This job isn't just a paycheck—it's my chance to give Leo the stable life he deserves. The only way forward is to prove James wrong. I need to show him I belong here, that I earned my position because of my intellect and experience, not through manipulation or deceit.

Decision made, I feel a bit better—until I remember the fake name he gave me in Malta.

Dick move.

I lift my head just as Nathan approaches, his lips pressed in a thin line. "Cora, you're shaking," he says softly. "What the hell happened back there?"

"Shhh," I hiss, glancing around. "Keep your voice down!"

Nathan leans in, eyes wide. "I've never seen James like that before. He looked livid, and that's saying something—his normal look is pissed off."

I cover my face with my hands. "Oh, Nathan, it's a complete disaster."

"What's going on?" he asks again, more impatient this time.

"I can't tell you here," I mumble.

"Fine, but you and me"—he points between us—"drinks after work, and you better spill."

"Okay, yes, let's do that," I whisper hurriedly.

His gaze lingers, uneasy, before he turns to leave. Though we've just met, his concern is unexpectedly comforting.

The rest of the day drags on painfully. I have no idea what I'm supposed to be doing and concentration is futile. By the time five o'clock rolls around, I'm more than ready to get out of here.

Nathan and I leave the office together and head directly across the road to Maxine's, a grungy bar filled with an after-work crowd.

"I'll get us some drinks, then you're going to talk," Nathan says, giving me a pointed look.

As I settle into a quiet corner, I consider how much to tell him. We've just met, so I can't be entirely sure I can trust him. I'm usually a good judge of character, but this situation is too sensitive. I decide to leave Eden out of the conversation for now.

Nathan returns with a tray of shots and cocktails.

"Did you forget it's a school night?" I laugh, despite myself.

"I have a feeling this is going to require a lot of alcohol." He hands me a shot. "To my new work wife," Nathan says with a wink, and we clink glasses. I throw back the shot, the tequila burning down my throat.

Four shots and two strong cocktails later, we're both well beyond tipsy, and my plan to keep certain things close to my chest has dissolved in a haze of alcohol.

"Wow... just... wow." Nathan's eyes are wide with bewilderment.

"I know, right?" I shout back, making Nathan wince.

"I knew we needed this tonight," he says, raising his martini. "I can't believe you fucked him… he's such a prick." He shakes his head.

After hearing most of my story—everything except for the identity of Leo's father—he shared his insights on the office culture. Having been with Hayes & Hayward Media for nearly a decade, Nathan has seen the company's internal dynamics shift dramatically. When the founders' sons stepped down unexpectedly and Dameon and James took over, swooping in from the US to save the struggling Australian branch, they brought a new energy to the company—but it wasn't exactly a good one. According to him, they are respected but feared, and completely out of touch with their employees. Upper management seems to be where the culture problems begin, yet no one dares to approach or challenge them.

"What are you going to do?" Nathan asks, snapping me out of my thoughts.

I sigh, feeling the weight of my situation. "I honestly don't know."

We sit quietly for a moment, the noise of the bar fading into the background, until my phone rings.

Thinking it might be Dad, I quickly fish it out of my purse and gesture to Nathan that I need to take the call. I head toward the bathrooms where it's quieter.

"Hello," I answer, just in time.

"Hi Cora, it's Madame Sophia. I'm calling to see how your trial went on Saturday and if you'd be interested in joining us on a permanent basis."

"I'm sorry, what?" I stammer, my alcohol-fogged brain struggling to understand her words. Surely there's been a mistake. I've been dreading this call, expecting her to be furious with me over what I did. I just hoped she wouldn't press charges for theft—after all, it'd be bad for business. Best case scenario, she'd accept my apology along with the money I stole, and we'd part ways.

"I wanted to see how everything went on Saturday night and if you enjoyed it," she repeats. "The client certainly did; he gave you a glowing review. We would love to have you on board."

Wait, James didn't report me? Why the hell not?

"Ah yes, it was a lot of fun. Love to do it again," I reply, slipping into a strange British accent. I squeeze my eyes shut, biting my lip as my cheeks burn.

What are you doing, you weirdo?

"Wonderful! Welcome aboard, Cora. Hailee will email your roster shortly."

I make a non-committal sound as she hangs up and slowly make my way back to our table. James's unexpected praise has thrown me. Why didn't he report the theft? It doesn't add up. Is he planning his own revenge? I need to figure it out before I walk into a trap.

Nathan looks up from his phone, his eyes narrowing slightly. "What was that about?"

I hesitate, trying to decide how much to share. But Nathan's already in this with me, and after everything I've spilled tonight, there's no point in holding back now.

"That was... work-related," I say slowly, still processing the conversation myself. "Madame Sophia. She was calling to offer me a permanent spot at Eden."

Nathan's jaw hangs open. "Wait, *what?* After everything that happened?"

"Exactly," I say, leaning in, my voice hushed. "I thought for sure James would've said something—hell, I was bracing myself for a criminal charge after his reaction this morning. But instead, she says he gave excellent feedback. Like... *glowing*."

Nathan's confusion mirrors my own. "That doesn't make sense. Why would he do that?"

"I have no idea," I admit. "He was furious today, accusing me of all sorts of things—blackmail, theft, being a hooker... but then he doesn't say a word to Madame Sophia?"

Nathan sits back, running a hand through his hair. "That's messed up. But it might give you some leverage, right? If he didn't report you, maybe he's not as eager to get rid of you as he's letting on."

"Maybe," I murmur, though the thought doesn't bring much comfort.

We fall into silence, both of us lost in the tangle of the mess I've created.

Nathan reaches across the table, giving my arm a reassuring squeeze. "You'll figure it out, Cora. You're a tough bitch—I can tell."

His words bring a smile to my lips. "Thanks, Nathan. I really appreciate that."

"Anytime." He grins. "Now, how about one more drink before we call it a night? God knows we could both use it."

I laugh softly, nodding in agreement. "Why not? After today, I think I've earned it."

Nathan heads to the bar and I take a moment to just breathe. I don't know what game James is playing, but I know one thing for sure: I'm not going down without a fight.

My thoughts drift to Leo, his little face flashing in my mind. What would happen if James found out about him? Tightness grips my throat, and I force down a hard, dry gulp.

I can't let my mind go there. I need to be focused to stay ahead of whatever James is planning. If he thinks he can scare me off, he's wrong. I belong at Hayes & Hayward Media, and I'll prove it—even if it means going head-to-head with Leo's father.

CHAPTER FOURTEEN

Cora

The pounding in my head is relentless, each throb like a hammer to my skull. I pry my eyes open, but the spinning room forces them shut again.

Am I still drunk?

Nathan and I didn't leave the bar until two, after drinking far more than we should have for a weeknight. It's been years since I stayed out that late—or had that much fun. Nathan's a blast to be around, undeniably cute, but there's no spark between us. No butterflies in my stomach, no heat coursing through me... not like a certain tall, dark, and infuriating CEO. The image of his smug face tightens the vice around my temples, intensifying the pain.

What the hell was I thinking? Getting wasted on my first day is a new low.

I drag myself into the kitchen, hoping that coffee might perform some miracle on my sorry state. Dad and Leo are finishing breakfast, both looking annoyingly bright and chipper.

"Morning, Momma!" Leo's cheerful voice cuts through my throbbing head like a knife, and I wince, forcing a smile that's more like a grimace.

"Morning, baby," I croak, reaching for the mug of coffee Dad's holding out.

"Good night?" Dad's smirk says it all.

"Yeah, until now," I mutter, taking a cautious sip. The strong, black coffee offers a small relief as it slides down my throat.

Dad chuckles. "Ahh, to be young again. Leo, get your things, pumpkin. Grandpa's taking you to kindy," he calls, his voice at an unnecessarily loud volume.

"Dad!" I snap. "For the love of God, you're killing me here!" I shoot him a glare, rubbing my temples as if that will somehow lessen the pain.

"Sorry, darling," he whispers with exaggerated softness.

As they leave, I consider how I'm going to survive the day when just standing here is a challenge.

I manage to make myself presentable—or at least somewhat less of a disaster. My white silk blouse is neatly tucked into my high-waisted pants, and I throw on a blazer for good measure, hoping it'll help me look more put-together than I feel.

Staggering into the building, the world sways. If I can reach my desk without passing out or puking, I might make it through the day.

I spot Nathan in the lobby, looking every bit as wrecked as I feel. His hair is a mess, stubble darkens his jawline, and his tie is hanging loose around his neck.

"Well, you look like shit," he jokes with a weak chuckle as I approach.

"You aren't exactly fresh as a daisy yourself," I retort, eyeing his untucked shirt.

Before he can respond, a familiar, deep voice booms behind us, making my blood run cold.

"You both look horrible."

Nathan and I spin to see James standing there, his gaze flicking between us with a mix of disdain and irritation. We must look like we've just rolled out of bed together.

Great, he already thinks I'm a hooker. Now, the office slut.

I close my eyes briefly, wishing I were anywhere but here. When I reopen them, James is staring directly at me, his expression unreadable.

"Both of you—my office in ten minutes," he snaps. The elevator dings, and he storms inside and jabs the button. "Get the next one."

As the doors close, Nathan grunts "fuck," and I can't help it—I burst out laughing. It must be the remnants of alcohol still flowing through me, because nothing about this situation is funny.

We manage to stifle our laughter as we step into the next elevator, both of us sobering up—mentally, at least—as we prepare for the inevitable lecture. We quickly stash our things at our desks and head to the top floor, determined not to make our situation worse by being late.

The top level of the building is a different world from the floors below. Where the lower levels are warm and collaborative, this floor is all business—pristine white marble, glass offices, and sleek, black furnishings that scream corporate efficiency. It's intimidating, to say the least.

Nathan approaches the receptionist, a woman in her late sixties with perfectly coiffed gray hair and flawless makeup that puts my feeble contouring skills to shame. She's dolled up in a bright red pantsuit, looking every bit the picture of competence and poise. In comparison, Nathan and I look like something the cat ate and regurgitated.

"Hey, Portia, we're here to see James as requested," he says, flashing that killer smile of his. It's amazing to watch—that smile would charm the pants off just about anyone. "This is Cora. She started yesterday," he adds, nodding in my direction.

Portia smiles warmly, a hint of pink coloring her cheeks. "James is expecting you both. Go on through."

"Thanks," I manage, returning her smile, though it feels like my cheeks might crack from the effort.

Why is everything so painful this morning? And why the hell are my cheeks sore?

I giggle quietly, the absurdity of it all catching up with me. *God, how much did we drink last night?*

As we approach James's office, I catch Nathan's eye, and he shoots me a look that says "what the hell are you laughing at?" But as soon as we step into James's office, the laughter dies in my throat. He's sitting behind a massive desk, and the air in the room feels like it's dropped ten degrees.

James looks up from his screen, his eyes narrowing as he takes us in. The silence stretches on, thick and uncomfortable, and I can't help but fidget. I smooth my hands over my pants, trying to ignore the way his gaze feels like it's cutting right through me.

Finally he breaks the silence. "Do you think it's appropriate to turn up to work intoxicated and disheveled?"

"No, sir," we answer in unison, and the ridiculousness of it hits me again. I bite back a giggle, but it's no use. Once the laughter starts, there's no stopping it. Nathan and I are soon bent over, tears streaming down our faces.

James waits, his expression unreadable, as we try—and fail—to pull ourselves together. It feels like an eternity before our laughter finally dies down, leaving us both wiping at our eyes, trying to compose ourselves.

"Consider this your first warning," he says coolly. "I'll be notifying HR to issue your official written warnings today. Nathan, you're excused. I need a word with Ms. Rossi."

A small, satisfied smile lifts the corner of my mouth when I hear him say, "Ms." One point to me.

Nathan gives me a sympathetic look, mouthing *Good luck* before hightailing it out of there, leaving me alone with Mr. Grumpy Pants.

The atmosphere in the room shifts the moment the door closes. James settles back in his chair, his thumb tracing his lower lip as he studies me in a way that makes my skin tingle. There's a new intensity in his eyes.

"This is going to be easier than I thought," he says, his tone almost mocking. "You've already earned yourself a warning, and it's only your second day. Two more strikes, and you're out. I have to say, I expected more of a challenge. Frankly, I'm disappointed."

"Admittedly, this isn't a great first impression," I start, raising my hands in a gesture of surrender. His eyebrows arch in response. "Okay, second impression," I amend, rolling my eyes.

Damn it, how could I have forgotten about taking his money?

"Don't roll your eyes at me," he snaps.

"Why, what are you going to do about it?" I retort before I can stop myself. Liquid courage must still be clouding my judgment, because the next words out of my mouth are nothing short of reckless. "Flip me over your knee and spank me?"

His eyes darken, and a slow, dangerous smile spreads across his face. "Careful, my sweet slut, you're treading on dangerous territory."

Hearing that name in this setting does things to me—wicked things I don't want to admit. My body reacts to his words, my breath hitching as my nipples tighten to hard peaks. I hate how easily he can affect me.

James rises from his chair, his movements slow and deliberate as he rounds the desk. He stops in front of me, his hand lifting to cup my cheek, his thumb brushing lightly over my skin.

"Cora," he murmurs, his voice softer now. "I'm assuming you're still drunk and therefore not entirely in control of what you're saying. So, let me make the situation clear for you. You have exactly one week to put together a strategy to improve company culture. If you don't deliver, you'll receive your second warning. Am I clear?"

His thumb continues to brush over my cheek, the gentleness of the gesture contrasting sharply with the threat he's just laid down. The proximity of him, the warmth of his hand, makes it hard to think straight.

I nod, the motion stiff and jerky.

"Good." His eyes hold mine for a moment longer, searching, before he steps back, the sudden absence of his touch leaving me cold. "Go home and come back tomorrow when you've sobered up."

I pull away, hating how much I miss his touch the moment it's gone. Without another word, I turn on my heel and head for the door, my shaky legs betraying me as I try to make a dignified exit. I can feel his eyes burning into my back, but I don't dare turn around.

As soon as I'm out of his office, I let out a breath I didn't realize I'd been holding. My head is still swimming from both the booze and his touch, and it takes everything in me to walk steadily to my desk. I gather my purse, avoiding eye contact with anyone, and make a beeline for the exit.

Christ, we're idiots.

I can't believe Nathan and I thought we could pull off a day at work while still drunk. I groan inwardly at our stupidity, vowing to make better decisions from now on—especially where Mr. Sexy Grumpy Pants is concerned.

Stepping into the thick morning air, I fight back the rising bile. I need to get home and sleep this off, but more than that, I need to figure out how the hell I'm going to survive this job.

One week. I've got one week to prove myself.

The thought of James's ultimatum sends anxiety surging through me like an icy current. I've never felt so out of my depth. But there's no way I'm going to let him win. I refuse to be the weak link he expects me to be.

My phone buzzes in my pocket as I start walking to the train station. Pulling it out, I see a message from Nathan.

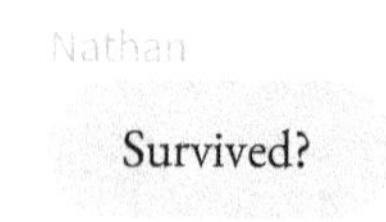

A small smile tugs at my lips as I type back a quick reply.

Barely. But I'm on my way home to sleep it off.

Nathan

Same. Let's not do that again anytime soon.

Agreed.

I slide my phone back into my pocket and let out a deep sigh. Today was a disaster, but it's over now. Tomorrow is a new day, and I'll be damned if I don't walk into that office ready to fight for my place. No matter what it takes.

At home, I drop my purse on the kitchen counter and head straight for my bedroom, stripping off my clothes and collapsing onto the bed. My head is still pounding, but at least now I can close my eyes and let sleep take me. Before I drift off, one last thought crosses my mind.

I need to stop thinking about him.

But even as I make that vow, I know it's useless. He's already under my skin, and there's no escaping him now.

CHAPTER FIFTEEN

Cora

When I wake up, it's with a clearer head and a renewed sense of determination. The hangover has dulled to a faint throb, and the embarrassment of yesterday lingers like a bad dream—one I'm eager to shake off.

I rise with purpose, the sting of yesterday's mistakes pushing me forward. Today there's no room for errors. I'm going to walk into that office, head held high, and show James Hayes exactly who he's dealing with.

On the train to work, I nibble on raisin toast between sips of coffee, my mind already buzzing with ideas for the strategy I need to create. I mentally map out my day, aware that every minute counts. First, I'll review the company's internal HR reports, then I'll gather feedback from employees. If I'm going to make a difference, I need to understand the problems from the ground up.

When I arrive at the office, a few curious glances come my way, but I brush them off. Nathan, looking much more like his usual self, waves from his desk, and I return the gesture with a slight smile.

Settling into my chair, I take a steadying breath. This is my chance to prove I'm not just some bad hire or worse, a threat. I dive into the reports, my focus razor-sharp, and the hours slip by in a blur as I start piecing together the challenges Hayes & Hayward Media is facing. The toxic culture, the palpable fear of upper management, the glaring lack of communication—it's daunting, but for the first time, a spark of excitement flickers to life within me.

I can do this.

By lunchtime I've made significant progress, but I'm far from done. As I consider interviewing employees, a thought strikes me—I need to figure out a way to do that without running into James. The idea of facing him again so soon makes my stomach twist. The memory of my stupid suggestion that he spank me makes me flush. Avoiding him is absolutely necessary at this point.

Why, just why?!

Determined to spare myself further humiliation, I decide to ask Dameon's permission to interview a few employees instead of risking another encounter with James. There's only so much embarrassment one person can take, and I've definitely hit my quota.

Entering the foyer on the top floor, I spot Portia at her desk, looking as fabulous as ever. "Hi Portia, I was wondering if

Dameon is available for a chat? I don't have an appointment, though."

"Sure, hon. Let me check for you." She picks up the phone, and while she's distracted, I glance toward James's office. The frosted glass walls hide him from view, but I can imagine him behind that large desk, his long, strong fingers tapping away at the keyboard. My breath stutters, and I shift my weight from one foot to the other.

"You can go on through; he's free now."

I let out a breath and head toward Dameon's office, relieved it's in the opposite direction. With a light knock on the door, I step inside. The office mirrors James's—a spacious corner office surrounded by windows and opaque glass walls, with a sitting area to the side and a commanding glass desk at its center.

Dameon rises from the couch, offering a firm handshake. "You must be Cora. Welcome to Hayes & Hayward Media. Please, take a seat."

We settle onto the couch, and I discreetly check him out. He's undeniably attractive, with sandy blond hair, vibrant green eyes, and a tall, broad-shouldered frame. There's a similar air of dominance and power around him, just like James.

"What can I do for you, Cora?" There's a trace of curiosity in his tone, as if he's still figuring me out.

"I'm putting together a strategy to improve office culture and perception," I begin in my most professional voice. "I'd like permission to interview staff on their thoughts about the current environment and what they think could be improved."

Dameon's eyes flicker with amusement. "I must say, I wasn't expecting that. You're quite the conundrum, Cora. I can see why you've gotten under his skin."

The comment catches me off guard. "Who? Mr. Hayes?"

"I know all about Eden, Cora. Let's just say James and I go way back. I know more about him than most people. We're not just co-CEOs."

The pit of my stomach drops, but I keep my composure, nodding slowly. "Oh... um, okay," I draw out, my mind scrambling to catch up. If the floor could open up and swallow me whole right now, I'd gladly welcome it.

"You're not here to blackmail him," he states, his head tilting slightly in thought.

"Look, I'm not exactly sure what he's told you, but I can assure you I'm not here under false pretenses. I just want to do my job to the best of my ability and prove that I belong here."

There's a long pause as Dameon examines my face, searching for any sign of deceit. Finally he nods, as if making a decision. "I believe you. I do. You're going to keep things interesting, aren't you?" he says with a chuckle. "Alright, so you want to interview employees. How many?"

Ignoring his first question, though I'm dying to know what he meant, I focus on why I'm here. "About ten or so—someone from every department and level of seniority."

"Absolutely. Let Nathan know, and he can help set it up."

"Thank you for being open with me," I say sincerely. "I really appreciate the opportunity to work here, and I promise I won't let you down."

Dameon holds my gaze with a steady confidence. "I know you won't."

As I leave his office, a small sense of relief settles in. Dameon truly believes I'm not here to cause harm, at least not to him or his co-CEO. If only I could convince James of the same.

I wait impatiently for the elevator, repeatedly pressing the call button as if it might make it arrive faster. The man himself suddenly emerges from his office, and my breath stills as I instinctively shrink back. He doesn't notice me as he heads toward Dameon's office, but I take the opportunity to admire him from afar. His black wavy hair is slicked back again, and the navy shirt he's wearing clings to his chest in a way that's both distracting and infuriating. His fitted suit pants only highlight his perfectly sculpted ass, and the way his sleeves are rolled up to reveal muscular forearms makes me weak in the knees.

Why isn't arm porn a thing?

As he disappears into Dameon's office, I step into the elevator and return to my floor. I can't help but think about the similarities between James and Leo. Both have the same dark, wavy hair, and their noses are practically identical—straight and perfectly proportioned. I only hope Leo doesn't inherit any of

James's more infuriating traits, though the stubbornness might already be showing.

The rest of the day passes in a rush. By some miracle, I managed to squeeze in three employee interviews in the afternoon—far more than I'd expected. But now that the clock has struck five, tiredness sinks into my bones. Recovering from a hangover is definitely not as easy as it used to be.

I slide my headphones into my ears as I pack up my desk, scrolling through the recordings from earlier. I'd kept my composure during the interviews, but now that I'm alone, I can finally indulge in the absurdity of what I heard. The moment the first employee's voice filters through my ears, a soft laugh escapes me.

"Dameon never remembers my name. I've been working in finance for three years, and he calls me Ashley. My name is Ellie! It's not even close!"

"I was speaking to James on the phone, and I ended the conversation with, 'Alright babe, love you, see you later.' That's what I always say to my husband—it wasn't meant for James! I panicked and said, 'Oh my God! I didn't mean that. I don't love you, I just like working for you... I mean, I'm married! I'm not hitting on you, I swear!' He hung up and reported me to HR the next day. But it was an accident, I promise!"

"James spilled his coffee in the boardroom. He held out his hand for the tissues, but I misunderstood and shook his hand instead.

The look on his face—God, I was so embarrassed. I had to take stress leave. I still can't look him in the eye."

I burst out laughing, clutching my stomach as mortification hits me again. My secondhand embarrassment is almost unbearable. At least they didn't suggest James spank them. My cheeks flush and I fan myself with my hand, still grinning as I replay the moment in my mind while I wait for the elevator.

I'm taking out my headphones when the elevator doors slide open, so I don't see who's inside straight away.

James.

He's standing at the back of the elevator, as composed and intimidating as ever. Our eyes meet, and for a moment, the air between us crackles. My pulse quickens, a flush creeping up my neck, but I force myself to keep a neutral expression as I step inside. Being this close to him is... distracting. His presence is a storm—intense, suffocating, thrilling.

We ride down in silence, the only sound the soft whirr of the elevator. My mind races, replaying the events of yesterday, but I shove those thoughts aside. I can't afford to let them rattle me.

When we reach the lobby, I step out first, eager to escape, but before I can make my getaway, James's voice stops me in my tracks.

"Ms. Rossi."

I turn to face him, my heart pounding. "Yes?" My tone is polite, professional.

He regards me for a moment, his expression unreadable. "I look forward to seeing what you come up with."

There's a challenge in his words, and despite the knot in my stomach, I offer him a hint of a smile. "I'm sure you won't be disappointed."

His eyes narrow, a brief look crossing his face that I can't pin down. And then it's gone. "We'll see," he says, and strides out. "Have a good night," he calls over his shoulder, leaving me standing there in his wake, a whirlwind of utter confusion.

No matter how many times he tries to throw me off balance, I'll keep standing.

I won't let him win.

I belong here.

And I'm going to prove it.

CHAPTER SIXTEEN

James

Dameon drops his tablet on the desk. "What are you looking at?" he asks, rounding my desk and leaning over to peer at my screen.

We've just endured a mind-numbing two-hour conference call with New York, and I couldn't tell you a single thing that was discussed. Their sign-off barely registered.

I don't answer right away. My eyes are locked on the CCTV feed of Cora's floor. She's sitting at her desk, a half-eaten sandwich forgotten beside her, typing with deep focus. The light of her screen highlights the curve of her jaw, the way she absentmindedly tucks a stray strand of hair behind her ear as she reads through her notes. It's mesmerizing.

"James," Dameon says, louder this time.

I tear my eyes away from the screen, but almost instantly they flick back to Cora, now sipping her coffee, completely unaware of my attention. "Nothing," I mutter, though the word rings hollow.

Dameon squints, and a slow grin stretches across his face. "Ahh... so that's what's had you distracted all week." His chuckle is light.

I force myself to relax back in my chair, trying to project an air of nonchalance. "I'm keeping an eye on her. Making sure she doesn't screw me—*us*—over." The words come out too quickly, the excuse flimsy even to my own ears. It's not entirely a lie—I *don't* fully trust her. But it's more than that, and we both know it.

"Righttt," Dameon drags out the word. "How long have you been watching her?"

"Just today," I lie through my teeth.

"Uh-huh," he says, clearly not buying my bullshit. He leans against the desk, arms crossed, his smirk deepening. "You realize how this looks, right?"

Of course I do, I'm not an idiot. I'm teetering on the edge of stalker behavior, but I don't give a shit.

Instead of answering, I minimize the feed and turn to face him, fingers steepled under my chin. "What do you know about Nathan?"

Dameon's brow furrows. "Nathan? From HR?"

"Yeah. I don't like the way he's been acting around Cora."

His tilts his head. "What are you talking about?"

"He's too... familiar," I say. My voice is sharper than I'd like. "Always at her desk, flirting, laughing. He's at her desk more than he's at his own. It's unprofessional, especially when we're trying to improve company culture. Harassment is harassment, even if it's under the guise of friendliness."

Dameon rolls his eyes. "James, it's not harassment to be friendly. You're reaching, and you know it."

"He's overstepping," I bite out. "And how productive can he be when he's always hanging around her desk?"

"You're jealous," Dameon states, the certainty in his voice hitting me like a slap.

I open my mouth to deny it, but the words don't come out. *Jealous? Me?*

That's ridiculous. I'm not some possessive boyfriend—I've never been possessive.

"Of course not," I growl, but even I hear the strain in it. "He's out of line."

"You're unbelievable." Dameon shakes his head with a low chuckle. "Besides, I'm pretty sure Nathan's not even interested in Cora. He's more into... your flavor." He gestures toward me with a casual flick of his hand.

I freeze. "What?"

"Yeah," Dameon says with a shrug. "He dated a friend of mine, Shaun, a few years back. They broke up, but... you know, they were together for a while."

I stare at him, the tightness in my chest easing a fraction, but my pride is too damn stubborn to let it show. Instead, I tilt back in my chair, gaze sliding away from Dameon's shrewd smirk. "And you're just telling me this now?"

He snorts, strolling back to the couch and flopping down. "What? His love life never came up before." He shrugs, clearly enjoying himself. "I figured you'd be secure enough in your own ego not to care."

I grumble "fucker" under my breath, shifting in my chair, filled with an unexpected sense of relief that I refuse to fully acknowledge.

Why should it matter? I've never been territorial. I play with a goddess, enjoy their submission, then move on. Simple.

But Cora's different. This past week, I've watched her every move, tracking her like a hunter fixated on his prey. It's unnerving how much she consumes my thoughts—the way her tongue slips out when she's deep in concentration, the soft focus in her eyes when she chews on the end of her pen. The way she smiles when Nathan makes her laugh...

"Are you going to report him for harassment, then?"

My fingers, tapping impatiently on the desk, go still. I glance at him. "Fuck off."

Dameon laughs, a deep sound that grates on my nerves. "You're full of shit, you know that? Come on, just admit it—you've got a thing for her."

"Drop it," I warn.

He sighs, standing up and stretching lazily. "Fine, fine. But seriously, you need to relax. How about we head to Eden tomorrow night? Grab a drink. We could both blow off some steam."

I hesitate. I can't keep going like this, watching her from afar, letting jealousy seep into my mind like poison. I need to regain control.

Dameon's right. Jealousy coils in my gut, unfamiliar and unwelcome. It doesn't fit—it never has. The best way to shake it off is to find someone new to play with.

"Yeah," I finally say, nodding. "Maybe you're right."

"Great," he says, making his way to the door. "I'll check to see if Zac and Carter can make it too." He stops in the doorway, fixing me with that infuriating grin. "And, James? Ease up on the Cora surveillance. You're starting to look like a creep."

I shoot him a glare that would make anyone else shrivel, but Dameon just chuckles and disappears down the hallway.

Alone, I turn back to my screen, my finger hovering over the mouse. I pull up the CCTV feed one last time, watching Cora's eyes light up in conversation with a colleague, oblivious to how much space she occupies in my mind.

With a definite click, I close the feed, slide back in my chair, and drum my fingers rhythmically on the armrests.

Tomorrow night, this ends.

CHAPTER SEVENTEEN

Cora

"What are we watching?" I drop onto the couch beside Dad, stifling a yawn that threatens to crack my jaw. My body feels wrung out—heavy limbs, aching muscles, exhaustion draping around me like a weighted blanket.

"*Bluey*," Leo mumbles, not bothering to tear his eyes from the screen. He's sitting cross-legged on the floor, a bowl of potato chips in his lap, and I'm pretty sure half of them have already found their way into the carpet. He's completely absorbed, eyes glued to the Heeler family as if the cartoon might vanish if he blinks.

I love *Bluey* too—thank God someone finally made a kids' show that's actually watchable for adults—but even its charm isn't enough to hold my attention for long. My eyelids burn, itching to close, but I fight the pull and sink deeper into the cushions.

This week was a total clusterfuck—far more taxing than I anticipated. The first week at a new job is always draining, but this? Navigating a new workplace is one thing, but throw in an ultimatum, high expectations, and the emotional hurricane of running into Leo's father, and it's a recipe for burnout.

It's a perfect lazy Saturday, and all I want is to cocoon myself in blankets, binge-watch mindless TV, and eat enough cookie dough to send me into a sugar coma. But that's not an option. Guilt nags at the corners of my tired mind—I haven't spent nearly enough time with Leo or Dad this week. I've been totally neglecting them.

Leo's giggles fill the room, and all I can think about is how I've missed hearing that sound all week. He's barely looked up from the screen, but can I blame him? I haven't been here. The shadows under Dad's eyes are darker than usual, and I wonder when he last had a proper rest—certainly not since I threw myself headfirst into work. He's been picking up all the slack—keeping the house running, looking after Leo, making sure there's dinner on the table—and I've been... absent. Lost in my work.

"You doing okay, Dad?" I ask, watching him closely, noticing the way his frame is hunched, like it's taking more effort than it should just to sit upright.

"Yeah, I'm fine. Just feeling a bit wiped, that's all." He attempts a smile, but it doesn't quite reach his eyes. I should be helping him, not the other way around. Yet here I am, practically falling asleep on the couch while he bears the load of my responsibilities.

"You should go lie down," I suggest, even though I know he'll refuse. "You need to rest."

He shakes his head gently. "I will, sweetheart," he says, patting my hand. "But I wanted to sit with you two first. I've missed seeing you this week."

I nod, guilt spearing through me. Dad's always there for me, always picking up the pieces. And I keep leaning on him, even when I shouldn't.

"I know this week's been a lot for you, and, well... I wish I could help more," he adds.

"You do way too much already, Dad," I say quickly. We've had this conversation a thousand times before. I force a smile, but the way his skin looks pale—almost translucent—has me worried.

Before I can say anything else, my phone buzzes. Reluctantly, I pull it from my pocket and glance at the screen. It's a message from Hailee. My stomach sinks as I read it.

Hailee

Hey Cora, just a friendly reminder - you're scheduled to work tonight in the lounge at 8 p.m. Don't forget to check your roster. X

Crap. Eden.

I completely forgot about my conversation with Madame Sophia. This week has been such a disaster that Eden wasn't even on my radar. I bite my lip, my mind racing. Do I really want to go back? Financially, I should—my job at Hayes & Hayward Media is far from secure, especially with James gunning for me. But do I *actually* want to work tonight?

The question hangs in my mind, but the answer comes with surprising clarity. A shiver runs through me, my pulse quickening at the thought of slipping back into that world. I could be someone else, just for a few hours. No pressure, no expectations. Just... freedom. Last Saturday night awakened a strange feeling in me, one I wasn't ready to fully grasp. The power dynamics, the anonymity... Maybe going back is exactly what I need.

"Are you up for looking after Leo tonight?" I ask, trying to keep my voice steady, swallowing roughly. "I... forgot I had a shift at the bar."

Dad looks at me for a long moment, concern etched into the lines of his face. He knows me too well. "Of course I can, darling," he says. "You know Leo sleeps right through. But... are you sure you're up for it? You've been running on fumes all week. I thought you didn't have to go back to that job?"

"I *don't* have to," I admit, my fingers twisting a loose strand of hair. "But... I don't know, it feels safer. Keeping my options open, you know? Just in case Hayes & Hayward doesn't work out." The words taste bitter as they leave my mouth, and I can't shake the fear lodged in my throat. The truth is, I'm not just keeping my options open—I'm hedging my bets. I could be out of a job in a week's time. But I can't tell him that.

And I don't just need Eden for financial security. I need it for me—for control, for some sense of power over my life. Because right now, it's like the ground is shifting beneath my feet and I can't seem to stop it.

"Alright." He nods. "Just don't wear yourself out. Promise me that."

"I won't," I assure him, offering a grateful smile. "Thanks, Dad. I owe you."

"My pleasure, darling." His hand rests on mine for a moment. Then he turns his attention back to Leo, who is still engrossed in *Bluey*.

I shoot Hailee a quick text.

> Thanks, I'll be there. See you tonight. X

I settle back into the couch, pretending to focus on Bluey and Bingo, but my mind is already at Eden. My fingers trace idle patterns on my thigh, fidgeting unconsciously, as I think about slipping back into that world, where I can shed everything else and just be... Cora. Not Cora the mother, Cora the employee, or Cora the daughter.

But Cora, the goddess.

CHAPTER EIGHTEEN

James

The moment I step into Eden, the noise of the outside world fades into silence. Market share, stock prices, investors—they melt away, replaced by a visceral need driving through my veins. Here, I don't think; I simply act.

Dameon, Zac, and I stride through the entrance, handing over our phones to security like we've done a hundred times before. The sense of being watched isn't new to me. Our presence is expected here, even revered. But tonight, my focus is elsewhere. The usual surge of pride I feel from the attention doesn't land the same. I'm scanning the room for just one person.

Cora.

Dameon's in his usual easygoing mood, chatting with Zac as we make our way through the club. I listen to their banter and can't help but feel lucky to have Dameon watching my back. Given our families' business partnership, our friendship was practically written in the stars, but when we discovered our shared taste for submissive women, it cemented our bond even further. Finding Eden a couple of years ago was like stumbling across paradise.

We met Zac at university. Back then he was dreaming of becoming a leading surgeon; these days he's buried under hospital admin and rotations most of the time. We rarely see him anymore. His life is chaos, much like Carter's, who's off on some endless world tour again. Fame has its perks, but I'll never understand the appeal of not being able to move freely. There's something to be said about anonymity, about being able to slip in and out of places unnoticed. Being based in Australia the past few years has meant that, for once, I've flown under the radar a little more. Fewer eyes tracking my every move, fewer paparazzi following me around. Out here, I'm just another face, able to go about my life without the constant glare of the New York press and the expectation that I'm always one misstep away from scandal.

But even as they talk, my mind is somewhere else. It's been there all week, in fact, ever since Monday morning when I saw her in the auditorium. I've been watching her—studying her movements, analyzing her every shift in expression. At first I tried to convince myself I was being cautious, ensuring she wouldn't fuck me over. But deep down, I know that's bullshit.

Dameon glances at me. "You're wound up tight," he comments. "Eden's supposed to be where you *unwind*, remember?"

I grunt in response, barely acknowledging him. My eyes are still scanning the room, searching for her. And then I see her.

Cora.

She's standing at the bar, her back turned to me, fingers lightly drumming on the counter as she waits for her drinks. The black satin gown she's wearing clings to her body, accentuating the soft slope of her waist, the line of her spine. The way her hair cascades down her back makes my fists itch with the need to grip it—to wrap it around my hand and pull. Fire surges through me, tightening every muscle in my body, my cock thickening in my trousers.

Beside me Dameon chuckles, noticing the direction of my stare. "Ah, there she is."

She commands my focus, every movement drawing me in deeper, like she's the only thing in the room that matters.

Then, as if sensing my attention, her body stiffens. Her fingers freeze mid-drum, and she slowly turns around, scanning the room. The moment our eyes lock, it's like I've physically grabbed hold of her. Her chest rises, lips part, and a delicious flush colors her throat. She's caught in my gaze, and she knows it.

"She's stunning when she blushes like that," Dameon murmurs. His eyes appraise her longer than I'd like. I shoot him a warning glance, but he just laughs under his breath. He's pushing me, testing the waters. But Cora isn't just another toy to be shared—not this time.

Without a word, I stride toward the bar, my pulse quickening with every step. I catch the bartender's eye as I approach, leaning in to whisper my request into her ear. She nods, casting a glance at Cora before moving to prepare our drinks. Dameon and Zac take their seats at the bar, but my attention stays solely on her.

I can sense her eyes on me as I make my way toward one of the couches at the back of the club. Taking a seat, I let my eyes drift over the room, casually scanning the crowd, but my attention keeps returning to her. She's been instructed to serve me, and the air between us tightens, like a cord pulled taut, vibrating with unspoken tension—dark, electric, and inevitable. At last, she moves, her hips swaying deliberately as she walks toward me. She's putting on a show, and I can't help but admire her boldness. She knows exactly what she's doing, and it's working.

Kneeling before me, she sets the whiskey down on the low table beside the couch. The sight of her on her knees triggers a deep, primal need within me. *Control. Power.* This is where she belongs—kneeling before me, waiting for my command. But there's also a trace of need beyond dominance. It's not just about control anymore. It's her. And that's dangerous.

"Can I get you anything else, sir?" she asks softly. Her voice is demure but her eyes flash with a hint of defiance maybe, or curiosity. Either way, I'm hooked.

I let the question hang in the air, savoring the way her posture tenses ever so slightly. Silence is often more powerful than words.

Slowly, deliberately, I bring the glass to my lips, letting the burn of the whiskey settle in my gut before I lower the glass. I lick my lips and lean forward.

"Nothing." My tone is cold and controlled, and the word drops between us like a stone, sinking into the silence.

Her eyelashes flutter, momentarily stunned. Clearly she was expecting a response—something, anything—but I gave her nothing.

Good. Let the frustration sink in.

Minutes tick by, and Cora begins to unravel. Her composure starts to slip, and when her eyes flick up to meet mine, I can see the fire in them.

"What the hell is your problem?" she hisses. Her voice is low, but the heat behind it burns hotter than her blush.

I chuckle, running my thumb over my bottom lip as I settle deeper into the couch. "That didn't take long," I murmur. "Breaking the rules already, are we?"

Her eyes are defiant, but she holds her tongue, waiting for my next move.

"You look perfect on your knees for me. That's where you belong, my sweet slut."

A sharp breath escapes her, her lips parting on instinct. Her body betrays her, drawn toward the authority of my voice like a moth to a flame. I can tell she hates how much my words affect her, and that's what makes it all the more satisfying.

I spread my legs, extending one toward her until the tip of my shoe touches her knee.

Let's see how far she'll go.

"Lift your gown," I command. "Kneel directly on the floor, knees spread apart."

Her fingers pause, gripping the satin fabric a little tighter than necessary. There's a slight hesitation before she moves, slowly gathering the gown and parting her knees, falling perfectly into place.

"Good girl," I praise. Her breath hitches at the compliment, her body trembling.

Slowly I slip the tip of my shoe beneath her gown, brushing it against her bare, wet pussy. The contact is light, teasing, but it's enough that a soft moan escapes her lips. The sound goes straight to my cock, making it weep in need.

"Shh," I murmur, watching her intently. "You don't want us to get kicked out, do you?"

She shakes her head quickly, her breath coming in shallow, ragged bursts. I drag the tip of my shoe along her slit, up and down, slow enough to make her squirm, to make her *want more.*

"Ride my foot," I growl, my tone as sharp as the command itself.

Her eyes widen and she frantically looks around. But she doesn't protest. She's too far gone for that.

"No one is looking," I reassure her.

Her hips move tentatively at first, testing, adjusting, but soon she's grinding against my shoe, her movements becoming more desperate, more frenzied. Her need is written all over her face.

Her eyes meet mine, silently begging for permission, for release.

"Come," I grant, my voice just above a whisper.

Her body shudders violently, a silent scream parting her lips as she comes hard. She clings to my leg for support, her forehead resting against my trousers as she trembles.

When she finally lifts her head, her face is flushed, her eyes glassy with the aftershocks of pleasure. Embarrassment flashes across her features, but I don't let it settle.

"Beautiful," I whisper. There's pride in the way I say it, like she's a work of art I've crafted with my own hands. "We're far from finished."

I glance at my shoe, which is now glistening with her arousal, and a wicked smile tugs at my lips.

"Lick it clean," I command. "You made this mess; now fix it."

Her eyes widen, a flush deepening across her cheeks as my demand sinks in. But this time there's no hesitation in her movements. She lowers herself again, bending down toward my shoe, her face inching closer. Her lips part and her tongue darts out, tentatively at first, tasting her own essence on the polished leather.

A deep satisfaction coils in my gut as I watch her on her knees, meticulously cleaning up after herself. She's fully committed, and as she arches her back, making a show of it, a quiet whimper slips from her throat. She's performing, knowing exactly what it does to me.

I lean back, savoring the control, the power of it all. The longer she continues, the more my body throbs with need. My cock is painfully hard, straining against my pants, but I don't move. I let her finish, aware of the effect this is having on both of us.

When she's done, she sits back on her heels, looking up at me with wide eyes, her breath still uneven.

Reaching down, I grab her chin between my thumb and forefinger, tilting her face up so that our eyes connect. The possessive heat in my gaze must be unmistakable because her pupils dilate, her lips parting again as if she's forgotten how to breathe.

"Give me a taste."

She crawls forward, leaning into me as I pull her up, our faces only inches apart. The moment our lips meet, the rest of the world vanishes. There's nothing but hunger between us, the way her mouth moves against mine, the taste of her submission mixed with the raw ache of my own need. I deepen the kiss, taking control of it, feeling her melt against me.

But as much as I want to lose myself in her, I know we can't. Not here, not like this. Reluctantly I pull back, ending the kiss far too soon, though the taste of her still lingers on my lips.

She's staring at me, her eyes glazed with lust, her chest heaving.

"Mmm... Delicious." I lick my lips, savoring the flavor of her submission.

Her eyes drop, and I follow it to my lap. The outline of my erection is painfully obvious, straining against my pants, begging for release. A small, teasing smile crosses her face.

"That must be painful," she whispers.

"You have no idea," I reply, my lips curving into a smirk. "But it was worth it."

Her smile widens, and for a brief moment, there's a spark between us that isn't just about power or control. It's more than just the dynamic of dominance and submission. It's the way she looks at me, the way her eyes linger on mine, but the moment passes as quickly as it arrived.

We're still in Eden, surrounded by others, and there are rules we have to follow. No matter how much I want to take this further, to push her even more, I know there's a time and place for everything. And right now, we've reached the limit of what we can do here.

I release her chin, sinking back into the couch, my eyes never leaving hers.

"Thank you, sir."

I dip my head, acknowledging her submission. This is just the beginning, and we both know it.

"Go," I say. "Before I decide to break any more rules tonight."

She stands slowly, her body still trembling. For a moment, she hesitates, as if she's waiting for me to call her back, to pull her into something more. But I don't.

She nods once, her cheeks still flushed, then turns and walks away. The sway of her hips as she moves has my jaw clenching, my body thrumming with desire. I watch her until she disappears through the employee door behind the bar, and even then, my eyes stay fixed on the space she occupied.

Cora Rossi.

I thought coming to Eden tonight would help me regain control, but all it's done is stir a deeper need inside me.

This isn't just about power.

This is about *her.*

Dameon and Zac settle into the couches beside me, shattering the hold my thoughts had over me. Zac raises his eyebrows, taking a slow sip from his drink. "Well, that was... intense."

I don't respond, my mind still lingering on Cora's flushed face, the way her body reacted to me, the way she looked at me afterwards.

"You're playing a dangerous game," Zac says quietly. "She's not like the others, and you know it."

Dameon leans back with that easy smile, but his gaze is sharp, like he's watching me more closely than usual. We've been through years of this—shared women, shared power—but Cora has made him curious. "She's different," he agrees.

I shoot him a look. I know exactly what he means, but I'm not in the mood to discuss it.

He chuckles. "Man, you're in for it now."

I already know that. And yet, I can't stop myself.

I don't want to.

My eyes drift back to where Cora disappeared, my pulse still racing. This is far from over.

Not by a long shot.

Chapter Nineteen

Cora

The soft whirr of the projector fills the boardroom as I fumble with the laptop, trying to get my presentation to sync. Nathan hovers beside me, hands in his pockets, offering the occasional useless suggestion with his trademark grin.

"Did you try turning it off and on again?" he offers.

I shoot him a dry look. "Thanks for that high-level tech advice, Nathan. I'm sure IT will be thrilled to know they can retire."

He snorts, leaning casually against the table. "Hey, just trying to help."

My fingers fumble over the keys, a fine tremor I can't control. The damn projector isn't the problem—it's my heartbeat pounding in my ears. My mind keeps drifting back to Eden, to James—the way his eyes bored into mine, the power in his voice as he called me his *sweet slut*. It's been impossible to forget.

I can still feel the touch of his foot between my legs, the way my body responded to his every command. And then, as if that weren't enough, *Dameon freaking Hayward* was *right there,* watching everything unfold.

A flush creeps up my neck. I've spent the entire morning trying not to think about it, but it's impossible. Every time my mind drifts back to James, to the way his voice enveloped me like velvet, I feel that same rush of heat. And then mortification follows. Because let's face it—Dameon *definitely* saw everything. And now I'm about to stand in front of both him and James, pretending that Saturday night didn't happen, pretending that I'm just another competent employee giving a presentation to senior management.

I glance at the clock: 9.55 a.m. They'll be here any minute.

I fiddle with the cord connecting the projector, and my presentation finally displays on the screen.

Thank fuck.

"Are you alright?" Nathan asks, tilting his head as he watches me scroll through the slides.

"Just nerves," I lie, forcing a smile. "Everything needs to be perfect."

Nathan leans in closer, raising an eyebrow. "Uh-huh. You're totally fine. Definitely not on the verge of a nervous breakdown or whatever." He rolls his eyes but thankfully drops it. "Well, at least you look like a boss. Vintage cream pantsuit, black stilettos? You're giving off some serious 'don't fuck with me' vibes today. Plus, the ponytail?" He mimes a chef's kiss. "You're killing it."

I laugh, the strain easing just a little. "Glad you approve, fashion police."

He grins. "You're lucky I don't have the power to fine you. With the amount of outfit repeating you've been doing, I'd be making a killing."

I smirk, shaking my head as I adjust the collar of my cream blazer, feeling a tad self-conscious. It's been years since I bought myself anything new to wear. "And here I thought you were just in HR for the paperwork."

"Hey," he protests, feigning hurt, "I'm multifaceted. Some days I'm a people person, some days I'm a fashion guru. Today, I'm both. I brought my A game."

"Clearly," I reply dryly, though his light-hearted teasing does manage to chip away at my anxiety, if only for a second. Nathan knows how to diffuse tension without making a big deal out of it.

I check the clock again. It's 9.58 a.m. Almost time.

Executives trickle in, taking their seats with the quiet efficiency of people accustomed to long meetings. Fingers tap rhythmically on keyboards, eyes flick between laptop screens and paperwork. A few thumb through their phones, barely looking up. The soft murmur of idle chatter mixes with the hum of the projector.

Nathan watches me for a beat, his grin fading. He leans in, dropping his voice. "You're going to be fine, Cora. You've got this."

I nod, grateful for the pep talk. I've prepared all week for this; I'm ready. Even so, the knowledge does little to calm the nervous flutter in my stomach.

"Thanks, Nathan." I manage a smile. "Hopefully I still have a job in an hour."

Before he can respond, the door swings open.

James strides into the room first, with Dameon close behind. Their entrance draws the attention of everyone already seated, the soft chatter instantly evaporating. My breath falters, the weight of James's presence constricting my lungs. I swear the air in the room shifts when he's here.

James is, as always, devastatingly handsome, his tailored suit fitting him like a glove. He exudes power with every step. But it's Dameon who makes my nerves spark to life. The glint in his eyes tells me everything I need to know—he hasn't forgotten Saturday night. He knows exactly what happened between James and me.

Heat rises to my cheeks, my mouth suddenly dry. I struggle to hold Dameon's gaze—it's like looking into the eyes of someone who knows all my secrets. I swallow hard, trying to keep my expression neutral.

James is all business, his face giving nothing away. But Dameon... his smirk is unmistakable.

Shit.

"Morning," James says coolly, his eyes sweeping the room before landing on me. "Cora, Nathan."

Nathan gives a nod, unfazed as ever, but I'm not nearly as composed. I force a smile, but it's stiff, like a mask barely holding together. My fingers dig into the sides of the projector remote, as if gripping it hard enough will keep my nerves in check. But when James looks at me, I feel it again—that slip of control, like trying to hold water in my hands.

"Good morning, Mr. Hayes, Mr. Hayward," I reply, my voice steady even though my pulse is racing.

Dameon shoots me a wink, his smirk growing a little wider.

Oh God. He's definitely enjoying this.

Nathan settles into the chair beside me at the front of the room, while James and Dameon take their seats at the far end of the table. James rests against the chair back, one arm resting casually on the armrest, but there's nothing relaxed about him. He's watching—waiting. His silence isn't passive; it's charged.

I clear my throat, gripping the remote again as if it's my safety net. All eyes are on me. The words are right there, on the tip of my tongue, but for a split second, everything freezes—James's steady gaze, Dameon's smirk, Nathan's silent support. It all feels like a pressure cooker, ready to burst. I force myself to breathe, to remain calm. "Now that we're all present, let's begin. Thank you, everyone, for your time today…"

I click the first slide into view, praying the presentation goes smoothly—and that I can get through the next hour without dying of embarrassment.

Cora stands at the front of the room, poised and professional, but all I see is the memory of her on her knees, submissive, *mine*. I shake my head slightly and refocus. Her cream pants hug her ass in a way that distracts me more than it should. That high ponytail? It's a temptation I can't ignore. I want to grab it, feel the smooth strands in my fist, yank her close. But it's more than that. It's the control, the power she gave me, and how easily she slipped into a subservient role. It unnerves me how much I crave it.

My heart races at the thought, and I have to force myself to remain still. But inside, it's chaos. That word—*mine*—echoes in my head. And it terrifies me how true it feels. I push down the possessive urge building in my chest. She's here to work, and today is her test.

I settle back in my seat, fingers moving to my chin as I focus on her. I'm here to see what Cora is really capable of. If she is here on merit or if this entire thing has been some intricately plotted manipulation. If she'll sink or swim. Though deep down, I already know—she'll swim. She has no idea how closely I've been watching her since she walked into my company. Today, this presentation, it's the final piece of her test. If she nails this, she stays. But trust doesn't come easily to me, and especially not with her. I've been blackmailed before. I've let women in, let them play their mind-games, and I've paid the price. I can't let Cora do the same. She might be beautiful and brilliant, but that doesn't make her trustworthy. If she's playing me, she could ruin everything. And I'll be damned if I let that happen.

I glance at Dameon. His smirk says it all—he hasn't forgotten Saturday night. Hell, it's his kink, watching people unravel. And I've been fully absorbed in her; I almost forgot he saw everything.

Almost.

Cora's words flow smoothly as she outlines her three-step strategy to improve company culture. She's calm, composed, the picture of professionalism.

As she clicks through the slides, I can't shake the thought: *She's too perfect. Too poised.* There's no hesitation, no nervous stammer, no visible crack in her armor. Is she really this good, or is this all part of her act?

My eyes narrow as I watch her closely. If she is manipulating me, she's doing a fine job of it. But then again, that's what makes manipulation effective, isn't it? The way it makes you doubt your instincts.

Beside me, Dameon crosses his arms, his attention fixed lazily on her, but I know him well enough to see his mind at work. He's taking in her every move, calculating. Cora's confidence doesn't faze him—if anything, it amuses him, challenges him. But my attention isn't on him right now; it's on her, on the cadence of her words and the flawless composure she maintains. She's undeniably talented. The strategy she's pitching isn't just well-researched; it's exactly what we need. But her suggestion that Dameon and I participate in employee training sessions is the last thing I want to be doing. It's more involvement than I'd prefer, but damn if it isn't effective. She's found the weak points, the gaps, and positioned herself to fill them with a perfect solution. She knows exactly how to play this.

She finishes with a confident, "Thank you," and waits, completely unruffled as the room fills with quiet murmurs of approval and applause. My executive team exchange glances, nodding to one another. She's done her job well. She didn't just swim; she blew everyone out of the water. She earned her place here. And now? I've got a whole new set of problems on my hands.

Dameon and I rise as everyone begins gathering their things. Cora makes her way over to us.

"Well done, Cora," Dameon says. "Can't wait to see you bring that plan to life."

With a deliberate wink, he turns and strides out of the boardroom, leaving Cora and me standing there as the rest of the team filters out around us.

Her cheeks flush a delicate pink as she quickly covers her face with her hands, but it's too late—it's obvious she remembers. I can see it in the way her eyes widen, the way she avoids looking directly at him.

Once the room is empty, she turns to me, her eyes wide. "Did he see *everything* at Eden?" she whispers.

I can't help but chuckle. "Trust me," I say, "Dameon didn't miss a thing. And knowing him, he enjoyed every second of it."

She groans, pressing her hands to her face again. "God…"

I grab her wrists, pulling her hands down and holding them in mine. My thumb strokes the soft skin of her knuckles, and I relish the contact for just a second. "You were amazing, Cora. There's nothing to be ashamed of."

She looks up at me, her eyes softening, and I can see it—the need for reassurance. I meant every word. She was beyond amazing. She exceeded every expectation I had. The way her body responded to me wasn't forced or calculated—it was instinct. It was real. And it was *us*—a perfect alignment of kinks. The way she reacts to praise, and exhibitionism with a touch of degradation, is beautiful.

I drop her hands, stepping back, distancing myself. There's no room for this here. Not now. "You were amazing in here too," I add. "Even though I'm not thrilled about spending time with my employees."

She laughs, her smile lighting up her face. For a second, my chest tightens.

What the hell is happening to me?

"So, does that mean I get to keep my job?" she asks, a playful smirk curling at her lips.

"For now," I tease, though there's more weight to my words than she realizes. I still don't know if I can trust her. There are too many unanswered questions. But one thing's for sure—I'm not ready for her to walk out of my life yet.

She laughs again, a sound that almost makes me smile.

"Really good work today, Cora," I remark, my words clipped and professional. I give her a tight smile and turn on my heel, making my way out of the boardroom. The door closes behind me with a soft *click*, but the smell of vanilla and citrus doesn't leave me.

I walk briskly to my office, my mind replaying her words, her expressions. By the time I sink into my chair, my mind is a fucking mess. Only one thought keeps running on a loop.

What the fuck am I doing?

I'm not used to this—this obsession. I pull up her HR file on my screen, willing something—*anything*—to stand out, to give me a reason to cut her loose. As I scan through it, a sense of relief hits me—she's out of Sinclair's reach now. And for a fleeting moment, a smug satisfaction settles in; she's here now, away from that prick and working under my roof.

Just as I'm about to shut the file, my phone rings, Sam's name flashing across the screen. Without hesitation, I snatch it up.

"Sam. Did you run the credit check on Cora Rossi?"

"Yes. And..." Sam hesitates for a beat. "She's in serious financial trouble."

As Sam runs through the details—medical bills, maxed-out credit cards, a mountain of debt—a knot forms in my gut. She's drowning in it. The pieces start to fall into place—why she's working two jobs, why she took my money.

"Who's the patient? Is it her?"

"No. A family member. Someone named Anthony Rossi."

My shoulders relax slightly. Family, then. Likely her father or brother. But that lingering question remains.

Can I trust her?

I hang up, staring at my screen. I'm no clearer than before. Financial trouble, family in the hospital—it all makes sense. Too much sense. And that's what's bothering me. What if it's all a cover? What if she's planted this story just to gain my sympathy, to worm her way in?

There's only one way to find out.

For now, Cora stays.

CHAPTER TWENTY-ONE

Cora

"So, what's the latest with you and the big boss man?" Nathan asks, spearing a piece of lettuce.

We're working through our lunch break at my desk, tying up loose ends for the leadership training session later this afternoon. Since my presentation went off without a hitch, I've settled into a more comfortable rhythm at work. It's gratifying to see my three-step plan rolling out. First up: modern leadership training for department heads and upper management.

"Well, he's finally gotten his head out of his ass," I deadpan, not glancing away from my computer screen.

Nathan chokes on his salad, eyes bulging as I pat him on the back. "I swear, one of these days, you're going to make me die laughing. That'll be on your conscience, Rossi."

I laugh, shaking my head. "You're a hazard in the office, you know that?"

"Yeah, yeah," he waves me off, taking a sip of water. "At least I'll die entertained."

The truth is, James has changed. The man who looked at me with nothing but suspicion and icy restraint has softened—though I'm not sure if it's due to the success of my presentation or what happened between us at Eden. Either way, the tension between us has shifted into something else. Something much more intimate.

I want to drop to my knees for him when he glances my way with that all-consuming heat in his eyes. I am stupidly attracted to this man.

Heat floods my cheeks, and I squirm in my chair.

"Your blush tells me there's more to the story here." Nathan points his salad fork at me with narrowed eyes.

"There's nothing to tell," I lie, quickly biting into my sandwich.

"Fine, fine. Keep all the juicy goss to yourself. Just so you know, though, I'm living vicariously through you."

I smile, fighting the urge to spill. There's no way I can tell Nathan about what happened between James and me at Eden. The memory of submitting to him in front of Dameon still burns, both thrilling and mortifying.

Nathan picks up on my silence and, with an intentional smirk, drops the subject.

"Hey, do you think this is the right approach for the second training session?" I ask, scrolling through the outline on my computer.

Nathan leans over my desk, reviewing the document. "Looks good to me, but you might want to add a segment on conflict resolution. You know how the execs love those buzzwords."

I nod, making a mental note. "You're right. Good catch."

"Anytime." He shoots me a wink. "Teamwork makes the dream work, Rossi."

Nathan might joke around, but he never lets me down when it comes to work. I'm lucky to have him in my corner.

We finish our lunch in relative quiet, the upcoming session looming over us both.

As the time nears, I head to James's office to make sure he shows. Portia looks up from her computer as I arrive and gives me a reassuring nod. "He's aware of the training," she says, lips quirking. "It's blocked off in his calendar."

I let out a small laugh. "Thank you." We both know he would totally blow it off.

Pushing open the door to his office, I step inside quietly. James looks up from behind his desk, his hardened features softening as his eyes land on me.

"Are you here to escort me, Cora?" he asks, his tone teasing, but there's a glint in his eyes—an undercurrent of dominance that always makes my core clench.

"Just making sure you come," I reply, the words tumbling out before I realize the double entendre. My cheeks flame, and I wish I could take it back.

His lips curve up in that infuriatingly sexy grin that weakens my knees. "Oh, my sweet slut, thank you for looking out for my needs."

His eyes sweep over my body like a physical touch, igniting a fire under my skin that instantly dampens my panties.

Just like that, I'm undone.

He crooks a finger, beckoning me closer. "Come here." His voice is like silk, dangerous and tempting, draping over me.

My body obeys before my mind catches up. Without thinking, I take a step forward, my heels clicking softly on the marble floor. The space between us crackles with electricity. As I approach, his eyes darken, filling with that familiar hunger that sets my body alight.

He picks up a small remote, aiming it at the door. The soft whirr of the frosted glass walls sliding into place fills the room, followed by the solid click of the door locking. We're completely alone.

The air shifts. The dynamic between us is undeniable, the power exchange evident.

"Are you wet for me?"

I swallow hard, my throat suddenly dry, and nod.

"Show me," he demands.

With shaky hands, I lift the hem of my skirt, letting the fabric bunch around my waist. The cool air hits my bare skin as I slide my thong down my legs, stepping out of it with deliberate care.

James picks up the scrap of lace, bringing it to his face and inhaling deeply. His eyes close as he savors the scent. "You smell fucking incredible."

My breath falters. I perch myself on the edge of his desk, leaning back on my elbows for balance. I spread my legs, placing my heels on the armrests of his chair, completely baring myself to him. The cold surface of the glass desk against my skin is an exquisite contrast to the heat building inside me.

His eyes, dark with hunger, sweep over my exposed pussy. He leans forward, trailing two fingers up my inner thigh, grazing my slick heat. He dips them inside me briefly before pulling them out, bringing them to his mouth. His eyes roll back as he sucks my essence from his fingers. "Delicious," he growls.

The low, guttural sound makes my pussy clench. Hard.

"I love how wet you get for me. So responsive." He thrusts his fingers back into me, then slides them out, offering them to my lips. "Taste yourself," he commands. "Taste how sweet you are."

I open my mouth, obedient, and wrap my lips around his fingers, swirling my tongue, cherishing the taste. I close my eyes, imagining it's his cock instead.

The cold glass beneath me does little to quench the fire burning between my legs. The thrill of being so exposed, of being watched, heightens every sensation.

I'm lost in the moment, my mind consumed by his touch, but then his phone rings, cutting through the haze like a sharp blade.

James's expression hardens as he reclines back in his chair. "Don't move."

I freeze, every muscle in my body tense, as he answers the phone. His eyes never leave my body, locked onto the sight of me spread open before him. As the seconds tick by, I start to squirm, my desire slowly dripping down my thighs and pooling beneath me. My hips shift, seeking relief.

His eyes flick up to mine, a warning passing through them. *Not an inch*, his lips mouth.

I bite my lip, forcing myself to still, the tension between us growing unbearable. I struggle to focus on his conversation. My body aches for his touch, to finish what he started.

With the phone still pressed to his ear, he leans forward and runs his tongue up the length of my slit. The sensation is too much. I gasp, my hands gripping the edge of the desk, trying and failing to keep quiet.

"I'll have to call you back." James's voice comes out muffled with his face buried in my pussy. I'm struggling to remain quiet as his words vibrate against my core and he hangs up just before I let out a loud breathy moan.

James dives in deeper, sucking my clit into his mouth, and I cry out. The anticipation, the denial, has built to the point that it only takes a few more strokes of his tongue before I explode, my body convulsing against his face as the orgasm rips through me. The room fades and I arch my spine, throwing my head back.

James's lips linger on my thighs as I come down from the high, every inch of me throbbing. The world feels like it's tilting, as though every sense has been heightened and sharpened by him. His mouth is still wet from me, his breath hot on my skin, and all I want is to keep him there. To stay in this haze. He pulls back, wiping his chin with the back of his hand, a self-satisfied grin firmly in place.

"Good girl," he murmurs.

Never in a million years would I have thought I had a praise kink, but sure enough, every time he says "good girl," I melt into a puddle.

I can't believe we just did that on his desk.

I blink, the reality of what just transpired crashing over me. We're at work. In his office. *He's my boss.*

My heart pounds for an entirely different reason now. I jump off the desk, smoothing down my skirt as panic creeps in. "Shit! They've probably already started." I glance at the clock, my heart sinking.

James pushes his chair back. There's a smug glint in his eyes as he drags his fingers through his tousled hair like he has all the time in the world.

"They'll wait." He shrugs, as though what we shared hadn't been both dangerous and delicious. "They'll survive without us for a few minutes."

"That was insane," I whisper under my breath, trying to pull myself together. My hands are shaking. "We're at work, James."

I struggle to catch my breath. The adrenaline is still running through my veins, but the reality of what we just did is quickly sobering me up.

I hold my hand out, palm up, waiting for him to return my thong. "Please?"

He arches an eyebrow, his smirk deepening as he slips my panties into his pocket. "Not a chance."

I blink, the flush creeping back up my neck. "James—"

"No panties for you." His voice is firm, final. He's already back in control. "If I have to sit through this session with a hard-on, bored out of my mind, I want your panties in my pocket and the taste of you on my tongue."

My mouth goes dry, heat flooding me all over again. "Are you serious?"

"Deadly." He stands, buttoning his suit jacket, looking entirely too composed. Like he wasn't just buried between my legs two minutes ago.

"I want you to sit there, wet and sticky, a constant reminder of where my mouth has just been."

My pulse leaps at his words. But there's no time to argue, and the way his eyes are burning into me says that I wouldn't win this fight anyway.

I take a breath, trying to focus. *I can do this.* It's just a leadership training session. Simple. Professional. Easy.

But as James walks around the desk, his hand brushing my arm, I realize nothing about this is going to be simple.

"Let's go, Cora." He presses lightly at the small of my back, guiding me toward the door. "We don't want to keep them waiting too long, do we?"

I exhale shakily, nodding as I follow his lead. What just happened hangs in the air like a fog, and I can't help but feel we've blurred a line we were never meant to cross.

The door swings open, and the cool air outside his office is like a slap to my flushed skin. I take a calming breath, trying to compose myself as I walk beside him, my heels clicking against the floor.

The walk down the hall to the elevator feels longer than usual, each step reminding me that I'm bare underneath my skirt, vulnerable. Each step is a reminder of the intensity between us, still lingering like a touch I can't brush off.

I can't believe he's making me go through with this.

We reach the boardroom, and I'm grateful it's already full. Everyone is seated, their eyes glued to their laptops or notebooks, oblivious to what just transpired. I slide into a seat at the back, the cold chair sending a jolt through me as I settle in, painfully aware of the dampness between my legs.

James takes the seat next to me, perfectly composed, as if nothing out of the ordinary has happened. I, on the other hand, am going to combust any second.

Nathan catches my eye from across the room, his smile easy as usual. He waves, and I force myself to smile back, hoping it doesn't look as strained as it feels.

You alright? he mouths, raising an eyebrow.

I give him a quick nod, knowing full well that I am anything but alright. My mind is stuck on the fact that James is sitting so close, his knee brushing against mine under the table. His presence is so potent I can sense his gaze on me even when I'm not looking.

The session begins and I try to focus on the speaker, but my thoughts keep drifting. Every shift in my seat, every subtle movement reminds me of the fact that I'm sitting here, completely bare under my skirt, while James watches me like a hawk.

He leans in close, and whispers against my ear. "What are you thinking about?"

My breath catches in my throat. "James—"

"I bet you're dripping for me right now." His tone is dark, teasing, his lips so close that they almost brush my earlobe as he speaks. "Aren't you, Ms. Rossi?"

I swallow hard, squeezing my thighs together in a feeble attempt to find some relief, but it only makes it worse. The pressure coils tighter, the heat spreading through me like a blazing inferno.

I glance around, praying no one notices the flush creeping up my neck, the way my body betrays me with every word he speaks.

Nathan shoots me a curious look from across the table. I force another smile, hoping it'll be enough to satisfy him.

James, of course, is completely composed, acting like it's just another meeting. But the hand he rests on my knee beneath the table tells a different story. His fingers slide up my thigh, the touch barely there but enough to drive me to the edge.

I grip the table, knuckles white as I struggle to keep my breathing even.

"You'll thank me later," he whispers, his fingers brushing the sensitive skin at the top of my thigh, dangerously close to where I need him most.

I bite my lip, trying to hold back the whimper threatening to escape, the world around me disappearing into the background. All I can focus on is James. His touch. His control.

But then the session wraps, and just like that, the room begins to stir. Laptops close, people shuffle papers, and I realize with a sudden rush of panic that it's over.

I stand, my legs shaky, my mind still reeling.

James rises beside me, his expression unreadable as he slips his hand into his pocket.

"Well," he says, that damn grin back on his face, "that was enlightening."

I glance at him, my cheeks burning, and mutter, "You're impossible."

He leans in, his lips close to my ear once more. "And you love it."

Before I can respond, he turns and strides out of the room like he owns the place.

And damn it, he does.

CHAPTER TWENTY-TWO

James

The training session was *excruciatingly* boring, exactly as I'd predicted. Motivating and inspiring teams, emotional intelligence, active listening—all valuable for my employees. But I had to sit there, nodding along like I didn't have a thousand more productive things to do.

What a monumental waste of time.

The only thing that kept me from losing it completely was Cora sitting next to me. I couldn't stop thinking about her, knowing she was bare under her skirt, wet and sticky. The power of that knowledge was almost enough to make the session tolerable.

I'll admit, the idea of making her wear a vibrator next time, letting me control her pleasure remotely, is tempting. Watching her squirm in need while trying to stay composed would definitely spice up these sessions. Hell, I'd probably attend willingly then.

But that's dangerous thinking. And Cora's already bringing out too much of that in me.

Before I can dwell too long on those thoughts, the door to my office opens, and *she* walks in, accompanied by Dameon. The moment she steps into my office, I feel it again—that unsettling pull in my chest, the one I can't name. It's not just lust; it's deeper, and it lingers too long after she's gone. Every time I see her, it claws a little further into me, harder to ignore, harder to shake. And I hate it as much as I need it.

Cora is radiant in a tight black dress that perfectly highlights every inch of her body. It's a battle to keep my composure, especially when all I can think about is bending her over my desk. If only Dameon would fuck off, I could do exactly that.

She takes a seat across from me, her beaming smile momentarily taking my breath away. God, she's beautiful. Too beautiful. The way her smile reaches her eyes messes with my head. I'm not here for feelings—I'm here for power, for pleasure. Yet, every time she looks at me like that, the foundation shifts beneath me, and it's a reminder that I'm not in complete control. Not of her, and sure as hell not of myself. This feeling is getting harder to keep buried. Whatever it is, I know one thing: I feel a hell of a lot more alive when she's around.

"Thank you for meeting with me today," she starts, her voice smooth and polished, though she flashes a sly smile my way. "And more importantly, thank you both for your active participation in yesterday's session." Her cheeks flush the faintest shade of pink, and it immediately sends blood rushing south.

I will never tire of making her blush.

She pulls out two reports from her bag, handing one to me and one to Dameon. I flip it open, but my focus is only half engaged—my mind is too occupied with thoughts of her spread across my desk.

"I've conducted my research and interviews," she continues, "and I've put together a formal recommendation regarding a few employees."

I set the report down. "Which is?" I ask, a darkness creeping into my voice. I don't tolerate any bullshit in my company, especially not when it comes to harassment or bullying. If that's what this is about, heads will roll.

"There are three employees in upper management," Cora says carefully, her gaze flicking between Dameon and me. "Jenny King, Allan Davies, and Alysha Holland. I believe they're at the root of the toxic culture and the workplace bullying that's responsible for the company's high staff turnover."

My blood pressure spikes instantly. *Those fuckers.* I had my suspicions, but with no concrete evidence, I'd been forced to let it slide. Now, though? I have all the proof I need.

"Consider them gone," I say coolly.

Cora nods solemnly. "Once they're out, you should see a significant improvement in morale."

"Excellent," Dameon chimes in, his eyes sharp. I know that look. He's thinking exactly what I am—losing their jobs isn't punishment enough. But there are limits to what we can do. Legally, at least.

Cora rises from her chair, smoothing her dress. "The next leadership session starts in ten minutes. I'll see you both there, yes?" She arches a delicate brow.

Dameon groans theatrically, making me chuckle. "Wouldn't miss it for the world," he drawls.

Cora claps her hands with exaggerated enthusiasm, a bright smile lighting up her face as she heads for the door. The scent of citrus and vanilla lingers in her wake.

Intoxicating.

When the door closes behind her, Dameon glances up from the report, his expression hard. "They shouldn't get away with this."

"They won't," I respond, my voice like steel. "They'll be blacklisted. I'll make sure they never work in media again."

For a moment we sit in silence, lost in our own thoughts.

"You know... I like her."

I frown, not following. "Who?"

"Cora," Dameon says, lacing his hands behind his head, watching me closely. "She's good for you."

I scoff. "She's good at giving me head, but that's about it."

Dameon quirks a brow. "Keep telling yourself that."

I roll my eyes, tilting back in my chair. "What? You want me to say I like her? That I care?"

He doesn't answer, just holds my gaze until I look away. I don't have time for this. For her. For... whatever the fuck this is.

By the time Dameon and I step into the auditorium, the session is already underway. I hate being late, but a phone call had been unavoidable. Still, when Cora's glare locks onto me from across the auditorium, arms crossed and brows drawn, a chuckle slips out.

She's even more beautiful when she's pissed.

Dameon takes his seat beside me, clearly just as amused by her annoyance, and we settle in as the speaker starts up again. Today's topic is something about giving and receiving constructive feedback in the workplace—complete bullshit, if you ask me. I'm not here to hold hands and sing *Kumbaya*.

Suddenly, the speaker's voice cuts through my thoughts. "Could I ask James to come up on stage?"

I freeze in place. Dameon laughs quietly beside me, attempting to hide his grin behind his hand.

Fuck you, I mouth at him, rising from my seat and reluctantly making my way to the front of the auditorium.

The next thirty minutes are absolute torture. Pure hell. I sit there while the speaker reads *anonymous* feedback from employees, each comment more infuriating than the last. The speaker then instructs everyone on how to communicate more effectively. A celebrity roasting would be more pleasurable. This is just brutal, like getting fucked in the ass with no lube.

The speaker reads aloud: "James walks around like he's always in a foul mood. Would it kill him to smile once in a while? Maybe he just needs to get la—" She cuts herself off abruptly, but it's obvious to me and everyone in the auditorium what she was about to say: *laid*.

An awkward silence fills the room as the speaker clears her throat. "Well then," she says, "remember when offering feedback to use phrases like: 'I see room for improvement here,' or 'The team could benefit from,' or perhaps, 'A better way to handle this might be...'"

I clench my jaw, glaring out into the audience, daring the asshole who wrote that to make eye contact. No one does, of course. They wouldn't dream of it.

But then I catch sight of Cora.

She's shaking with laughter, her shoulders trembling as she tries to hold it in. I narrow my eyes at her, silently promising retribution.

She will pay for this.

The second the session ends, I'm out of my chair, moving fast. My anger builds, gaining momentum with each deliberate step in her direction. Cora's smile dies quickly when she realizes I'm headed straight for her. Her wide eyes snap onto mine, and for a moment, I feel like a predator about to devour my prey.

When I finally reach her seat, I lean in, bracing myself on the armrests, trapping her beneath me. Our faces are close—too close in this public space—and I can feel the sharp inhale of her breath against my skin. My voice is low, just for her. "Get your ass to my office. *Now.* I've got one-on-one *constructive* feedback to give you."

The heat in her eyes is unmistakable. Without another word, I straighten up and walk out of the auditorium, confident that she'll follow.

Less than five minutes later, there's a soft knock on my door.

"Come in," I bark, already loosening my tie. The door swings open, and there she is, standing just inside my office, her chest rising and falling with each breath, her lips parted slightly.

I reach for the remote, frosting the glass walls and locking the door behind her.

"Seems I need to get laid," I deadpan. Her lips twitch, trying to hide a smile, but it's no use. Her eyes sparkle, and the corner of my mouth pulls upward before I can stop it.

"Well, if it'll help improve company morale, sir..." she teases, biting her lip in that way that makes me feral.

"It'll improve a lot more than that," I utter, a dark note threading through my words.

Her smile falters for a second, replaced by an expression that's far more heated. And just like that, we're back in dangerous territory.

"Bend over my desk," I command.

Without hesitation, Cora sashays toward me, her hips swaying provocatively. She's playing this game just as much as I am, and fuck, she's good at it.

She bends over the desk, flashing me a coy look over her shoulder, and I nearly lose it right then. Her ass, perfectly framed in that dress, looks even better than I imagined.

Fuck.

I can barely hold back as I rise from my chair. The fantasy I've been entertaining all morning, all through that mind-numbing and humiliating session, is becoming a reality. And the only thing on my mind is how good she's going to look with my handprint on her ass.

My eyes are fixed on the curve of her hip as I grip the hem of her dress and yank it up, exposing her smooth, bare skin. She's wearing black lace panties, and just the sight of them is enough to push me past my limit.

I pull open my drawer, fingers scrambling for a condom as I unbuckle my belt with the other hand. My breath is already ragged. The anticipation, the desire, thrums through my veins like fire.

Once I've rolled the condom on, I waste no time. I grab the thin lace of her panties, pulling them to the side with one hand,

and run my fingers along her slit. She's already drenched—*so ready for me.*

"Good girl," I growl, unable to stop myself praising her.

She moans softly, arching her back just enough to offer herself to me completely, and that's all the invitation I need. I position myself behind her, my cock hard and throbbing as I thrust into her with a single, deep stroke.

She gasps, her body jerking forward, and I still for a moment, letting her adjust to my size.

The tight heat of her sears me, delivering a rush of ecstasy that nearly unravels my control. But when she pushes back against me, her body telling me she's ready, I start to move. I grip her hips hard, holding her steady as I drive into her with relentless force. The sound of skin slapping against skin fills the office, mingling with her breathy moans.

Her moans—*fuck.* They're the most intoxicating thing I've ever heard. She's so responsive, so eager. Every movement, every sound she makes fuels the fire burning inside me.

Her hair slips easily through my fingers as I gather it in one hand, tugging just hard enough to make her gasp. The sound—it's everything I need. Her body reacts instantly, arching against me, trembling as I drive into her harder, deeper. Every moan, every sharp intake of breath pushes me closer to oblivion, but I hold back, savoring the way she quivers beneath me, how she's helpless against the force of her own pleasure.

"Look at me." I turn her head until her eyes meet mine. They're wide, glazed with need. "You like this, don't you?"

She doesn't answer with words—she doesn't have to. Her body answers for her, clenching around me with a tight, slick heat that makes my head spin.

She's close. So close.

The sensation of her pulsing around me, the way she's completely mine in this moment—it's too much. Yet it's not enough.

With my free hand I slap her ass, hard, and the sharp cry she lets out sends another shot of electricity to my balls.

I could do this forever.

"You ready to come for me?" I grit out.

"Yesss," she wails.

Her body tenses, her muscles contracting as she hurtles toward the brink. I pick up the pace, thrusting faster, harder, chasing that moment when she falls apart in my hands.

And then it happens—her body convulses, her pussy gripping me in a tight vice as she shudders through her orgasm. The sight, the feel of her coming around me, is enough to push me over the cliff with her. With a final, deep thrust, I explode inside her, groaning through my release as pleasure surges through me.

For a few moments, the only sound in the room is our shuddering breaths. My chest is heaving, my mind reeling, struggling to make sense of anything beyond the fog of pleasure.

Slowly I pull out, careful not to hurt her, and after tossing the condom, I grab a few tissues from my desk drawer. Cora stays bent over the desk, her body still trembling with aftershocks as I gently wipe her clean. When I'm done, I pull her panties back into place and smooth down her dress, my fingers brushing over her flushed skin.

She doesn't move for a second, catching her breath, but when she finally pushes up and turns around to face me, there's a serene smile on her lips, and her eyes are half-mast.

God, she's beautiful.

Before I can stop myself, I lean in, pressing my lips to hers. The kiss is soft—too soft. It's not the way I planned for this to end. I pull back quickly at the realization that maybe she's starting to mean something to me. The look in her eyes makes me want to dive back in.

"Dinner. Tonight." The words slip out, more an order than a question. But there's a vulnerability beneath the command, a silent plea that I hope she doesn't notice.

She pauses, eyebrows slowly rising, then her face breaks into one of those bright, beaming smiles that steals the air from my lungs. "Is that an invitation or a demand, sir?"

My breath returns with a shaky inhale. "Does it matter?"

CHAPTER TWENTY-THREE

Cora

Looking at my reflection in the mirror, I can't stop smiling. It's foreign, almost strange, to be this excited about a date. A real date. The kind where you're wined and dined, and the banter is flirtatious and fun. My conversations these past few years have mainly featured phrases like "Put your shoes on, Leo" and "Take that out of your mouth, please." I chuckle, shaking my head. I once caught Leo trying to eat dirt from one of my indoor plants when he was younger.

But this—tonight—is different. It's been so long since I've been on a proper date that my hands tremble as I rummage through my wardrobe, looking for the perfect outfit to knock James's socks off.

I've spent way too much time on my hair and makeup, carefully recreating the sultry look from Eden. My long hair flows down my back in soft waves, and the eyeliner frames my eyes just right.

It's been a while since I've felt like this—alive, desirable, more than just a mom with a to-do list a mile long. I've forgotten what it's like to be seen as a woman, to be looked at the way James looks at me. There's a glint in his eyes that awakens an unfiltered need. Dangerous. Addictive. And I'm not sure how to balance that with everything else.

As I apply my lipstick, my complicated feelings for James resurface. There's no denying we have an intense sexual connection, but beyond that, what else is there? Do we have anything in common other than the fact that we share a child?

I hate that I'm even asking myself these questions. It's not like I have room for complications right now, not with everything I've got on my plate. But James... he's not just another guy. I can't ignore the pull between us, no matter how hard I try. And that's what scares me the most—letting him in. Letting him see the parts of me I've kept hidden. What if I let him too close, only to get burned in the end?

The questions grip me, and my hand falters, leaving a smudge of lipstick on my cheek. I quickly wipe it away, but the thought remains, heavier than before.

Then there's the elephant in the room—Malta. Leo. How do I even bring that up? *Hey, have you ever been to Europe? Oh, you have? That's great! Fun fact, I spent some time in Malta. Oh, you did too? Here's a story: I hooked up with a ridiculously hot guy one night and got pregnant. Pretty sure that guy was you. Surprise!*

The thought makes my insides clench. I can't tell him tonight. I can't risk seeing his face twist in shock, then maybe fall in regret. What if he doesn't want kids? Or what if he freaks out about the scandal of it all and rejects Leo? I don't want to face it—not tonight. I'm not ready to share Leo with anyone—not even his father. Not yet.

The sound of small footsteps makes me smile, and I turn just as Leo bounds into the room. His wide brown eyes light up when he sees me all made up.

"You look so purty, Momma."

I grin, crouching down to plant a big kiss on his forehead, leaving a perfect lip print behind.

"Ew, gross!" Leo scrunches his nose, trying to wipe the lipstick away with the back of his hand.

"Go see what Grandpa's up to," I say, gently nudging him toward the door.

Once he's gone, I slip into my black lace lingerie—a matching bra and panty set, complete with garter belt and stockings—which I haven't worn in ages. It feels strange and exhilarating all at once. I pull on an emerald satin dress, which leaves just the right amount of cleavage on display, and slide into my stilettos. When I look in the mirror, I can't help but do a little happy dance. I feel... beautiful. Alive.

Stepping into the living room, I do a dramatic twirl for Dad and Leo, who are lounging on the couch.

"Wow, you look stunning, darling." Dad rises to give me a warm hug.

"Momma!" Leo adds, his little voice filled with awe.

I laugh, feeling lighter than I have in months. "Thanks, boys."

Dad pulls back, holding me at arm's length and looking me over with a soft smile. "Enjoy tonight. You deserve it. Don't worry about anything."

His words hit me harder than expected, making my throat tighten. I've been carrying such a big load these past few years—raising Leo, taking care of Dad through his illness, the financial stress. One night of freedom feels like a gift.

"Thanks, Dad. I'll try." I blink back the sudden tears threatening to spill and give them both a playful warning. "Alright, behave yourselves and don't stay up too late."

Leo giggles, and they both respond in unison, "We won't!"

Their cheeky smiles make my heart swell, and I leave the house excited for the chance to be a woman for a few precious hours.

When the driver drops me off in front of James's gated mansion, I suck in a quiet breath. This isn't just a mansion—it's an estate. The kind you only see in movies or magazines. The gates swing open, and a man in a black suit seated in a golf cart greets me, introducing himself as security. He escorts me up the long driveway, and as we approach the house, my jaw goes slack.

Venetian-inspired architecture. Manicured gardens. Expansive views of the harbor. It's all stunning. Overwhelming, even. I've stepped into a world where I don't quite fit—a world of privilege.

As we near the entrance of the villa, I spot James waiting for me. Our eyes meet, and my breath escapes in a rush. He looks incredible—dark jeans, a black shirt with the sleeves rolled up, showcasing his powerful forearms. His hair is slicked back, still damp from the shower, and the sight of him sends a flutter of nerves through me.

"Hey." His smile is breathtaking as he reaches for my hand, helping me out of the cart. His eyes rake over me appreciatively. "You look gorgeous."

I bite my lip, feeling the heat rise to my cheeks. "Don't sound so surprised," I tease.

"Not surprised. Just impressed." He keeps my hand in his as we walk toward the villa. "Want a tour?" he asks, amusement dancing in his eyes.

"Oh my God, yes! This place is insane," I reply, glancing around in awe.

James guides me around the estate, and I'm not sure what impresses me more—the grandeur of his home or the way he seems genuinely relaxed, like the weight he carries day in and day out has lightened. As we stroll through the lavish rooms, our hands remain clasped, his thumb brushing over mine in a way that feels intimate, natural. I steal glances at him, marveling at the softer side he's letting me see. This isn't the cold, guarded man I've gotten used to. This is someone else—someone kinder, more open, yet still exuding that undeniable dominance. This is my stranger from Malta.

The tour ends in the courtyard, where a table has been set up under the stars. The soft glow of candles casts a warm light over the scene, and I'm struck by how beautiful it all is.

"I didn't know what you'd like, so I had the chef prepare a little of everything." James gestures to the table overflowing with food from seemingly every cuisine.

I let out a soft laugh. "Wow, you weren't kidding. It looks delicious, but I'm not sure how much you think I can eat."

He grins as we take our seats and pours us both a glass of wine.

The conversation starts light, flowing effortlessly. Until James asks, "So, tell me about your family. The Rossi clan?"

I tense, trying not to show it. The question is innocent enough, but it touches on dangerous ground. I'm not ready for that yet.

"It's just my dad and me," I say, keeping my voice steady. "My mom passed away a few years ago. Car accident." The words are easier to say now, but they still sting. "And Dad's battling cancer, but he's doing well. They caught it early."

James leans forward, his fingers brushing mine. "That's great news. I can't imagine how hard that must've been for you." There's a flicker in his eyes, a flash of pain.

I nod, offering a small smile. "Yeah. He's strong."

His hand retreats, and his jaw tightens slightly, almost imperceptibly. There's a momentary shift in the air between us, like he's somewhere else for a heartbeat. "What about you?" I ask.

He eases back into his chair, smiling, though it doesn't quite reach his eyes. "I've got a younger sister and an adorable niece and nephew. My parents are obsessed with them. Can't get enough."

The warmth in his eyes returns, and for a second, the strain fades. The way he talks about his family makes my heart squeeze. There's a tenderness there, a love that's hard to miss.

We fall into easy conversation after that, talking about everything from our favorite foods to childhood memories—everything except the one thing looming between us: Leo. Malta. But that's fine by me. I'm not ready to deal with that just yet.

By the time we've finished our second bottle of wine, the sexual tension has become distracting. My thoughts are no longer on the conversation but the way his gaze lingers on my lips.

Suddenly I'm standing, moving around the table to straddle him. His words trail off as I settle in his lap, my dress riding up to reveal my garter and stockings.

"Hey there." His hands cradle the back of my head, pulling me closer.

"Hey yourself," I whisper, our lips brushing.

There's no need for more words. I press my lips to his, deepening the kiss as my hand works to undo his jeans. I trail kisses down his neck, tasting the salt of his skin, and he groans when I finally free his hardness from the confines of his jeans.

Not wanting to lose the heat of his body against mine, I slide my panties aside, my breath catching as I position myself over him. I don't wait for a condom. I know it's risky—considering what happened five years ago—but I can't wait another second. I just want him, every inch, just us. The pill will have to be enough. With a slow inhale, I sink down onto him, the slick warmth of my body letting me take him all at once.

I rock against him, my hips moving instinctively, grinding down on his lap. The delicious stretch is all-consuming, and the feel of him buried deep is a sensation I'm becoming addicted to. I arch my back, leaning into the pleasure as his hands tighten on my waist, guiding my movements, controlling the rhythm.

"Fuck," he groans. His fingers dig into my hips, pulling me down harder, faster, the need between us escalating.

I don't care that we're out in the open, the remnants of our dinner still spread across the table and his staff no doubt lingering in the shadows. Nothing matters except this. His touch is fire, and I'm burning alive for him.

His mouth finds mine again, the kiss deep and demanding. I moan into his lips, the pressure coiling tighter with every thrust. The steady slapping of our bodies coming together echoes in the night air. His hands slide up my thighs, brushing the garter straps, before one hand tangles in my hair, pulling me closer. He slaps my ass hard as I bounce on his cock and the sting of pain is exhilarating.

But it's not enough. I need more.

I pull back, my breath hitching. "I need... deeper," I whisper, thick with desperation.

He doesn't hesitate. With a grunt, James stands, lifting me effortlessly as I cling to him, our bodies still locked together. In one swift motion, he sweeps his arm across the table, knocking plates and glasses to the ground in a clatter. The sound is jarring, but I hardly register it, too focused on the clenching in my core.

He lays me down on the edge of the table; his eyes predatory, as he looms over me. With a rough thrust, he hits a spot that has me gasping for air.

"Oh, fuck," I cry out, trembling.

His jaw clenches, his hands gripping my thighs as he pounds into me, each thrust more powerful than the last. The heat in my core intensifies until it's almost unbearable. I dig my nails into his forearms, holding on as the tide breaks.

My body convulses, and for the first time in my life, a gush of liquid releases from within me. My eyes squeeze shut and I let out a strangled moan, my entire body shaking with the force of my orgasm.

The wetness between us is undeniable, soaking my panties and his jeans, but I don't care. All I can think about is how good it feels—how good *he* feels, filling me, claiming me.

James's lips curl into a wicked grin as he thrusts even harder, driving into me with renewed strength. His breath is ragged, the muscles in his arms taut as he pushes us both toward the cliff.

"You're so fucking perfect," he growls low and rough. "Mine. You're mine."

His words send another shockwave through me, and I tighten around him, strangling his cock. He's relentless, his hips slamming into mine with a pace that has me on the verge of another climax. My hands grip the edge of the table, desperate for something to hold on to as he pushes me higher and higher.

"Come for me again," he orders.

I bite my lip, trying to hold back, but it's no use. My body obeys, shuddering as another orgasm rips through me, my pussy clenching around him in pulses. It's too much, too tender, and I can barely breathe as I cry out his name, my voice hoarse.

James isn't far behind. With one final, powerful thrust, he buries himself deep inside me, his body trembling as he finds his release. He throbs inside me, unloading, filling me up as he groans into my neck, his breath hot against my skin.

For a few moments, we stay like that—his body pressed against mine, our breathing labored, hearts racing. The world feels hazy, distant, as we come down from the high, still locked in the afterglow of the moment.

Slowly James pulls out, careful and gentle. The loss is immediate and a soft whimper escapes my lips at the emptiness left behind. His seed trickles out, and I reach for a napkin on the table to clean myself up, but his hand catches my wrist.

"No," he barks. "Leave it."

My eyes widen, but the look in his eyes has me frozen in place.

"I want you to feel it. To feel *me*," he murmurs, his thumb brushing over my swollen clit, making me jolt. "I want you to feel my cum slowly drip down your thighs and be reminded of who owns this pussy."

His words send tingles dancing across my skin, and I nod. My heart races again, a fresh wave of arousal washing over me, despite the fact that I've just come twice.

"I hope you recover quickly," I say, breathless, my lips curling into a playful smile. "Because *your* pussy is hungry again."

"Greedy little thing, isn't she?" His eyes gleam, but beneath the shine, I can still see the lust lurking. "Your wish is my command."

Without warning, he lifts me into his arms, my legs wrapping around his waist as he carries me inside. The smashed remnants of our dinner are forgotten, left behind in the courtyard, but I don't care. All that matters is the feeling of James's strong arms around me, the press of his lips against mine, the promise of more to come.

As we stumble into his bedroom, I laugh against his lips. For the rest of the night, we lose ourselves in each other, our fucking shifting from rough and frantic to softer, sweeter, almost reverent. We don't stop until the early hours of the morning, when exhaustion finally catches up with us.

As dawn breaks, I slip out of James's estate, my body sore in all the best ways, my heart still fluttering from the night we shared. But as I slide into the back of the taxi, the real world begins to worm back in. I rest my head against the cool window and watch the city rush past as we weave through the quiet streets. No matter how much I try to cling to the euphoria, there's a quiet fear I can't quite shake. James is dangerous—not just in the way he touches me, but in the way he makes me feel like I'm his. Like I could fall, and there'd be no coming back. Keeping him out of my heart is going to be harder than I thought. And I'm afraid it might be too late. I have to protect my heart from this man. Because he has the power to destroy it.

Utterly annihilate it.

Chapter Twenty-Four

Cora

His touch lingers, etched into my skin like a phantom. The dull ache in my thighs, the ghost of his breath on my neck—it's all there, refusing to fade. A reminder of everything that happened last night, and everything it could mean.

I sit at my desk with sunlight streaming through the windows and a smile dancing on my lips. It's strange, this feeling—this happiness. Almost like I'd forgotten how it felt.

Last night wasn't just mind-blowing; it was deeper. James let me into his world, beyond the guarded mask he wears at work. Now our dynamic has shifted. But where do we go from here? We've crossed a line and I want more. But a relationship with James isn't just complicated—it's a risk I can't afford to take.

Dread coils within me at the thought of anyone at work finding out. If they knew I was sleeping with the CEO, how would they look at me? Worse, how would they look at the changes I've been fighting for? All the progress I've made to improve the toxic culture would be overshadowed by whispers about how I got here. I've worked too hard to be reduced to a cliché—a woman sleeping her way to the top. And yet, here I am, falling deeper and I can't seem to stop.

He's absolutely irresistible, the way he looks at me like I'm the only woman in the room, the way he seems to trust me—both at work and in those quiet moments we've shared. I have a feeling not many people get to see this side of James, and now that I've glimpsed it, I don't want to let it go.

But ever since our eyes met on my first day, when he stalked across that stage, I've been content to keep my head down, bury the past, and protect Leo from any potential fallout. It felt safer that way. I didn't know the man, and I wasn't about to invite a stranger into our lives. But now... everything's different. I've held onto Leo's secret, convinced it was the only way to protect him. With every moment James pulls me closer, that secret becomes heavier, more suffocating. It's not just guilt weighing me down—it's the fear of what will happen when I finally speak the truth. Will I lose control of the one thing I've kept safe?

Every time I think about telling him, a knot tightens inside me, a mix of fear and dread. What if he's furious? What if he hates me for keeping Leo a secret?

Or... what if he wants to be a father, to be *involved* in Leo's life? I'm unable to let go of the image of James, not just as a powerful businessman, but as someone who could reshape our entire world. His wealth, his influence—it's light-years away from the life Leo and I have built together. And once James knows, there's no going back. Everything would shift, and the possibility circles me like a rising tide. As if on cue, my computer pings. I glance at the screen, and a smile curls my lips when I see James's message.

James
Lunch with me?

I quickly type back.

Be there in five.

Maybe this is the right moment to figure out where we stand. To talk about last night. About us.

I gather my things and head to James's office. When I reach the door, I pause, smoothing my dress and taking a calming breath before walking in.

"Hey."

James looks up, flashing a lazy, sexy grin that makes my stomach flip. "Thought we could have lunch together. I ordered Thai." He gestures to the take-out boxes spread across his desk.

"Perfect." I grab a couple of boxes and head toward the couch, but before I sit, his phone rings.

"Shit," he mutters, frowning as he checks the caller ID. "Give me a second?"

I nod, settling on the couch with my food as he answers the call. At first, I focus on laying out our lunch, but the low timbre of his voice keeps drawing my attention. His brow furrows as the conversation drags on, and I can tell it's going to be more than a second.

An idea sparks—a wicked one. Without overthinking it, I set the food aside and slide off the couch, lowering myself to the floor on all fours. The cool marble against my palms sends a shiver up my spine as I slowly crawl toward him, arching my back just enough to draw his attention.

His eyes flick down, and when they meet mine, desire flares in them. I stop between his legs, sitting back on my haunches, and his gaze drops to my cleavage spilling out of my dress. His hand tightens on the phone, but he doesn't stop me when I reach for his belt, loosening it like I did last night. I tug down his pants just enough to free his hardening cock and eagerly wrap my hand around his length. James inhales sharply, adjusting his position in the chair as I slide my hand from the base to the head, squeezing the tip. His eyes meet mine, and he raises an eyebrow in question, a silent dare. Smirking, I lean forward, my lips brushing the tip of his cock before taking him in my mouth.

He jolts at the contact, his free hand gripping the edge of his desk. His eyes close briefly, and when they open again, they're a shade darker. I continue lapping at his cock like a lollipop, and I'm doing it on purpose to drive him insane.

He hits the mute button. "Stop teasing," he snaps. "Suck me like a good girl."

I love it when he makes demands. My body responds instinctively, the desire coiling tight inside me. I know exactly what he wants, and the thrill of it—of giving in—makes my pulse race.

I coat his shaft in saliva, bobbing my head up and down in the rhythm that he loves. I know exactly how to please him, and the low groan that escapes his throat tells me I'm doing just that.

But then, in a move that surprises me, James puts the phone down on his desk, unmuting the call.

I pause, confused, but his hand on the back of my head urges me to keep going.

Really? He's putting this guy on speaker while I'm sucking him off?

I glance up at him, eyes wide, and he brings a finger to his lips, signaling for silence. The challenge in his expression sends a burst of adrenaline through me, and I can't help but smirk.

Game on.

The voice on the other end of the line drones on about budget reports or something equally boring, but I couldn't care less. All I can focus on is the heaviness of James in my mouth, the taste of him, the way his breathing catches every time I take him deeper. I increase the pressure, swirling my tongue around his head before sliding down again. His fingers tangle in my hair, guiding me, controlling the rhythm.

"Fuuuck," he whispers.

I glance up and his eyes lock on mine. His hand tightens in my hair as I suck harder. The wet sounds of my mouth on his cock fill the room, obscenely loud against the conversation happening on the speakerphone.

"I'll need to speak to marketing…" the voice drones on, but I can tell James isn't listening anymore. He's close—very close.

With a faint audible groan, he manages to cut the call short. "Report back on Monday." And with that, he hangs up, just in time. His climax crashes through him, and he comes hard in my mouth, his body tensing as he spills down my throat. I swallow everything, savoring the taste of him, and when I pull back, his eyes are glazed.

He drags me up onto his lap, kissing me hard, not caring about the salty taste of himself on my lips. "That was fucking hot," he murmurs against my mouth.

I laugh, breathless. "Consider it my contribution to the workday."

"You always this dangerous?" His grin is sinful.

"Only when I'm bored," I tease, brushing my thumb over the corner of my lips.

He groans, tipping his head back. "You're going to be the death of me."

We spend the next hour eating lunch, stealing kisses between bites. I should ask him where we stand, to define this thing between us, but the words stick in my throat. I can't bear to say it, not yet—not when the answer might be something I'm not ready to hear. Maybe I'm not ready to know if this is just lust for him. For now, I want to enjoy the moment. The calm before the storm.

Later, back at my desk, my phone buzzes. I glance at the screen, expecting it to be Dad sending me a cute picture of Leo, but the name "Hailee" flashes instead. I bite my bottom lip as I open the message.

Hailee

You're on for Saturday. Le Jardin. X

I stare at the words, a sinking feeling creeping in. Setting the phone down, I run a hand through my hair, trying to steady my breathing.

Le Jardin.

A dull throb builds behind my eyes as the questions pile up, each one more suffocating than the last. I rub my temples, trying to fend off the headache that's threatening to ruin the rest of my day.

I should tell James about Le Jardin. But now I'm second-guessing myself. Maybe it's because I don't even know if

I have the right to feel guilty. As far as I know, this thing between us is casual. We haven't defined it—we still haven't put words to whatever this is.

So why do I feel like I'm betraying him? Why does the idea of working on Saturday make me feel like I'm doing something wrong? The logical part of me knows I need the money. Leo, Dad, the bills—they all demand more than I can give. Eden has been a blessing for me, and yet, the thought of stepping back into that world now, knowing James is tied to it... it feels different.

But why should I feel guilty for doing what I need to survive, when James is the one paying an exorbitant amount of money for a membership there? For all I know, he's been back to Eden, picking someone else. I don't even know if he's seeing other women, or if he views the goddesses at Eden as a mere distraction. Maybe he still sees me that way.

The questions whirl inside me like a tornado. What if I show up on Saturday and he's there, watching? Choosing someone else? The thought makes my fingers clench into fists. And the worst part is, I don't know if I could handle it. The idea of him seeing me with another man, or of me watching him with another woman... makes me feel almost sick.

Whether I like it or not, James has a hold on me, and I'm not sure I know how to untangle myself from him.

I take a steady breath and expel it slowly, my thumb hovering over the buttons. The moment I hit Send, a cold wave of dread washes over me. There's no going back now.

I could tell him everything—about working Saturday, about Leo—but once I open that door, there's no closing it. Nothing will be the same. And I can't afford to make the wrong move.

I'm teetering on the edge, just waiting to tip over. If I step forward, if I go to Eden on Saturday, something will break. Maybe it's my heart. Maybe it's his.

Or maybe, it's us.

Chapter Twenty-Five

James

The amber liquid swirls in my glass, catching the dim light of the living room as I tip it back and take another slow sip. The scotch burns down my throat, its heat a poor distraction for the tension clawing at the base of my skull. The alcohol is supposed to help, supposed to clear my head of Cora, but instead, it only sharpens the memories of her.

Her laugh. The flush that deepened in her cheeks when she smiled. How the sunset lit the flecks of honey in her eyes just before we...

Fuck.

I slam the glass down harder than I mean to, almost shattering the crystal. I run a hand down my face. It's not supposed to feel like this.

She's in my head. Even now, sitting alone at home on a Saturday night with half a bottle of scotch down, she's everywhere. The memory of her lingers—her hair spilling over my pillow, the way her body felt under my hands.

She looked perfect in my home. Fucking perfect.

The thought makes my throat tighten. A relationship wasn't part of the plan. Hell, none of this was. It was supposed to be casual. Simple. I wasn't supposed to care this much.

I let out a deep breath and flip my wrist to check the time. Too late to join Dameon at Eden. Not that I need another reminder of her. Eden only brings her back into focus. I swipe my phone off the table, desperate for a distraction, and hit video call on the only person who knows how to pull me out of my head—Larissa.

The phone rings once, twice, before her face pops up on screen, framed by the chaos of her kitchen. My niece and nephew are running around in the background, a blur of pajamas and energy.

"Hey!" Larissa chirps, her warm smile instantly easing some of the pressure behind my tired eyes. "You look like hell. What's going on?"

I let out a dry chuckle. "Thanks, Lars. You look... uh, busy."

She rolls her eyes, throwing a thumb over her shoulder as Oliver and Emma wrestle near the fridge. "You have no idea. I can't get these two to bed for the life of me. They've been bouncing off the walls all night."

"Looks like you've got your hands full," I say, rubbing my hand over my chin. "What's their deal tonight?"

"Oliver's been on this weird reptile kick. Keeps talking about snakes and spiders. You know how much I hate snakes." She pulls a face, then yells over her shoulder, "Guys, seriously, I'm on the phone!"

I laugh, for real this time. "Want me to take him to the zoo again? He can terrorize me with snake facts instead."

"God, yes. You'll save me from another lecture about how 'snakes are misunderstood.'" She mimics Oliver's voice, and it makes me smile.

"Alright. I'll take them soon. Promise."

"Thank you, seriously." She sighs, looking genuinely relieved. But then her smile falters as she studies me. "Wait, you called me. You okay? You look... off."

I hesitate, running a hand through my hair. How the hell do I explain this? Without giving too much away?

"I'm fine," I lie, the words coming out too quickly. "Just wanted to check in."

Her eyes narrow. "Alright. But call me soon. We'll figure out the zoo thing. And hey—don't be a stranger."

"Yeah. Sure. Tell the kids I'll take them soon."

"Will do. Alright, kids, say goodnight to Uncle James!"

"Night, Uncle James!" they call in unison, their voices a chaotic jumble that makes me grin, despite everything.

I hang up and exhale slowly, staring at the empty screen. For a moment, I'm steady. But it doesn't last.

My phone buzzes with a message.

Dameon

Get down to Eden. NOW.

Cora's in Le Jardin tonight.

What. The. Fuck?

My blood goes cold, then hot in the span of a second.

Le Jardin?

What the fuck is she doing in Le Jardin?

Without thinking, I grab my keys and storm out of my villa, shooting off a quick response to Dameon.

On my way.

The engine roars to life, tires squealing as I speed out of the driveway. The city flies by in a blur of red lights and asphalt, each passing second feeding the fire burning in my veins. Every mile stretches endlessly, though I push harder on the accelerator, hardly noticing the speed.

By the time I skid into Eden's underground garage, my blood pressure has hit a new high. I fling the car door open without a second thought, shoes pounding against the polished concrete as I race inside.

Dameon is leaning casually against a window in the foyer, his arms crossed.

"Where is she?" I demand.

"Jesus, would you calm down?" he hisses, glancing nervously at the security guards. "You're going to get us kicked out."

"Anyone who touches her, dies," I growl, fists clenched tight. The possessiveness in my voice shocks me, but I don't give a shit. *She's mine.*

Dameon doesn't flinch. Instead, he gives me a measured look. "You can't go barging in there like a lunatic. You'll blow everything. Just listen for once."

I glare at him, my heart pounding against my ribcage. "You don't understand—"

"I do." Dameon cuts me off. "I'm registered for Le Jardin tonight. I'll pick her."

Does he have a death wish?

The words hit me like a punch to the gut. *Dameon.* Picking *Cora.* Rage surges through me again, but before I can snap, Dameon steps closer, lowering his voice.

"Listen, I'll pick her, then we'll switch. No one else touches her. But if you blow up now, if you walk in there, guns blazing, you'll ruin everything."

I breathe hard through my nose, trying to rein in the storm building inside me. The thought of Dameon being the one to pick her, even if it's just for show, twists something in me, but the logic is starting to sink in. Slowly I unclench my fists.

"Fine," I bite out. "But this better work."

"It will," Dameon says evenly. "Wait here. I'll come get you when it's done."

The minutes stretch on like hours. I pace the foyer like a caged animal, my heart beating a wild, erratic rhythm in my chest. Every second feels like an eternity. My phone and ID have already been handed over to security, so all I can do is wait, the walls of Eden closing in around me.

At last, Dameon emerges and slips me a key.

"Room six," he says.

I snatch it from his hand without a word and head down the hallway, my breath coming hard and fast. By the time I reach the door, my pulse is a roar in my ears. My hand trembles as I turn the knob and push it open.

Cora is standing by the bed, her body half-lit by the soft light spilling across the room. She spins around, startled, when I enter.

"What are you doing here?" she asks.

I don't answer right away, my eyes dragging over her naked form, anger knotting together in my gut.

"What the hell do you think *you're* doing?" I snap.

Her eyes flash, and she grabs the sheet from the bed, wrapping it around herself. "I'm doing my job, James. What does it look like?"

"Not anymore, you're not." I take a step toward her, my jaw tight. "I forbid you from working here."

Fire flashes in her eyes as she steps closer, her chin lifting. "You *forbid* me? What the hell gives you that right? You don't own me."

Her words hit hard, but the truth of them stings worse. My possessiveness is getting the best of me, but I can't stop. I can't let her slip out of my control, out of my life.

I close the distance between us until we're chest to chest, our breath mingling in the charged air. "If this is about money, I'll pay you whatever you need. You don't need to fuck men for money."

Her face hardens, hurt flickering behind her eyes before she blinks it away. "Don't you dare judge me, you prick. You pay a ton of money for your membership here so you can fuck women. I'm here doing a job. Sex work is real work." She pauses, her jaw tightening as she takes a breath. "And don't be stupid. I'm not taking your damn money, James." She rolls her eyes like it's the most ridiculous thing she's heard. I arch an eyebrow to remind her that she's taken my money before. Without my consent. While I was asleep. She flushes and adds, "It's not only about money. I'm not your property. I don't belong to you."

"The fuck you don't," I snarl, grabbing her wrist, pulling her closer until her breath is hot against my skin. We're inches apart now, both of us trembling.

Her breath comes faster, her breasts rising and falling beneath the sheet, but she doesn't back down. "You don't get to control me." Her voice is quieter now, but still defiant. "I make my own choices. You—you don't get to just walk in here and decide what I can and can't do."

"I'm not asking you. I'm telling you. This isn't happening again."

The tension between us is palpable, electric, and for a moment, neither of us moves.

CHAPTER TWENTY-SIX

Cora

The air between us crackles, like all the oxygen has been sucked out of the room. James stands before me, towering, his shoulders tense, as though holding back a torrent of energy beneath his skin. His hair is tousled, his jaw clenched so hard I can almost hear his teeth grinding.

On the surface, he's furious—intimidating, even—but I know him better. I see the tension rippling through him, barely masked by anger.

It's not just fury. It's something wild that he doesn't know how to control.

And James? James always needs control.

The man standing before me now isn't the same man who gently held my hand over dinner, who smiled at me like I meant more to him than just another conquest. No. This is James the dom, the one who commands, who expects nothing less than full submission. His eyes are on mine with a force that makes it hard to breathe.

I swallow hard, my pulse quickening. Heat crawls up my neck, my body reacting to the power radiating off him in waves. I hate that he can do this to me—how easily I soften under his dominance. How part of me craves this.

"I'll prove you're mine," he growls, deep, rich, and filled with a hunger that makes my knees weak.

Before I can respond, his hand wraps around my throat—not tight enough to hurt, but enough to send a jolt of electricity down my spine. My body surrenders, and his smirk tells me he feels it too.

In one fluid motion, he spins me around and pins me against the wall, his grip still firm around my neck. The cool surface presses into my back, but it's nothing compared to the heat radiating from his body, now inches from mine.

"Let's see if your body knows who it belongs to," he murmurs.

Before I can process his words, he tears the sheet from my body, leaving me bare. His fingers thrust into me without hesitation, driving deep, and the shock of it rips a gasp from my throat.

I'm wet, embarrassingly so.

"Ahhh," he chuckles, a wicked gleam in his eye. "Just as I expected. Look at you—your cunt is already dripping, begging to be fucked."

His fingers pump in and out, his thumb brushing over my clit in maddening circles. I'm falling apart, the pressure building too fast, too strong, and I can't stop it. I can't hold back. I come hard, my body shaking, my moans filling the room.

He pulls his fingers out and holds them up, showing me the evidence of my surrender, his mouth twisted in a snarl. I should be embarrassed, humiliated even, that he made me come so quickly, but I'm not. James knows my body better than anyone, and he knows exactly how to use that power.

"See?" he taunts. "Your body knows its master. Your mind just needs to catch up."

He crashes his lips against mine, devouring me in a kiss that's more like a battle. It's not gentle or soft—it's demanding, a claim. My head spins as I melt into it, my legs trembling. When he lifts me and presses me harder against the wall, I wrap my legs around his waist instinctively. His lips never leave mine as he fumbles with his zipper, freeing his cock.

He thrusts into me in one powerful stroke, filling me completely. My head falls back, a low, animalistic sound escaping my throat. He pauses, deep inside me, his breath hot against my neck. God, I'll never get used to this—how he fills me, how perfectly we fit together.

He grips my jaw, forcing me to meet his gaze. "Who do you belong to?"

My core pulses, desperate for him to move, to create the friction I crave. But I can't give in. Not yet. I refuse to give him the satisfaction.

"I belong to no one," I whisper, daring him even as my body betrays me.

His eyes flash and without warning, he drives into me again, harder this time. His thrusts are punishing, each one sending shockwaves through my body.

"My cock inside your tight little pussy says otherwise," he grinds out, each word punctuated by a deep, harsh thrust. "From now on, no one else will touch you."

"Dream on, asshole," I bite back, but even as the words leave my mouth, I know I'm losing the battle. My body is giving in, clenching around him as pleasure builds, overwhelming, consuming.

With a swift motion, he pulls out, slides me down and turns me to face the wall, guiding my hips as he bends me forward. I brace my hands against the wall for support as he presses close, sliding back inside me. His palm lands on my ass with a sharp, stinging slap. The sound ricochets off the walls, followed by my breathless moan.

"Wrong answer," he grunts. His palm meets my skin, harder this time, the sting sending pleasure and pain coursing through me. My body trembles, my resolve weakening.

"Try again, my sweet little slut." His tone drips with authority, and I'm losing myself—losing the battle. "I won't stop until you give me the answer I want."

I shake my head, whimpering. "You don't get to tell me what to do."

"Watch me."

Three more slaps, each one more brutal than the last. My body is a mess of pleasure and pain, and I begin to slip, my defiance crumbling with every punishing thrust.

I'm clenching around him so tightly now, teetering on the brink of a violent release that could shatter me.

"You're soaking my cock, just from a few slaps on that pretty little ass," he taunts. "Tell me, Cora, who do you belong to?"

I bite my lip, fighting the words that threaten to spill from my mouth. I can't give him what he wants. I can't—

"Asshole," I mutter through gritted teeth, even though I'm on the verge of breaking.

He chuckles darkly, running his thumb along the curve of my ass, teasing before sliding lower until it brushes against the sensitive skin of my back hole. "You mean this cute little one? I can't wait to fuck you here." His voice is rough like gravel, and the thought alone nearly sends me over the edge.

But then, just as I'm about to fall, just as I'm ready to let go... he stops.

He pulls out of me abruptly, leaving me shaking on the brink of release.

"What the fuck?" I gasp, spinning to face him, my body still quaking from the sudden loss of him.

He steps back, zipping up his pants with deliberate slowness, his eyes never leaving mine. "You don't come unless you accept it," he says coldly. "You don't come unless you accept you're mine."

The words cut the air between us like a blade. I know what he wants. I know I'm his. And I know he's mine. I know it with every fiber of my being. But I can't say it. Not yet. The words stick in my throat, tangled up in my pride and fear.

"But I'm not yours," I whisper, the lie slipping weakly from my lips.

For a split second, hurt flashes across his face, but it's gone before I can fully register it. He nods, the cold mask slipping back into place. His silence is louder than any words he could have spoken.

Without another glance, he turns and opens the door, stepping out into the hallway. He doesn't slam the door, doesn't make a scene. He just... leaves. Quietly. As if he's walking out of my life.

When the door closes softly behind him, I collapse to the floor, my knees finally giving out.

My hands fly to my face, the tears coming before I can stop them.

What have I done?

CHAPTER TWENTY-SEVEN

Cora

The dressing room feels as empty as I do, a hollow silence where there's usually chatter and laughter. I trudge toward my locker, my body heavy, my mind heavier, replaying the night on a loop.

"Cora, are you okay?"

I whip around, startled, to see Hailee standing by her locker, gathering her things. I hadn't even noticed her there—too caught up in my own head, drowning in everything I'm trying not to feel.

"Yeah, I'm fine," I mumble, though the words feel thick on my tongue. I'm not fine. I haven't been since James walked out of that room, leaving me in a wrecked heap of emotions I haven't been able to process. But I can't unpack that here, not now.

Hailee frowns, watching me as I slowly get dressed. "What happened? I saw you got picked by Mr. Voyeur. God, he's ah-mazing." She fans herself dramatically, her eyes glazing over with some daydream about Daemon she's clearly entertained before.

A small, bitter laugh slips out. "Yeah, amazing," I echo. "He, uh... had to leave early."

Hailee's eyes snap back to me, her playful expression fading as she takes a closer look. "You sure you're okay? You look a little down."

Down? That doesn't even scratch the surface. I'm gutted. But I don't want to dump all of that on Hailee. She doesn't need to know about my tangled mess with James or how my stupid pride always gets in the way of what I want, wrecking everything in the process. Every time I close my eyes, I see the hurt on his face. I hate it.

I force a smile, weak as it is. "Yeah, just tired, I guess."

But even I don't believe the lie.

Hailee eyes me for a long moment. Then, her face lights up. "You know what? You should come out with me tonight. I'm meeting some friends in the city. It might help take your mind off things."

My first instinct is to say no. I'm an introvert at heart, and the idea of making small talk with strangers is my personal definition of hell. What I really want is to go home, curl up in bed with a cup of tea, and disappear into a book. But I know where that will lead—endless hours of replaying my night with James, obsessing over what I should have said, what I should have done differently.

Hailee jangles her car keys in front of me, her grin widening. "Come on! I'll drive."

I hesitate, then sigh. "Fine. Give me five minutes."

"Yes!" Hailee claps her hands together, practically skipping toward the door. "I'll wait for you in the foyer."

Once she's gone, I finish getting dressed, pulling on my summery dress and a pair of heels. My reflection in the mirror stares back at me, eyes shadowed with fatigue, but I force a smile. It doesn't reach my eyes. I run a hand through my hair, smoothing it down, and make sure my makeup is intact. I look the part—put-together, confident—but inside, I'm anything but.

Fake it till you make it, right?

With a final glance in the mirror, I grab my purse and head out to meet Hailee, ready to let the night drown out everything I don't want to feel.

The Pink Diamond is perched on the fortieth floor of a skyscraper in the heart of Sydney. As we weave our way through the crowd, the first thing that hits me is the view. From up here, the city glitters like a sea of lights, the Opera House and

Harbour Bridge illuminated in the distance. The bar itself is sleek, with dark wood and floor-to-ceiling windows. There's a three-piece jazz band in the corner, playing something smooth and soulful.

"Isn't this place great?" Hailee shouts over the music, her eyes sparkling as she leads us toward a round table in the back where her friends are already seated.

I nod, though my mind feels detached from everything around me. The views are breathtaking, the music is good—but there's a numbness settling over me.

As we reach the table, Hailee introduces me to the group. "Everyone, this is Cora."

She rattles off names—Orlando, Harper, Liz, Brent, and Dave—but they blend together in a haze. I give a small, awkward wave and take a seat, hoping no one expects me to keep track of who's who.

"Espresso martinis for the ladies," Orlando—*I think*—says, handing Hailee and me a drink each when a waitress sets them down on the table.

I don't hesitate. I down mine in one go, the strong mix of coffee and alcohol burning my throat. I shudder as it hits my stomach like a brick, but it's exactly what I need. Hailee lifts a brow at me, clearly impressed, and I shrug with a small grin before signaling the waitress for another round.

"Damn," Orlando chuckles, shaking his head. "Someone had a rough day."

"You could say that," I mumble, already feeling the alcohol numb my frayed nerves.

By the time I'm on my third martini, the buzz has fully set in. My head is light, my limbs loose, and for the first time all evening, thoughts of James have faded into the background. Hailee's friends have welcomed me into their group, and the conversation flows easily. Between the drinks, the music, and the breathtaking view, I've managed to keep my mind off our disastrous encounter and the hurt I caused him.

But when a fourth martini lands in front of me, I hesitate. The room is starting to spin and my stomach clenches in protest. I take a sip, but the bitter taste makes me grimace. I've hit my limit.

I glance around the table. Hailee is deep in an animated story, her arms swinging wildly, nearly knocking over a few glasses. Her friends are laughing, clearly having a good time, but they've all sailed past their limit a couple of drinks ago.

I need to get out of here.

I push back from the table, my legs wobbling slightly as I stand. Just as I'm about to slip away, Hailee catches sight of me and jumps up, pulling me into a sloppy hug.

"You know I love you, riiight?" she slurs. "Are you feeling betterrr?"

I can't help but laugh. "Yeah, Hails. I'm good. But I'm heading off now."

"Nooo, you can't go yet!" She pouts dramatically, swaying on her feet. Then, as if she's had an epiphany, her expression shifts. "Wait... I should go too. I'll come with you."

I chuckle at how quickly she changes her mind. "Alright. Let's get out of here."

After a quick round of goodbyes to her friends, we stumble out of the bar and into the cool night air. The crisp breeze should sober me up, but instead, it makes everything worse. My head spins, my stomach churns, and I feel hot—too hot. My body is burning up like I've been engulfed in flames. A wave of nausea rolls through me, and I groan, wishing I was already home and curled up in bed.

Why haven't they invented teleporters yet? I mean come on, it's the twenty-first century!

I fumble for my phone, ready to call us a rideshare, when Hailee stops me.

"Wait! I can't leave my car here. Can you drive it back to my place? It's just around the corner, pleeeaaase?" She clasps her hands together, giving me the best puppy-dog eyes I've ever seen. Even better than Leo's.

I blink at her, trying to process her request through the alcohol fog. My stomach lurches, and I swallow the saliva pooling in my mouth, fighting the urge to be sick. The last thing I want to do is get behind the wheel of a car right now. But Hailee's eyes are wide, pleading, and then she drops the kicker.

"I need it to take my sister to the doctor in the morning," she adds, her voice small and desperate.

Shit.

I know what it's like to have a family member who needs you. Taking a slow breath, I nod. "Okay, but it's really just around the corner, right?"

"Yup! I swear," she promises, wobbling on her heels.

I help her to the car, my stomach flipping with every step. Then I slide into the driver's seat and grip the steering wheel, my knuckles white as I fight to keep the world from spinning. I close my eyes for a second, hoping that will help.

When I open them again, I start the ignition and carefully pull out onto the street. Soft snores fill the car and I glance over at Hailee. Of course she's passed out. Her mouth is hanging open and a thread of saliva drips onto her shoulder.

I tap the "home" button on the car's navigation system, relieved to see she wasn't exaggerating—it's only a few minutes away.

I keep my focus laser-sharp on the road, willing myself to make it without throwing up or passing out. But just as I start to relax, the shrill sound of a siren blares behind me.

Oh, no.

I glance in the rearview mirror and see the flashing lights of a police car. My heart drops to my feet.

Fuck.

I quickly signal and pull over to the side of the road, my hands shaking on the steering wheel. My head is pounding, and nausea twists my insides.

I wait... and wait.

I look in the rearview mirror again.

What the hell are they doing?

I'm sweating profusely as my body burns hotter than the sun. Sweat is dripping down my back and in between my boobs as my stomach twists in agony.

The officer finally approaches the car and I roll down my window. He leans down to peer inside, his eyes narrowing at the sight of Hailee slumped in the passenger seat. I can feel the bile rising, but I clench my teeth, willing it back down.

Not now. Please, not now.

"Ma'am," he starts. But before he can say anything else, my body betrays me. I lean out of the window just in time to vomit—violently—over the officer's shoes.

Oh. My. God.

He swears under his breath, and I want to disappear, to sink into the earth and never come back. But I can't stop retching. When I'm finally done, I slump back in the seat, mortified, my head spinning. I'd give my left tit to be anywhere else right now. After a few seconds, I know I can't delay the inevitable any longer, so I gradually open my eyes. The officer stares at me, his expression a mix of horror and concern.

"Ma'am, please step out of the vehicle."

CHAPTER TWENTY-EIGHT

Cora

James strides into the police station like he owns the place. Each crisp clack of his shoes on the linoleum carries an air of authority that immediately turns heads. There's a subtle, commanding swagger in the way he moves, and it's impossible not to take note. Even the police officers at the front desk look up, their posture stiffening as if they've been caught slacking off. The line of civilians waiting for their turn at the counter doesn't faze him. James bypasses them all, heading straight to the front of the queue.

No one questions him—not the people in line, not the officers, no one. They recognize power when they see it. He is the kind of man people don't confront.

I slouch in the corner of the waiting room, the hard-plastic chair digging into my back. The scent of stale coffee and disinfectant hangs in the air, and the fluorescent lights overhead buzz like a swarm of flies. I feel safe watching him from a distance. But my heart gives an involuntary jump the second his eyes land on me. There's a hint of something in his gaze—relief?

But then his jaw tightens, and his eyes travel over my body, inspecting me. Once he's satisfied, he locks onto my eyes, and I'm caught in the power of his stare.

My pulse quickens. There's a promise in that look—punishment. My skin heats at the thought. I shift uncomfortably in my seat, suddenly all too aware of how horrible I must look—my makeup smudged, hair tangled with remnants of vomit, bloodshot eyes. I must look like shit.

But still, the mental image of James bending me over his knee and pulling my panties down to spank my ass red sparks a dark thrill in me. Pressure builds within me, anticipation prickling along my skin. His lips twitch into a knowing smirk as if he can read my filthy thoughts.

God, of course he knows.

He turns back to the officer he's speaking with, nodding curtly. Even while he's focused on the conversation, his gaze flicks to me every few moments, keeping me pinned. I can't look at him any longer—I'm too mortified. I drop my eyes to the floor, my cheeks burning.

This is rock bottom.

After what I'm now referring to as "spew-gate," the officer—Carl—woke up Hailee and escorted us both to his patrol car. Hailee had apologized profusely, sobbing in the backseat, but I was too sick and too humiliated to care. I just wanted to crawl into a hole and disappear.

At the station, Carl handed me a breathalyzer, and I held my breath, praying. When the number blinked just under the legal limit, relief hit me so hard I almost staggered. I'd been stupid, reckless—if I hadn't thrown up, I'd probably be in a cell right now, facing charges, maybe even losing my license.

Instead, I got a warning. Extremely lucky, considering how it could have turned out. I shouldn't have gotten behind the wheel in that state. It was dangerous and stupid. I promised myself I'd be better, that I'd make smarter choices, yet here I am, sitting in a police station at three in the morning, waiting to be picked up like a reckless teenager. Shame curls inside me. It's not just about the vomiting or the breathalyzer. It's about how easily I could've lost everything—my freedom, my safety, my son. I can't let this happen again. I can't keep making stupid, reckless decisions like this. Leo deserves better. I deserve better.

James finishes his conversation and stalks toward me. He looks as polished as ever, despite the early hour and the fact that he's still wearing his suit from earlier. He stops directly in front of me, towering over me, forcing me to tilt my head back. He runs his thumb over his bottom lip and studies my face. He's slipped his mask back on, but the frustration and disappointment that flares in his eyes is hard to miss. Whether that's from earlier in the evening or from now, I don't know. Take your pick.

"Come on, let's go." Without sparing me another glance, he turns and walks toward the exit, expecting me to follow.

I jump to my feet, irritation simmering under my skin. His cold indifference is starting to piss me off. By the time we reach his car, I can't hold back anymore.

"Get in," he says.

"No." I cross my arms over my chest, refusing to budge.

James freezes, his hand on the passenger door handle. He turns slowly, his eyes narrowing. "Excuse me?"

"I know I asked the officers to call you," I say, "and I'm grateful that you came. But I'm not a child, and I won't be treated like one." The words spill out faster than I expect.

His face clouds over. "Well, stop acting like one."

The sharpness of his retort slices through me, but I hold my ground. "I screwed up, okay?! I made a mistake, but that doesn't give you the right to treat me like an idiot!" I plant my hands on my hips, only just containing the urge to tap my foot like a petulant child.

His eyes blaze, anger finally breaking through his icy exterior. He steps closer, his body practically vibrating with fury. "An idiot? You *are* an idiot!" he bites back, his voice rising with each word. "You could've killed someone! Or worse, *you* could've been killed!"

His hands grip my upper arms, like he's going to shake some sense into me. "You could've been hurt, Cora. Do you understand that?" His voice breaks on the last word, and for a moment, the emotion on his face is raw and unfiltered.

"When the officer called and asked if I knew a Cora Rossi," he says, quieter now, almost broken, "I—I just..." He trails off, lowering his head, his grip loosening. His vulnerability is breaking my heart.

God, he's right. I'm such an idiot.

"Please, Cora." He lifts his head, not quite meeting my eyes. "Just get in the car."

I nod, my throat too tight to speak, and slip into the passenger seat.

The car door slams behind me, making me flinch. James stalks around to the driver's side and slides in without a word, the leather creaking beneath his weight. His knuckles turn white as they clamp down on the steering wheel like he's trying to crush it. The air in the car is thick, silence pressing in on us as Sydney's streets race past the window. I notice we're heading toward my neighborhood, but I don't dare ask how he knows my address.

Finally, when we're a block away from my house, he breaks the silence, making me jump in my seat. "Do you have a problem with alcohol?"

"What?" I whip my head around to look at him. He's serious. Deadly serious. "No! Of course not." I scoff, but the accusation stings. Sure, I like to let loose once in a while, but I've never been *this* drunk or sick from alcohol before. Never. His words from five years ago bubble to the surface: *I don't fuck drunk chicks.*

James says nothing, his eyes fixed on the road ahead. His grip on the steering wheel remains firm, his jaw clenched tight. The silence stretches between us and I gaze at him again, studying the hard lines of his face.

He's so gorgeous.

Even now, it's impossible to ignore. That strong jawline, those sharp cheekbones—they're almost unreal, like they were sculpted with precision.

When we pull up outside my house, he still won't look at me. He sits there, staring straight ahead, his entire body rigid. I wait for him to say something—anything, really—but he doesn't.

I sigh heavily; talking to him right now is pointless. With a huff, I open the car door and slam it shut behind me. I don't look back as I walk up to my front door. I hear his car drive away as soon as I step inside.

I slump against the door, close my eyes, and shake my head at my stupidity.

Fuck.

I want to collapse into bed and forget this whole night ever happened. But the pungent, sour smell of vomit in my hair hits me like a slap, making me grimace. There's no way I can sleep like this.

Somehow I peel myself off the door and drag my feet toward my bedroom, the wooden floorboards creaking under my heels. But as I pass Leo's room, instinct kicks in. My feet stop of their own accord, and I hover outside his door, staring at the faint light of his nightlight spilling into the hallway.

For a moment, I consider skipping it. I'm too tired, too wrecked. But then I think about his little face, his peaceful expression when he's sleeping, and I can't resist. I turn the knob and push the door open, just a crack.

Leo is curled up under his dinosaur blanket, one hand gripping his stuffed giraffe. His tiny chest rises and falls with each gentle breath, his face serene, completely unaware of the chaos his mother has just brought on herself. Watching him like this, so peaceful, so innocent, a lump forms in my throat. For a moment, I hate myself. I hate myself for being reckless, for almost making tonight a disaster, for being a woman with vomit in her hair instead of someone he can count on.

I step inside, my heels sinking into the carpet as I approach his bed. Leaning over, I gently brush a lock of dark hair off his forehead. I press a soft kiss to his temple, the catastrophe of the night momentarily slipping away.

"I'm sorry," I whisper, though he's too deep in sleep to hear me. "I'll do better."

Straightening up, I back out of the room and pull the door quietly behind me, leaving it slightly ajar. The moment I step into the hallway, though, exhaustion hits me. I'm running on fumes, my body aching for rest, but I still need to clean myself up.

The bathroom light is blinding, and I wince at my reflection in the mirror. Mascara streaks down my cheeks like black tears. My skin is blotchy, red patches blooming across my face, and the dark shadows under my eyes make me look like I haven't slept in days.

But the worst part is the hair. The vomit. *Ugh.* It's clumped in chunks near the ends of my curls, and the smell makes me gag all over again. I should shower, but the mere thought of standing under hot water is too much right now.

Instead, I settle for the bare minimum—pulling off my clothes and dragging a damp towel through my hair to clean out the worst of it. The towel comes away stained, and I cringe, throwing it into the laundry hamper with a sigh.

At least the smell isn't as overpowering now.

I shuffle out of the bathroom in my underwear and pull an oversized T-shirt from my dresser. It's soft and comforting against my skin, exactly what I need. I collapse into bed with a groan, burying my face in the pillow, but the events of the night keep playing on my mind, refusing to let me rest.

James.

The way he looked at me in the police station, his anger, his fear, the vulnerability in his voice—it all replays on a loop, cutting deeper each time. And then his question. *Do you have a problem with alcohol?*

I don't. Do I?

I squeeze my eyes shut, desperate to hold back the flood of memories of Nathan, our reckless, drunken night and our foolish attempt to work the next day. But tonight wasn't like that. Tonight was just... a stupid mistake. A one-off.

But still, I can't shake off James's words, the way his hands gripped my arms like he was scared to lose me.

Scared to lose me.

That thought sticks.

He cares.

And somehow, that makes everything worse.

I groan again, louder this time, pressing my face harder into the pillow as if that might block out the mess in my head. Sleep won't come easily tonight. Not with everything swirling around me like this. Not with the hurt I caused James still fresh in my mind, and the fear that I might lose him for good hanging over my head like a dark cloud.

Eventually the exhaustion wins. My body gives in, and I drift into a restless, uneasy sleep, haunted by the chaos I caused.

Chapter Twenty-Nine

Cora

I wake with a dull pressure building behind my eyes. My head feels sluggish, and the events of last night play in my mind like a broken record. I can't stop hearing James's voice, the sharp hint of fear in it: *You could've been hurt, Cora.* The way he looked at me. The disappointment in his eyes. It clings to me, refusing to let go.

I stare at the ceiling, struggling to clear the fog of exhaustion. Last night was a disaster. I can't afford another mistake—Leo needs me to do better.

With a measured breath, I push myself out of bed, my legs heavy, like they're wading through thick mud. The sun is just beginning to rise, its pale light filtering through the curtains.

I shuffle down the hall, the cold floor biting at my bare feet. Leo's door is cracked open, just like I left it last night. I peek inside and see him still fast asleep.

My throat tightens, and I turn away, guilt settling over me like a thick cloak. I can't undo last night, but I can make sure today is better. I'll make today perfect—for him. I'll be the mother he deserves, not one who ends up in a police station in the middle of the night.

The kitchen is cold in the early morning light. I fill the kettle with water, the familiar sound grounding me, giving me something to focus on. Anything to keep my mind from spiraling back to the mess I've made.

I pull down Leo's favorite cereal and set out his bowl and spoon, placing everything neatly on the table. He'll wake up soon, and I want to be ready. I want everything to be just right.

No matter how hard I try to focus on the little details, my mind keeps circling back to James—his fear, his hands gripping my arms. *You could've been killed, Cora.* His voice echoes in my mind, sending a shiver through me.

Stop. Focus on what you can control.

I grab Leo's lunchbox from the counter and start packing it, slicing an apple into neat, even wedges. If I can just keep moving, maybe I can distract myself long enough to give my mind a reprieve.

As I finish packing the lunch, soft footsteps sound behind me. I turn to see Leo standing in the doorway, his hair a messy halo around his sleepy face.

"Morning, pumpkin." I say softly.

Leo rubs his eyes and wanders over to me, his small hands reaching for me. "Morning, Momma," he mumbles, glancing at the lunchbox. "Where are we going?"

I crouch down, pulling him into a hug, sneaking a kiss on the back of his neck. "I thought we could have a picnic at the Botanic Gardens today. Maybe get some ice cream after. What do you think?"

He nods, a sleepy smile spreading across his face at the mention of ice cream. "Yeah!" He shuffles over to the table and climbs into his chair, grabbing his spoon.

As he eats, I make myself a coffee and busy myself wiping down the counters, straightening things that don't need straightening. I can't sit still. My mind is racing, full of everything that could've gone wrong last night. How close I came to losing it all.

The sound of the back door creaking open wrenches me from my tireless thoughts. I glance up to see Dad shuffling into the kitchen. He looks more tired than I've ever seen him, making him seem much older than he is. He moves slowly, as if every step takes effort.

"Morning," he says on a yawn, rubbing a hand across his unshaven face.

"Morning, Dad," I reply. "What are you doing up so early? You okay?"

He waves me off, his hand trembling slightly. "Didn't sleep well. Thought I'd go for a walk." He reaches for the kettle, but I step in before he can grab it.

"I'll get that," I say, taking the kettle and pouring him a cup of tea. "We're going to the Gardens today for a picnic. Do you want to come with us?"

He shakes his head. "No, no. You two go ahead."

I frown, watching him closely as he sits down at the table, his movements slow and cautious.

"What time did you get home last night?" he asks suddenly, his eyes flicking up to meet mine.

I swallow. "Uh... late," I admit, avoiding his gaze. "Around three."

He nods, taking a slow sip of his tea. "That's late even for you."

"I know," I say quickly. "It was a rough night at work."

I turn away, not wanting him to see the shame creeping across my face.

Dad doesn't say anything else. He just finishes his tea and slowly gets up from the table, giving Leo's head a gentle pat as he shuffles out of the room. I watch him go, an ache blooming inside me.

"Let's finish getting ready, okay?" I say, forcing a smile for Leo.

I help him get organized, focusing on the simple things—tying his shoes, gathering the picnic basket—small tasks to distract me.

We step outside, the crisp morning air brushing against my skin. I grip Leo's hand a little tighter than usual as we make our way to the car, the quiet stillness of the morning peaceful around us.

But even as I buckle him into his car seat and start the engine, last night's mistakes refuse to let go. I came so close to losing it all. I glance at Leo in the rearview mirror; he's humming a song, oblivious to the chaos inside me.

I'll make today better. But secretly, I wonder if it's just a matter of time before I let him down again.

CHAPTER THIRTY

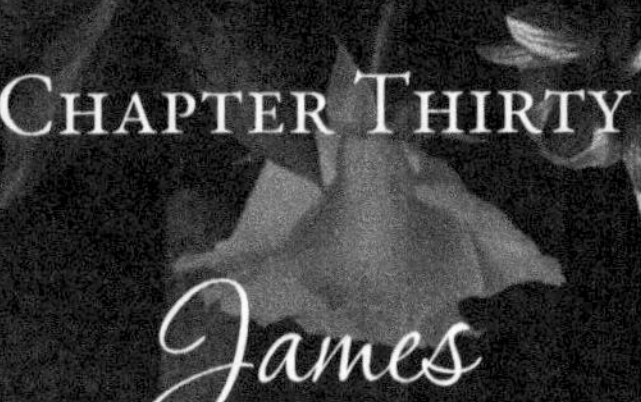

James

"You ready for tonight?" Dameon barges into my office at four o'clock, his grin so wide that I want nothing more than to wipe it off his face. He knows everything that went down two weeks ago—the standoff with Cora at Eden and the call from the police station. He's been enjoying this far too much.

I exhale heavily, reclining in my chair and pinching the bridge of my nose. "Honestly... no."

He sniggers. Of course he's eating this up. Over the last couple of weeks, he's been the one working closely with Cora on tonight's gala—Hayes & Hayward Media's first company-wide event, the final step in her grand strategy to overhaul our corporate culture. The fact that he's been the one at her side irritates me more than it should.

"Have you spoken to her?"

I glare at him. "You know I haven't."

Two weeks. Two agonizing weeks without hearing her laugh, without feeling her presence. I've seen her in passing—usually with Dameon—but she's been avoiding me, and I haven't exactly gone out of my way to fix that. I'm still pissed about her reckless behavior that night. *How could she put herself at risk like that?* That whole night was a clusterfuck—her working Le Jardin and refusing to acknowledge her feelings, then getting blind drunk and endangering herself and her colleague.

No one has ever made me feel the way Cora does—out of control, like I'm on a rollercoaster with no brakes. One minute I'm furious, the next I can't stop thinking about how much I need her. It's maddening.

Dameon laughs, shaking his head. "God, I'm loving this."

I narrow my eyes. "Eat shit, dickhead. Your time will come. When you meet a woman who turns your life upside down, I'm going to enjoy every second of it."

"Nope, not gonna happen." He backs toward the door. "I'll see you at seven."

I arrive at the Crest Hotel at seven-thirty, intentionally late to annoy Dameon. The gala is already in full swing, and I have to admit—the place looks incredible. Cora's done a fantastic job. The room is decked out with elaborate floral arrangements, waiters roam with platters of finger food, and there's a live band playing in the corner.

I scan the crowd, my eyes searching the sea of suits and dresses, but she's nowhere to be seen. Forcing a polite smile, I nod at a few familiar faces.

The sleek fabric of my Tom Ford suit fits like a second skin, every detail tailored to perfection. As I move through the room, I can feel the glances from the women and jealous stares from the men. But I keep my focus forward, letting their attention roll off me like water.

After a few minutes, I get trapped by Roger, our CFO, who launches into a long-winded story about his grandkids. I nod along, pretending that I give a flying fuck, but my attention is on sweeping the room.

And then I see her.

My jaw drops. She's standing near the bar, a vision in sapphire, her gown hugging her body perfectly, her hair flowing down her back. The sight of her steals the breath from my lungs. I hadn't realized how much I missed seeing her like this—radiant, effortless, and utterly captivating. She's with a group of colleagues, smiling at something one of them said. It's only then that I see Nathan standing close to her. Too close. His hand rests on the small of her back.

A low growl escapes my throat before I can stop it.

I excuse myself abruptly from Roger, who looks startled by my sudden exit, but I don't give a fuck. My focus narrows, zeroing in on Cora and the way Nathan's hand lingers on her.

By the time I reach them, Nathan has spotted me and pulled his hand away, but the damage is done.

Cora looks up at me, surprised. Her gaze drifts over my suit, and a faint blush rises in her cheeks.

Good. She likes what she sees.

"Good evening," I say coolly. "Would you excuse Cora for a moment?"

The group falls silent, exchanging glances. Cora narrows her eyes at me, clearly unimpressed, but steps away and follows me down a quiet hallway, away from prying eyes. We stop in a secluded alcove just past the bathrooms, the noise of the party fading behind us.

When I turn to face her, my muscles tense, my pulse drumming in my ears.

"What are you doing?" she asks, crossing her arms. "That was completely obvious. Now they're going to think something's going on between us."

"I don't give a shit what they think," I snap, stepping closer. "Nathan was practically fondling your ass in front of the entire office. That's not obvious?"

Her eyes flare. "He's just a friend, James."

"I don't care if he's your brother. No one touches you like that. No one."

Her breath hitches at my words, the shift in her body language subtle yet unmistakable. Her nipples tighten beneath the fabric of her dress, and my mouth waters with the aching need to taste them.

Two weeks ago she would've kneed me in the balls for saying she was mine. But now...

I step closer, lowering my voice. "Are you wet for me, Cora?"

Her eyes widen as I reach out, my hand gently circling her throat, backing her against the wall. A delicious pink blush creeps across her cheeks. "Do you like being my sweet slut? My good girl?"

A soft whimper escapes her lips; her body trembles.

My hand slips beneath the high slit of her dress, tracing the edge of her thong. She's soaked, just like I knew she would be. I pause for a moment, enjoying the way her body responds. Her breath quickens and her eyes flutter shut, anticipation thrumming between us like a taut wire. I could rush this, take her quickly like I want to, but this moment demands more—demands that I make her feel every second of it.

"Perfection," I murmur, slipping two fingers inside her, relishing the heat that envelops me. Her head falls back against the wall and her lips part in a soft gasp. I pick up the pace, curling my fingers to hit that spot that makes her fall apart.

Her body moves against my hand, her nipples straining against the dress. The sight of her like this—so vulnerable, so desperate—makes me snap. I tug the fabric of her dress down, exposing her breasts, and take one nipple into my mouth, biting gently at the tip. Her taste drives me mad. I pin her against the wall, feasting on her as she rides my hand. Anyone could walk past the bathroom to our little alcove and see us, but I couldn't care less. She's riding my hand like her life depends on it with her tits exposed, bouncing up and down. I want everyone to see her being pleasured by my hand and mouth, to know who she belongs to.

"Are you mine, Cora?" I rasp against her skin.

"Yesss," she hisses, her body trembling, her climax close.

"I didn't hear you," I taunt, curling my fingers deeper inside her.

"Yes!" she cries out, her voice breaking as she unravels.

"Atta girl." I smirk, watching her come undone, her body arching, her walls tightening around my fingers as she crashes over the cliff. I milk every last wave of her orgasm, reveling in the feel of her in my hand.

As she comes down, her breath heaving, I watch her. She's stunning—flushed, and completely wrecked in the best way. Every time I'm with her, I feel it—the pull, the need to be near her. Two weeks apart felt like a lifetime, and now, standing here with her, I know I can't let her go.

Maybe this is love, this aching need to be close to her. Maybe I'm too far gone to care.

Cora opens her eyes, giving me one of those smiles that makes my heart clench. Her cheeks are flushed, her body glowing. I crash my lips to hers, kissing her with all the pent-up desire and frustration I've held in for weeks.

Footsteps echo down the hallway, snapping us apart and back to reality. I pull my fingers from her pussy, helping her smooth her skirt while she tucks her tits back into her dress. Her hair is a mess, her lipstick smudged. She's perfect.

"We got lucky," she whispers, her eyes wide as the footsteps veer off into the bathroom.

I chuckle. "Very lucky." My cock throbs painfully, but we don't have time. "As much as I'd love for you to walk around with my cum on your tongue or dripping from your gorgeous pussy," I murmur, adjusting myself, "we don't have time. The scent of you on my fingers will have to be enough."

She shoots me a sultry smile before slipping into the bathroom.

Forcing myself back to the party, I swipe a drink from a passing waiter and join Dameon, who's deep in conversation with the senior management team. I nod along, pretending to care, but my mind isn't here. My eyes keep drifting to the hallway, waiting for my brown-eyed goddess to reappear.

Finally Cora steps out, looking flawless—her gown smooth, hair fixed, and that post-orgasm glow still lingering. Seeing her like this, surrounded by people who have no idea she was just pleasured by my hand, sets fire to my blood all over again. The urge to claim her, to pull her back into that hallway and mark every inch of her skin with my cum consumes me. I might control her body, but it's a fragile illusion. The way I crave her, the way my world narrows when she's near—it's not control. It's surrender. Whether I like it or not, I'm already hers.

Dameon, ever the observant bastard, catches the direction of my gaze. He lets out a low whistle, leaning in close enough that only I can hear him.

"Looks like someone made up."

I smirk, lifting the glass to my lips. "You could say that."

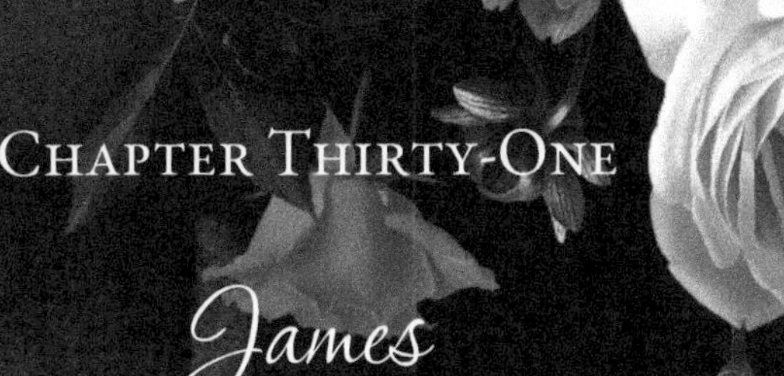

CHAPTER THIRTY-ONE

James

"Knock, knock," I call out as I step through the front door of my sister's place. It's Saturday morning and I'm on uncle duty. I peer into the living room and see Emma and Ollie glued to the TV, their little faces lit by the glow of cartoons.

"Hey, kids," I call, louder this time.

"Uncle James! Are we going to the zoo today?" they shout back, their mouths full of cereal.

"Sure are, kiddos."

"Yesss!" Ollie pumps his fist in the air, his excitement contagious.

Chuckling, I head to the kitchen, where I hear the familiar clatter of mugs and dishes. "Hey, Lars—" I stop mid-sentence as I take in her appearance. Dark circles weigh down her eyes, her hair resembles a bird's nest, and she's still in pajamas. "Wow. You look like shit," I say with a grin.

"Gee, thanks," she replies dryly. "And you look"—she pauses with her coffee cup halfway to her mouth, eyes narrowing—"good, actually. More like... like you used to. Like him," she adds softly. The comparison lands harder than it should, but I shrug it off.

She's right, though. I'm not one to smile without reason, and today I can't seem to help it.

Last night at the gala, Cora and I played our parts seamlessly, orbiting each other, tethered by that invisible pull we can't seem to break. And afterward, when I texted asking her to stay with me tonight, she accepted without hesitation. Knowing I'll see her again in a few short hours... yeah, it's hard not to smile.

"Come on, spill," Lars demands, pulling a mug from the cabinet. "What's her name?"

I lean against the counter, smirking. "Cora."

"And...?" she prods, eyes gleaming with curiosity.

I don't want to get into the details. Telling my sister I met Cora at a brothel? Not happening. "What time do I need to have the kids back?" I ask, casually checking my watch.

"Nice dodge," she says, handing me a coffee. "Not before five. Adam and I need a day to ourselves."

"Message received." I give her a mock salute. "Emma, Ollie! Shoes on, we're leaving in five!"

The sun beats down as we make our way to the zoo's reptile exhibit. Ollie is mesmerized, his breath fogging up the glass as he studies every snake and lizard. His fascination with the scaly creatures makes me chuckle. Emma, though patient, is clearly getting restless, but she doesn't complain.

"Time for a break, kids," I announce, patting my stomach. "Uncle James is starving."

Ollie groans. "Oh, what? Already?"

"Yep, kiddo. Let's grab some snacks and check out the rest of the zoo. If there's time, we'll swing back through the reptile house before we head home."

"Okaaay," Ollie whines, but follows along.

The kids race ahead, their energy boundless, as we follow the path to the café. They immediately press their faces and hands to the display case, ogling the cakes inside. There's no chance they're getting any of that sweet shit. I draw the line at being the fun uncle when it comes to food. Dealing with the fallout from a sugar high is above my paygrade.

I'm scanning the café for a free table when I spot a familiar figure.

Cora.

She's sitting with a little boy who's trying to stuff an entire donut into his mouth with both hands. She hasn't noticed me yet, too focused on him. Casual in jeans and a low-cut T-shirt, she looks worlds away from the glamorous woman who owned the gala last night. And yet, just as stunning. I weave through the tables toward her, but as soon her eyes find mine, something shifts.

Her entire body goes rigid, like she's been caught out. She stands so fast her chair topples over with a loud crash. The sound echoes through the café, making heads turn, but I hardly notice. My focus is on her pale face, her wide eyes.

"James," she breathes, soft and shaky.

I stop in my tracks, her reaction completely throwing me. "Cora?"

Her hands fidget at her sides, her fingers twisting in the hem of her shirt.

Something is wrong.

Before I can ask what's going on, a small voice pipes up from beside her.

"Momma, what's wrong?"

I blink, my attention shifting to the boy. He's a cute kid—dark hair, big brown eyes. There's something... *familiar* about him, but I can't place it. Then the word hits me like a hammer to my brain. And suddenly, everything tilts.

Momma.

A son. She has a son.

And she never told me.

My fists clench, knuckles whitening, as my pulse pounds in my ears. I try to speak, to demand answers, but the words won't come. Instead, I take a step back, my mind racing, and all I can think is, *why? Why didn't she tell me?*

My eyes snap back to Cora, trying to make sense of it. She's still standing there, frozen, her eyes wide.

"James, wait—" Her voice is desperate, but it feels distant, muted by the rush of blood in my ears. My feet are already moving, heading toward Emma and Ollie, who are still glued to the dessert display.

"Come on, kids. We're leaving," I say.

They look at me, confused, but I crouch down to their level, forcing myself to remain calm. "Sorry, kids. Something came up. I've got a work emergency, but I'll make it up to you, okay? You can have as many treats as you want back at my place."

"Yay!" They high five each other, already forgetting about the zoo.

I lead them out of the café, every step I take like moving through quicksand. Like the earth beneath me is pulling me down, slowing everything except the pounding of my heart.

I don't look back.

I can't.

Safe at home, I set the kids up with an ungodly amount of candy and turn on the TV, hoping it'll keep them distracted long enough for me to deal with the anarchy in my head.

My mind is a chaotic mess, full of questions and suspicions, none of which I have answers to. But one thing is clear—I need to figure this out. Now.

Once they're settled, I head straight to my office, taking the stairs two at a time. I pull out the old family photo album from the bottom drawer of my desk. It's dusty and worn, the edges frayed from years of neglect. I haven't touched it since Jonathon died. I haven't wanted to.

But now... now I need to.

Flipping through the pages slowly, the smell of old paper hits me, stirring up memories I've buried deep. There we are—Jonathon and me, identical in every way. Two peas in a pod. Always together. Always the same. But the image of that boy at the café keeps flashing in my mind.

When I find the photo I'm looking for—the two of us at our fourth birthday party—air stalls in my lungs. The resemblance is undeniable. That boy, her son, looks just like we did at that age.

Same dark hair. Same big brown eyes.

This isn't a coincidence. Cora's son doesn't just look a little like me and my brother. He's got our DNA.

I close the album and drop my head into my hands as the brutal truth digs its claws into me. And it hurts like hell.

She thinks I'm Jonathon.

I should have picked up on it sooner. She called me Jonathon when I confronted her at work that first day. I shrugged it off back then, assuming it was part of her plan somehow. Another attempt to get into my head. Now it all makes sense. And she must have thought I didn't recognize her, or worse, that I was pretending not to know her.

Of course she did. Jonathon and I were identical. Same face, same voice, same everything. We even shared the same women when we got older. Hell, no one could tell us apart unless they knew us well, and even then it was hard. And Cora... well, it's obvious now. She didn't know me at all.

I close my eyes, groaning as the pieces fall into place. I let her in, piece by piece. I fell for her.

Was it even real? Or was it all just a game? A way to get something from me? *Money?* She's up to her ears in debt, so it's not a stretch. I should have trusted my gut instinct about Cora; it's never wrong. Now everything feels like a lie. She didn't trust me enough to tell me about her son. *My nephew.* And now I'm left wondering if anything we had was real.

My heart is being split open, an ache so deep it's as if it's being torn out.

Jonathon wasn't just my twin—he was half of me, the part that made everything make sense. And when he died, that half of me died too, leaving a hollow space I've never been able to fill. I wasn't there when he needed me. I wasn't there to stop the car, to save him. And now, losing Cora, realizing she never trusted me—it feels like I'm losing him all over again. The pain, the betrayal, the emptiness—it's all the same.

My thoughts drift back to that little boy.

Jonathon, what have you done?

My phone buzzes in my pocket. I pull it out and see Cora's name flashing on the screen. For a moment I consider answering, demanding answers, explanations. But then the anger surges, hot and biting. She lied. She hid the most important part of her life from me. If I didn't see her today, would she have ever told me?

I stab the Decline button, watching her name disappear from the screen, but the questions remain. I shut my phone off, trying to bury the anger, the hurt—the pain in my heart that no amount of rage can smother. She lied, and I let her in. I don't want her excuses. I just want it all to stop.

Now.

Forever.

Chapter Thirty-Two

Cora

Lying in bed, I stare at the ceiling, the cracks in the plaster blurred by my tears. I've been here for hours, but the ball of dread in my stomach sits just as heavily as it did when I left the zoo.

My palms are clammy, my skin slick with cold sweat despite the warm room. Each breath feels like a struggle, the air too thick to fill my lungs. I'm gasping, my chest tight with that old, familiar fear. The panic I've fought to suppress for years is creeping back, inch by inch, sinking its talons into me. It hasn't been this bad since... since Mom died. Back then, I thought the worst had passed. But now? Now it's suffocating me. I can feel it crawling under my skin, coiling tighter, ready to pull me under.

My fingers dig into the bedspread as though it might anchor me to this moment, as though I might hold myself together through sheer willpower. But it's slipping, unraveling—like the rest of my life. And no matter how hard I try to hold on, the rush of emotions overwhelms me. Guilt. Shame. Fear.

The phone sits like lead in my hand, its screen dark and cold. I've checked it every few minutes, my thumb hovering over the Call button each time. Over two dozen calls. Half a dozen voicemails. Countless texts. And not a single response from James.

Why would there be?

I fucked up.

If he could only hear my voice—if he could hear how desperate I am, how much I need him to listen—maybe he'd talk to me. Maybe he'd understand.

But what if he doesn't? What if it's just more silence? The thought makes my stomach lurch, anxiety winding tighter and tighter until I might be sick.

I close my eyes, fighting back the flood of tears, but they slip through anyway, hot against my cheeks. How did I let it come to this? How did I let fear—my own stupid fear—ruin everything?

I press my hand against my chest, trying to steady the wild thumping of my heart. Every time I think about his face—how it twisted from confusion to realization, from hurt to fury—I unravel all over again. His eyes... They'll haunt me forever.

It's clear now: I should have told him sooner. I should have trusted him. But fear kept me silent. Fear of losing him, fear of how he'd react, fear of what it would mean for Leo.

For the thousandth time, I think about calling him. I'm afraid the silence will keep stretching between us, growing wider and darker until it consumes me. I'm falling into the abyss, and there's no way out unless I do something.

The sheets are tangled, damp from restless tossing. I kick them off and sit up, my head spinning. Lying here, drowning in misery, won't fix anything. The only way out is to face him. He has to let me explain. He has to see how much he means to me.

A plan is already forming in my mind as I grab my purse from the dresser. It's a flimsy plan, reckless even, but I don't care. I'll beg him if I have to. I'll fall to my knees and make him listen. I won't let it end like this.

I hurry into the living room, where Dad is sitting on the couch with Leo.

"Dad, can you watch Leo for an hour?" I force myself to sound calm. Leo is coloring, absorbed in his crayons and paper, blissfully unaware of his world crumbling around him.

Dad glances up from the TV, frowning slightly at the urgency in my voice, but nods. "Of course. We're just hanging out, aren't we, pumpkin?" he says, nudging Leo's shoulder affectionately.

"Yup!" Leo replies, his face still buried in his drawing, his little hands moving quickly across the paper.

I watch him for a moment. How can I look him in the eyes, knowing I've denied him the one thing he deserves most—a father? And for what? A bitter knot of regret lodges in my throat. He deserves more than I've given him, more than I've allowed him to have. But can I fix this?

After James backed away from me in the café this morning, Leo looked at me with eyes wide, asking, "Who was that man, Momma?" My throat tightened when I answered, "Just a work friend." The lie tasted sour, wrong.

I swallow the lump in my throat. "Thanks, Dad. I'll be back soon."

Without another word, I head out the door, releasing a jerky breath. The humid air sticks to my skin as I flag down the first taxi I see. There's no time to waste. No time to think. I have to fix this.

I slide into the back seat and rattle off James's address, my voice shaking. As the taxi pulls away, my hands start to tremble. What am I even going to say when I see him? *Will* he see me? What if he turns me away?

The city rushes by outside the window, but all I can focus on is the fear crawling beneath my skin. James deserves to know the truth, and I should have told him sooner. But telling him meant accepting that my entire world could collapse.

What if I've not only ruined my life, but his too? James didn't deserve this. He didn't deserve the lies, the half-truths, the betrayal.

What if he can't forgive me?

The thought makes me want to scream. *No*. I can't think like that. I have to believe that if I explain everything—if I tell him how scared I was, how much I've wanted to tell him but didn't know how—he'll understand. Maybe there's still a chance.

The taxi comes to a stop outside James's estate. The gates loom in front of me, taller than I remember. Anxiety flows through me as I climb out of the car and stand before the intercom.

My hands shake as I press the Call button, the dial tone loud in the still air. I stand there, waiting, with only the sound of my own jittery breaths for company.

Seconds stretch, each heavier than the last, and with every breath, my hope frays a little more. My fingers tighten around the strap of my purse as I try to imagine James just inside those gates. Maybe he's pacing, thinking. Maybe, like me, he's desperate to fix this, to hear me out. My heart swells with the faintest hope that when the gate swings open, he'll be there, his eyes soft, his arms ready to pull me in.

But there's no movement. No sign of him. The seconds tick by, and with each one, my hope dies a little more.

Then the intercom crackles to life, and I nearly jump out of my skin.

"Hello. How can I help you?"

I take a deep breath, trying to steady myself. "Hi, it's Cora. James... he's expecting me. I'm just a little early." The lie stings as it leaves my lips, but I'm desperate. I was supposed to spend the night with him anyway—before everything went wrong. Maybe if the guard thinks I'm expected, he'll let me in.

There's a long pause and I bit my lip.

"I'm sorry, ma'am," the guard's voice says, cutting through the silence like a knife. "Mr. Hayes has requested no visitors today."

I close my eyes, trying to hold back the tears that are already burning at the corners of my eyes. I knew this was coming, but it still feels like the ground has dropped out from under me.

"Please," I whisper, my words almost lost in the silence. "I just need to talk to him. It's important." I press my hand to my stomach, trying to calm myself. I glance up at the camera on the gate, hoping, praying that James is there somewhere, listening, watching. That he'll change his mind.

"I'm sorry," the guard says again. "I know who you are, but I can't let you in. James's instructions were very clear."

He knows who I am. James told him. He doesn't want to see me.

I knew he was angry, but this... this feels like a final door slamming shut in my face. I blink hard, trying to push back the tears.

"I understand," I mumble, though the words feel hollow.

I turn away and slip back into the taxi, which had been waiting for me. I didn't even realize I hadn't paid the driver, I was so caught up in my frantic need to fix things. My last chance has slithered through my fingers, vanishing as quickly as I was dismissed.

The taxi pulls away and I turn and watch the gate grow smaller as the distance between us stretches wider than ever.

James is behind those cold iron bars, shutting me out of his world. My heart, my limbs—everything aches, and I pull my arms tight around myself, as if I can physically hold the pieces of my life together. But no matter how hard I cling, they're slipping away. I'm slipping away. And there's no one left to catch me.

Chapter Thirty-Three

Monday morning hits like a sledgehammer, leaden with the burden of everything unsaid. My hands shake as I drop my purse at my desk, determination and dread warring in my mind. I can't eat. I can't sleep. Not until I face James. I won't leave this building without talking to him.

My mind races through a thousand worst-case scenarios—*he hates me, he never wants to see me again, he's already moved on.* I swallow hard, forcing down the panic clawing at my throat. I have to stay focused.

My pace is quick, my heart pounding in time with each step as I swipe my security pass in the elevator and press the button for the fortieth floor. But nothing happens. The red light stays on, mocking me.

I swipe the card again, harder this time. No green light. No movement.

My heart drops.

No... he wouldn't.

I hurry back to my desk, collapsing into my chair as I snatch up the phone and dial security.

"Hi, this is Cora Rossi. My pass isn't working for level forty. Could you please check that for me?"

There's a pause on the other end, the sound of someone chewing. "Hold on a sec."

My fingers drum against the desk, impatience bubbling up inside me. After what feels like an eternity, the voice comes back.

"Looks like you don't have access to level forty."

"What? I had access last week."

A heavy sigh. "I don't know what you want me to say... you don't now."

I hang up before I scream at the poor guy.

I knew it. What an asshole.

My fingers curl into fists as I glare at the elevator.

Fine. He can block my access, he can shut me out—but he can't avoid me forever. We need to talk. I won't let this go.

Nathan strolls in a few minutes later, coffee in hand, oblivious to the hurricane raging inside me.

"Morning! Hey, congrats on the event Friday. You killed it," he says with a grin.

"Oh... thanks," I mumble, struggling to mask the desperation brewing. The gala feels like a lifetime ago now. My mind races, scrambling for a plan. Suddenly, an idea clicks—one that makes me feel lower than I've ever felt before, but right now, I'll do anything.

Nathan sips his coffee, raising an eyebrow. "You okay? You look... off. Coming down with something?"

"I'm fine, just tired." I force out a weak smile.

He smirks, leaning in. "Has our favorite tall, dark, and brooding boss been wearing you out?"

Despite everything, a laugh escapes me. And I hate myself for what I'm about to do next.

"Actually, speaking of James..." I glance around as if I'm about to share a secret. "I've got a meeting on level forty in a few minutes to debrief the gala, but my pass is acting up. Can I borrow yours? Security's sorting me out a new one, but I don't want to be late."

Nathan doesn't hesitate. "Sure thing!" He pulls the lanyard from his neck and hands it over without a second thought.

Guilt pierces through me. Nathan trusts me, and here I am, lying to his face. But once again... desperate times, desperate measures.

I swipe Nathan's pass at the elevator. This time, the light turns green. I blow out a deep breath as the elevator climbs, carrying me toward the confrontation I'm both dreading—and craving.

When the doors open on the top floor, I'm relieved to see Portia isn't at her desk. I move quickly on my tiptoes so my heels don't make a sound as I approach James's office. The frosted glass walls shield him from view, but I know he's in there.

My hand hovers just above the handle, a bead of sweat forming on the back of my neck.

Just go in. Just explain.

I grip the door handle, determined to make him listen, to make him understand that I never meant to hurt him. But the fear of seeing anger in his eyes paralyzes me.

I can't back out now.

I force myself to push the door open, every part of me braced for the worst.

Please... just let him listen.

I open it just far enough to peek inside. James sits behind his desk, looking like hell. Dark circles hang under his eyes, and his usually slick hair is a mess. He's clearly had as little sleep as I have. But the moment his eyes snap to mine, his entire demeanor hardens, the exhaustion replaced by cold fury.

"I see you've managed to lie and manipulate your way up here," he snarls.

The venom in his voice stings, but I swallow my pride and step fully into the room, closing the door behind me. "We need to talk."

"The time for talking was weeks ago. I'm not interested in anything you have to say now." His tone is like ice, each word a dagger meant to cut me down.

I step up to his desk and force myself to meet his eyes. "James, please. Just let me explain."

"Explain what, exactly? How you lied to me?"

"I-I didn't lie," I stammer. His piercing glare makes my resolve falter, but I push forward, desperate to explain. "I withheld the truth, yes. I should've told you about Leo sooner. But I never manipulated you. What we had—what I felt—it was real, at least for me..." I trail off. "I never expected to fall for you." The weight of my confession lingers in the air between us.

James shifts back in his chair, arms crossed, his expression unreadable. "Omission of truth is still a lie, Cora."

The words slice through me, and my heart feels like it's being squeezed. "I know," I whisper, my voice cracking. "I know, and I'm sorry. But I was scared. I wanted to protect my son. I didn't even know who you were for a long time, and when you didn't recognize me at Eden... it threw me. I wasn't sure what to think, or if I could trust you. I didn't want to let you into our lives without knowing more about who you are. I made mistakes—I kept Leo from you, and I'll never forgive myself for that. But everything I did was to protect him. I never wanted to hurt you."

Tears burn at the corners of my eyes, but I blink them away. This isn't the time for weakness.

James's expression doesn't soften. If anything, he seems even more closed off. Silence stretches between us, thick and suffocating.

Finally, he breaks the quiet with a bombshell.

"He's not my son."

The words hit like a thunderclap. For a moment, the world narrows, the air thinning, and I'm standing on the edge of a cliff.

His words echo in my ears, but my mind refuses to grasp them. *Not his son?* The thought swirls around, chaotic and senseless. I'm falling, even though I haven't moved.

"That's... impossible," I gasp. "You—" My voice breaks, choking on the confusion. "You're wrong."

But James's expression doesn't change. He's turned to stone—cold, immovable.

"Leo isn't my son," he repeats, almost too calmly, as if the words are just facts and not a wrecking ball. He watches me, waiting for the impact to land.

I blink, the world slanting beneath me.

Is this some kind of sick joke?

Some twisted form of revenge for not telling him sooner? Or does he not want to be part of Leo's life so he's denying it?

"I don't understand." I shake my head, stumbling back. My eyes search his face, pleading for something that might make sense of this nightmare.

I collapse into the chair behind me, my legs giving out. My mind spins, trying to grasp what he's saying, but it doesn't make sense. It can't be true. This conversation was never going to be easy, but I didn't expect him to outright deny it. I thought he had more honor than that.

"You've mistaken me for someone else. For Jonathon—my *brother*. He's Leo's father."

My mouth opens and closes in shock. I can't help but wonder if this is a sick scheme, a way for him to dodge responsibility.

But as James looks at me, I see the truth in his eyes, the anger, the pain.

This is no joke.

"Jonathon?"

"My twin." His voice is detached, like he's talking about a stranger.

I blink, my heart crashing against my ribs.

"What... where is Jonathon?" I whisper.

James flinches, the first crack in his icy facade. "He's dead."

The words feel like a noose tightening around my throat. My mind blanks, scrambling for meaning. I want to scream, to shake him, to demand that he take it back—to admit that it's some cruel joke. But the look in his eyes is like a hammer, driving the truth deep into my chest.

"No—no," I breathe, my hands trembling, my pulse wild in my ears. "This can't be real. Jonathon can't be..."

But he says nothing. His eyes, clouded with grief, lock onto mine, and I know—he's telling the truth. The world spins violently around me.

Dead? Leo's father... is dead? Leo's father is gone, and I never told him. My son will never meet his father.

James has reached inside my chest, grabbed my heart, and set it on fire. I struggle to breathe as my eyes and the tip of my nose burn with tears. But if I start to cry now, I'll never stop. If I let go and accept his words, the grief will consume me completely.

"When... how?" I manage to ask. The words scrape against my throat, the question forcing itself out despite the terror twisting inside me.

He looks away, his jaw tight, a muscle in his cheek ticking.

"Five years ago. Hit and run in Malta," he murmurs.

Malta? His voice sounds garbled as if coming from miles away, the distance between us morphing into an unbridgeable chasm.

"What date?" I croak out, shaking. The question hangs in the air, but I'm terrified of the answer.

James hesitates, his eyes flicking back to mine, confusion creasing his brow. "Excuse me?"

"What. Date. Did. He. Die?" I say, forcing each word through clenched teeth, as if speaking them slower will lessen the blow.

His stare sharpens, and for a brief moment, I wonder if he'll tell me. The silence is unbearable.

"Twenty-sixth of May," he finally says.

The world stops. My blood turns to ice in my veins; my lungs refuse to take in air. The date ricochets through my mind, making connections I don't want to acknowledge. The numbers circle like vultures, tearing through the haze until only one fact remains: *That was the day after...*

A sob rips out of my throat. "That was the day after we slept together," I whisper.

James recoils as if I've struck him, his face paling. His own devastation mirrors mine, but it's worlds apart. My breath tears out of me in gasps, and the truth—so horrifying, so impossible—crashes over me with brutal force.

The day after. It wasn't just a coincidence. It wasn't some random tragedy happening miles away, disconnected from my life. *I was there.*

Another sob claws its way up my throat, and I press my hand harder over my mouth to stop the flood of grief breaking free. My entire body trembles, the weight of it too much to bear.

I want to scream, but no sound comes out. I'm drowning in the enormity of it all.

James looks away, his face twisted with devastation. He doesn't speak, doesn't move. Maybe he feels it too—what this means. But even if he does, it's not enough to bridge the canyon between us.

I'm sinking, collapsing under the truth, the guilt, the horror that there's no going back.

Tears stream freely down my face now, and I can't hold back anymore.

I need to get out.

Shaky legs carry me out of his office, but I don't know where I'm going. Each step feels like it might be my last. Everything I've done, every lie, every secret, has led to this. My vision blurs, and I stumble into the elevator. My world is collapsing, and I have no one to blame but myself.

By the time I reach my desk, I'm hyperventilating. I must look a mess with snot and tears running down my face.

I don't care who sees me. I just need to escape.

I quickly drop Nathan's security pass on his desk, grab my purse, and make a break for the exit. Tears continue to blur my vision, and the world feels like it's crumbling beneath my feet.

Jonathon is dead.

Leo's father is gone.

And I'm the one who'll have to tell him.

Chapter Thirty-Four

Cora

The cracks in the plaster have become my constant companion. I haven't budged from my bed in three days. I trace them with my eyes, following the jagged lines as they stretch across the ceiling, splitting and branching like veins. They remind me of how fragile everything is— one wrong move, and it all breaks apart.

I blink, but my eyes are dry, raw from the tears I no longer have the energy to shed. This time the heartbreak cuts deeper, and more final.

It's not just James—although his absence has left a gaping hole in my heart. It's Jonathon too. I didn't know him, not really, but the loss is still sharp and real. My chest hurts when I think about him, how his life was cut short the day after we created a child. It's a vicious kind of cruelty, one that digs deep and twists, leaving its mark on my soul. And Leo... My sweet boy will never know his father. The thought churns in my stomach, nausea creeping up the back of my throat. For all these years, I've held onto a quiet hope that Jonathon might reappear. That one day I'd tell Leo, "This is your father." Now that hope is gone, crushed under a truth that can't be undone. Hope is a nefarious little bitch that will get you every time.

I haven't eaten. I haven't slept. Every time I try to close my eyes, I see James. His face, twisted with anger, then hollowed with the revelation of Jonathon. The devastation in his eyes wasn't just about me. It was about the brother he lost, and the future he never knew he'd been deprived of. The loss was shared, but we're not grieving together. James has shut me out completely. Not a single text, not one call. Nothing. The silence is deafening.

I turn onto my side, curling into the fetal position, clutching the pillow as if it might anchor me to reality. But even that feels futile. How do I go back to work, to the same building where I'll see him every day? How do I move on when the mere thought of James feels like a knife twisting deeper with each breath?

God, I miss him.

The only thing that's kept me tethered these past few days is Leo. He's sneaked into my room a few times, climbing into bed beside me, his tiny body warm and comforting against mine. He doesn't know why I'm sad, just that I am. And in his innocent way, he's tried to make me smile, showing me drawings, telling me stories. But even his visits can't keep me upright for long.

Thank God for Dad. He's been picking up the slack—feeding Leo, taking care of him, keeping our lives running while I fall apart. But I can't keep this up. I can't lie here forever. The world is moving on, whether I like it or not.

And deep down, I know I need to be a mother again. My son deserves better than a hollow shell of a parent. He deserves me—whole, present, fighting. For him, if nothing else. The thought carries me through the fog of despair, but it's like dragging myself through sludge.

When Saturday rolls around, I force myself out of bed, weak legs carrying me to the bathroom. I glance at my reflection in the mirror, wincing at the pale, gaunt version of myself staring back. My eyes are hollow, rimmed red from exhaustion.

I splash cold water on my face, hoping it will jolt me back to life. I don't have the luxury of wallowing anymore. My boys need me. Life needs me.

Eden has been a godsend, but the place reminds me of James. Every corner of that club is linked to him, and the thought of going back there makes me uneasy.

But I've got debts to pay. A future to secure for Leo. And if that means working two jobs, gritting my teeth, and facing James again... so be it. My family comes first, always.

As I get ready for my bar shift at Eden, I go through the motions mechanically. I only hope that I can make it to the end of the night without breaking down into a blubbering mess.

Waiting for my rideshare in the living room, I pull out my phone and start sifting through work emails. The thought of returning to the office on Monday turns my insides sour, but the emails piling up in my inbox demand my attention. I've only been away for five days, but I already have sixty unread messages. I let out a huff, deleting half of them and responding to the rest.

Crossing paths with James is inevitable. But I'll handle it. I have to. I can't avoid him forever. But if I'm honest with myself, the very idea of seeing him again—those cold, detached eyes—rips me apart. And yet, I know I can't run. Not anymore.

After finishing my work emails, I switch to my personal inbox. Most of it is junk—sales offers, newsletters I never signed up for. But one email stands out, from an unfamiliar sender. White & Day Lawyers.

My heart stops for a beat, and before I even click on it, dread coils tight inside me. I know what this is. I know without even reading it that James is making his move. My hands tremble as I open the email, the subject line making my blood run cold: Re: Leonardo Rossi—Legal Notice.

The words blur as I try to focus, my breath hitching in my throat. I force myself to read it. Slowly. Carefully. Each sentence is a slap to the face.

Mr. Hayes has initiated legal proceedings to establish paternity of Leonardo Rossi through a court-ordered DNA test. Pending confirmation of Jonathon Hayes's paternity, arrangements will be made for a formal trust fund for Leonardo Rossi. Furthermore, Mr. Hayes will be seeking visitation rights and partial custody as Leonardo Rossi's paternal uncle.

My vision swims and I drop my phone onto my lap, my hands clenching into fists.

He didn't even call me.

Not a conversation, not an attempt to sort this out between us like adults—he went straight to the lawyers.

Anger boils through me, but it's the overwhelming sense of powerlessness that pisses me off. James knows exactly what he's doing. He's rich, powerful, and connected. And me? I'm just scraping by, working two jobs, trying to keep my head above water. What am I supposed to do against someone like him?

I pick up the phone again, forcing myself to read the email a second time, though it doesn't change. My eyes catch on the words *trust fund* and *partial custody*. He's not asking. He's telling. He's dictating how this is going to go.

A strangled laugh escapes my throat, but there's nothing humorous about it. How could he do this without even talking to me? The email is clinical, impersonal—like this is just another business transaction for him. Just another item to tick off his list.

But this isn't just business. This is my *son*. My entire life.

I press my fingers to my temples, trying to will away the throbbing in my head. The thought of James entering Leo's life this way... it feels wrong. And yet, I can't stop him. Even if I wanted to fight this, I know I can't. I don't have the resources, the money, or the power to stand up to him.

A bitter taste rises in my throat as I realize what this really means: I'm trapped. Legally, financially, emotionally—there's no escape. I can't afford a lawyer who could even begin to challenge James's legal team. He could take Leo from me piece by piece if he really wanted to.

I squeeze my eyes shut and the email appears behind my lids, as if it's been burned into my retinas. The DNA test doesn't bother me—that's a formality. But the rest... visitation, custody—James has all the power now. And I hate him for it.

How dare he use his money to force his way into Leo's life like this? How dare he reduce us to legal proceedings when all he had to do was pick up the phone and talk to me?

The anger rises again, laced with a darker force. Fear. Because I know this is only the beginning. James is asserting his dominance—claiming his territory. And it doesn't matter that I would have willingly allowed Leo to know his uncle, would have worked something out if he'd just *asked*.

But that's not what this is about. This is about control. This is about him making sure I know my place—that he holds all the cards now.

I blink back the tears gathering in my eyes, the frustration and hopelessness burning inside me. My mind spins, thinking of all the ways this could go wrong. What if he pushes for more? What if he tries to take Leo from me entirely?

No. I won't let that happen. I can't.

Without thinking, I grab my phone and open my message thread with James. My fingers fly over the screen, the words spilling out before I can second-guess them.

Next time, just ask! I would have happily introduced you to your nephew. Oh, and I'm doing okay by the way... thanks for your concern.

The passive-aggressiveness barely scratches the surface of what I want to say, but it's all I can manage. The three little dots appear, showing that he's seen it, and for a second, my heart leaps into my throat. He's going to respond.

Please, just say something.

Anything.

But then they disappear.

I blink, gripping the phone so hard my knuckles turn white. Seconds drag by, and I find myself staring, willing the dots to reappear, willing him to care enough to respond.

But there's nothing. Just the empty screen staring back at me, a reflection of the void between us.

He's really not going to answer.

The rideshare pulls up outside, and I throw my phone into my purse, fighting back tears of anger threatening to spill.

What an asshole.

As I climb into the car, I know this battle is only just beginning.

Chapter Thirty-Five

Cora

The scent of freshly brewed coffee fills the kitchen as I wrap my hands around my mug, savoring the warmth seeping into my fingertips. After a long night at Eden, I'm drained, mentally, emotionally, and physically.

I glance over to the living room, where Leo's busy narrating the epic saga of his monster trucks, his voice rising with each "crash!" and "boom!" He's lost in his own world, oblivious to mine, and right now, that's all I can ask for.

Dad shuffles into the kitchen, yawning as he drops into the chair across from me, his T-shirt crumpled and his hair mussed. "Is there coffee in that pot for an old man?"

"Always." I get up and pour him a cup, watching as he takes it in both hands and breathes in the steam.

"You look worn out, darling." His eyes crinkle with worry as he studies my face.

I give him a tired half-smile. "Long night."

He looks at me with that piercing gaze, the one that makes me feel like he can read every thought I try to bury. "You've been pushing yourself too hard. Running on empty."

I shrug, staring down at my cup. "I just... I don't know, Dad. I'm terrified that James will try to take Leo away."

Dad's expression softens, and he reaches across the table to cover my hand with his. "We'll fight," he says, his tone strong and steady. "We'll fight with everything we have."

"But what if that isn't enough?" I whisper, voicing the fear that's been gnawing at me.

He squeezes my hand, his thumb brushing across my knuckles. "We may not have his money, but we have something better—love, stability, and a home. That's what Leo knows, and that's what truly matters."

Dad falls silent, a far-off look in his eyes like he's replaying a memory only he can see. "I think about your mother often, you know." His thumb absently rubs his wedding ring. "She had that same fierce protectiveness, that same fire that you have. She'd do anything to shield her family. And I know she'd never want Leo to be dragged into a world that could change who he is."

The lump in my throat grows and I swallow hard. "I worry about that too. James's world—it's full of privilege and entitlement. And Leo... he's just a kid. He still gets excited over finding worms in the garden, still believes that everyone tells the truth. What if that world warps him, turns him into someone I wouldn't even recognize? Someone who thinks money can buy happiness or respect?"

Dad nods. "It's true—growing up with that much privilege can mess with a person. They start to feel like the world owes them something, that they're above the rules that ground the rest of us. I've seen it happen before. Wealth and power have a way of tempting a person, changing what they value. But it doesn't have to be that way."

He pauses, tapping his fingers on his mug as if contemplating his next words carefully. "But if James is truly committed to being a father figure, if he wants to earn his place in Leo's life and respect the life you've built for him, then maybe there's hope. Maybe he won't let his world change Leo."

A small part of me wants to believe that, but I can't shake the doubt. "I don't know. James hasn't even tried to show he's serious. It's like he thinks he can just step in and take over, like Leo's a piece of his estate or something."

Dad chuckles, though there's no humor in it. "That's his world, Cora. People like him, they're used to control, having things fall into place just because they say so. But Leo's not something he can control. He's a person, a child, with his own mind, his own heart. James might think he has all the power, but he'll have to learn that Leo isn't just another piece on his chessboard."

Hearing those words makes it easier to breathe. "You really think he could come around?"

Dad nods slowly. "If he wants to be part of Leo's life, he'll have to make the effort. And if he can't respect the life you've built for Leo, then he doesn't deserve to be in it—simple as that. No matter how much money he has."

I close my eyes, letting those words sink in. "Thanks, Dad. Sometimes I just feel so... overwhelmed. I don't know if I'm strong enough for all of this."

He tightens his grip on my hand. "You're stronger than you know. And you're not alone. I'll be right here with you every step of the way. You have me, and you have Leo."

At that moment, Leo bounds into the kitchen, his face bright with excitement. "Mom! My truck did a flip! You gotta see it!" He holds up the truck, and his joy fills the room.

I smile, even as tears prick at the corners of my eyes. "That's awesome, pumpkin. I bet it was a great flip."

Leo beams, dashing back to his trucks.

Dad watches Leo with pride. "He's a good kid, Cora. And that's all thanks to you." His voice soft but sure. "And if James has any sense at all, he'll come to understand that love can't be bought."

I nod, Dad's reassurance a balm for the fears that have been eating away at me.

Leo's laughter rings out from the living room, and it's a sweet reminder of what truly matters.

CHAPTER THIRTY-SIX

I lower my sunglasses, getting a clearer look at Cora's house from the safety of my Aston Martin.

What a shithole.

My heart sinks. I knew it'd be bad, but this? This is worse than I imagined. A lot worse.

It's not the first time I've been here, but it's the first time I've really *seen* it. When I dropped Cora home after the police station, I was too furious to take anything in. But now, in broad daylight, it's clear this neighborhood is from a different world—a world where time has stopped. It's crumbling with neglect and decay. Paint peels from the walls of every house. Fences, rusted and leaning, look ready to collapse. A house across the street has plywood for windows, and the street itself is littered with trash and God knows what else.

This is where Jonathon's son has been growing up?

Cora's house is one of the better ones on the street, but even still, the front porch looks like it's seconds from giving way, and the paint is flaking like dead skin.

How has she been living like this?

I run a hand through my hair, pulling on the ends. How did I not know? How did I let my nephew grow up in this? And what kind of mother could let her child live like this? My anger spikes, sharp and bitter, but beneath it, there's a deeper emotion I don't want to acknowledge.

A movement in the rearview mirror draws my attention. Two men are having a loud argument in the middle of the street. I can't hear what they're saying, but the wild gestures and unhinged eyes tell me everything I need to know. Drugs. It doesn't take a genius to figure it out.

My hand drifts to my phone. Part of me wants to call in child protection services right now.

Leo doesn't belong here.

He doesn't deserve this.

I climb out of the car and lock the doors behind me. The Aston Martin stands out like a neon sign, and in a neighborhood like this, it's practically begging to be keyed—or worse. I step over a used syringe in the gutter and shake my head in disgust. This place... This isn't a home. It's a trap. And I'll be damned if I let Leo grow up in a place like this.

I walk through the rusted gate and knock on the door.

I'm not just angry with Cora for keeping Leo from me—I'm angry with myself for not finding him sooner. But all that anger needs to wait. I'm here for Leo today.

After a moment, the door creaks open, and there she is.

The emotions hit me all at once—anger, need, hurt. There's no denying the pull I still feel toward her, even now. Even after everything. But she looks different. Tired. Pale. The dark circles under her eyes and the way her collarbones stick out tell me more than words ever could. She's been suffering too.

But I can't think about that now.

"Come in," Cora says, her voice flat. "Leo's in the living room."

I follow her inside, down the hallway, glancing around at the small, worn room. Everything is mismatched and old. The furniture looks like it's been picked up from secondhand shops, maybe even off the street. But at least it's clean. She's doing her best. But is her best good enough for Leo?

For the first time, I wonder what she's gone through. Has she been fighting to keep it all together? Or was this all a choice? A calculated choice to cut me out, to raise Leo in this rundown neighborhood, when I could have given him everything?

I want to hold on to the anger. It's simpler that way. But seeing her now, it's not that easy. She looks to be hanging on by the thinnest thread.

Maybe she had her reasons. Maybe she thought she was doing what was best for Leo.

I clench my jaw, shaking the thought away. No. She doesn't get a pass for this. She made her bed, and now she can lie in it. I'm not here to fix her mistakes or get dragged into her mess. I'm here for Leo. For Jonathon.

An elderly man approaches me, and Cora introduces him. "This is Anthony, my dad."

His handshake is weak, and he looks gaunt, as if a strong gust of wind could knock him over.

"Good to meet you," I say, keeping my tone neutral as I shake his frail hand. He gives me a tight smile.

"I spoke to Leo last night," Cora continues. "I explained who you are... and what happened to his daddy."

She chokes on the last word, and I look away, unable to face her grief.

I can't deal with her pain on top of everything else.

And then I see him. Leo.

He's sitting in front of the TV, chuckling at some silly cartoon on screen, oblivious to the strain in the room.

The breath leaves my lungs. It's like seeing a ghost. His hair, his eyes, even the shape of his jaw—they're all Jonathon's. He's a living, breathing replica of my twin. The resemblance is so strong that, for a moment, I'm transported back in time.

I blink, trying to focus on the present, but the memories flood in, uninvited.

Jon was the outgoing one, always the first to throw himself into anything that felt even remotely like freedom. He had no interest in the family business—Hayes & Hayward was always my responsibility, my path, not his. He'd laugh about it, calling me "the good son," while he had his sights set elsewhere, determined to become an architect, to design his own world.

I was the boring one, the heir to our family legacy, while Jon would be... well, Jon.

As kids, we used to switch places just for fun, just to throw everyone off. He'd always push things too far, daring me to keep up with him. He was fearless that way, like he could shape the world with just his smile. And most of the time, he did.

For a split second when I gaze at Leo, it's like I'm looking at Jon. I see the same light in his eyes, that same adventurous spirit my brother had. I can almost hear Jon's laugh, daring me to race him down the beach, to see who could dive into the waves first.

Fuck, I miss him.

It's a bone-deep ache, a pain that doesn't fade with time. Some days, I still expect him to come strolling through the door, flashing that easy grin, ready with some new scheme. But he's not here. He's never coming back.

And yet, in some impossible way, here he is.

Leo.

It's like Jon's reaching out through space and time, reminding me that a piece of him is still here. Alive.

How could Cora keep this from me? From all of us?

If Jonathon were still here, he'd want to be in Leo's life every damn day. He'd want to be there for every scraped knee, every soccer game, every school play. And now it's up to me to do that. *To be what Jonathon would have been.*

I'm not just doing this for Leo. I'm doing it for Jon. Because this boy—this little kid who's already wormed his way into my heart—is all I have left of him. And I'll be damned if I let anyone—*anyone*—take that away.

I squat down to Leo's level, studying his face, and the familiarity makes me swallow hard. I see Jonathon in him so clearly it hurts.

"You look just like your dad, you know that?" I whisper, the words catching in my throat.

Leo stares back, his small face creasing in confusion as he shifts uncomfortably, clearly oblivious to the meaning those words carry.

I've already lost Jonathon once. I'm not losing him again.

Cora walks over to Leo, kneeling beside him as she turns off the TV. "Sweetheart, this is your uncle. Say hi to James."

"Hi," he says shyly, then beams. "I've never had an uncle before."

His words cut through my pain, and for the first time today, the tension eases. "That's right, buddy. I'm your uncle. I'm really happy to meet you. Would you like to meet your cousins? Emma and Ollie can't wait to play with you."

"Yay!" Leo jumps up. "Mommy, can I go? Please?"

Cora pulls him into a tight hug. "Of course, baby. Just be good for Uncle James, okay?" Her chin trembles. "See you in a couple of hours," she whispers, embracing Leo for just a moment longer.

She's holding back tears. I can see it in her eyes. And for a moment, I want to say something, to ask her if she's okay, but I bite my tongue. Now isn't the time. She hands me Leo's backpack and I nod, leading him out the door.

We walk around the syringe in the gutter, and I glance back at Cora's house one last time. *How has Leo been living like this?* I can't wrap my head around it.

I help Leo into the booster seat I picked up earlier and settle behind the wheel. "Ready to meet the family?" I ask, turning to look at him.

"Can I have a milkshake when we get there?" he asks, his eyes lighting up.

"Of course. Any flavor you want." His face brightens, and my heart clenches. Something as simple as a milkshake, and he acts like I've promised him the world.

On the way back to Rose Bay, I keep glancing at him in the rearview mirror. His excitement, his innocence—it's heartbreaking. It's a reminder of everything he's been missing, everything I can give him.

Leo is chasing Emma and Ollie around the garden, their laughter filling the air. My parents are playing with them too, lit up as if they've been given a second chance at life. It's been years since I've seen them this happy.

When my father chose to step down early as CEO after Jonathon's death, it was unexpected but entirely understandable. Losing Jonathon shifted everything for him, casting a new light on what really mattered. His priorities changed almost overnight—board meetings and market shares were suddenly second to family. The people he'd once sacrificed everything for but hardly had time to enjoy now became his focus.

So he made the move to Australia, intent on being an active presence in Emma and Ollie's lives, especially with my sister having settled here with her husband. He wanted to be there for all the little milestones—taking them to swim meets, helping with their science projects, and showing up for weekend camping trips. It was the life he'd spent years building but never truly enjoyed. I knew he needed this, a chance to finally live for himself and to be the husband and grandfather he'd always planned to become. And I couldn't blame him for wanting that, not one bit.

Taking his place at the helm was a responsibility I didn't take lightly, but the legacy he built? It was one I'd do anything to protect and uphold.

"Kids, ten more minutes!" I call out, but they ignore me, caught up in their game. It's almost time to take Leo back, but I don't want to. Leo is everything I never expected—sweet, kind, full of energy. My parents were an emotional wreck when they first laid eyes on him. Tears filled their eyes as they pulled him into a hug. A small part of Jonathon lives on in him, and for that, we're all grateful. But with every minute that passes, my anger toward Cora burns hotter. How could she hide him from us? From me?

I take in his clothes, a size too small, and the shoes, worn down and on the verge of falling apart. I have money—enough to give Leo the world. And yet, he's been living in a house that looks ready to collapse, in a neighborhood where syringes litter the streets.

My jaw tightens. This isn't right. I can provide for him better than Cora ever could.

Lars hands me a glass of lemonade and flops into the chair beside me. "I see that look on your face. What's going on in that head of yours?"

I take a sip, watching the kids play. "Leo doesn't belong there, Lars. Not in that house. He deserves more. He should be here—with us."

Lars raises an eyebrow. "You think just because you have money, you can swoop in and fix everything? It doesn't work that way, James."

"No, it doesn't. But you didn't see it. You didn't see the way he's living. That neighborhood, those streets—there's syringes lying in the gutter! And Leo... he's wearing clothes that don't even fit him. Cora can't give him what I can. How am I supposed to just walk away from that?"

Lars sighs. "I'm not saying she's doing everything right. But taking Leo from his mother... You're talking about ripping him out of the only life he's known. That's not protecting him, James. That's traumatizing him."

"She kept him from us, Lars. She kept Jon's son—*my* nephew—from his family. What kind of mother does that? And for what? Pride? Is that worth more than Leo's safety?"

Lars is quiet for a moment. "I get it. You're angry, and you have every right to be. But this isn't about punishing Cora. You think throwing lawyers at this will make it better for Leo? You really want to turn this into a fight?"

I shake my head, my resolve hardening. "I'm speaking to my lawyer. Leo deserves better."

Lars places a hand on my arm. "James, don't do something you'll regret. You're angry with Cora, and I get that. But don't let your anger drive you to make a decision that could hurt Leo in the long run. It'll only end in tears and heartbreak."

"It's already ended in tears and heartbreak," I confess quietly.

I look back at Leo, who's now running toward me with a huge smile on his face.

"Time to go home, buddy." I lift him onto my lap and his small arms wrap around my neck. "Did you have fun?"

"Yes! I love it here! Can I come back? Please, Uncle James?" His face lights up, and warmth blooms in my chest—raw and protective.

"You'll come back." My voice is softer than I expected. I clear my throat. "You'll come back as often as you like, Leo. I'll make sure of it."

He smiles, and it's that innocence—his trust in me—that tips the scale. As I hold him close, the decision solidifies, hardening into something unshakable.

"Uncle James?" he whispers, like he's sharing a secret. "Can I have my own room, like Ollie and Emma?"

Those words slice through me, and I swallow hard. He's already imagining a life with us. He doesn't understand what he's asking, but I do. I turn to Lars, my eyebrows raised.

How can I send him back? Back to that house, that neighborhood? Back to a life where he's missing out on everything I can give him?

Lars catches my eye, her expression serious. I know she's telling me not to rush this, not to act out of anger, but something's shifted. It's not just anger anymore. It's responsibility. It's love. And it's Jonathon's blood running through Leo's veins.

I hug Leo tightly. "Of course you can."

I say it with finality. It's not a promise. It's fact. And Cora... Cora will have to understand.

She has no choice.

Chapter Thirty-Seven

James

"Good morning, Portia. How was your weekend?" Portia looks up, startled, as I pause by her desk on my way to my office. It's rare for me to ask Portia about anything outside of work. Hell, it's rare for me to ask anything remotely personal at all.

"Very good, sir," she replies, smiling. "I spent the weekend looking after my grandkids."

I look closer and notice she seems a bit tired; her face is paler than usual and there's a large coffee cup on her desk. I wonder briefly what her life is like behind the scenes—children, grandkids, everything in between. For a moment, it's hard not to think about Cora. *How much has she been juggling?*

"You had your hands full, I take it?" I offer a forced chuckle, trying to break the stiffness that always seems to linger between me and my employees.

Portia beams and her tired eyes sparkle. "Yes, but I don't mind at all. They're sweet little cherubs."

I nod and continue walking toward my office. That was the first non-work-related conversation I've had with Portia since she started, what, eight years ago? How disconnected have I been? My mind flashes to Leo. Does Cora's father describe him as a "sweet cherub"? Does he take care of Leo like Portia does her grandkids?

Settling behind my desk, I shake the thoughts away. I need to focus. My computer hums to life, and my inbox fills the screen. The email from my lawyer stands out like a beacon.

I click it, my pulse already quickening.

Mr. Hayes,

As instructed, we have prepared a case for temporary placement of the child, Leonardo Rossi.

The case is founded on the claim that Ms. Cora Rossi is an unfit guardian. We cite her inability to provide safe living conditions, as her home resides in a high-risk neighborhood with evidence of drug activity. Furthermore, Ms. Rossi holds significant debt and works two jobs, one of which involves prostitution, leaving the child under the care of her terminally ill elderly father, Anthony Rossi. Mr. Rossi is not a suitable guardian due to his serious health condition.

Our case is strengthened by Ms. Rossi's recent detainment for driving under the influence. Although no formal charges were brought, her behavior indicates probable substance abuse issues.

We believe the court will grant temporary placement of Leonardo

Rossi under your care, pending Ms. Rossi's completion of a drug and alcohol rehabilitation program, and the improvement of her living conditions.

Upon your approval, we will file this motion, and the process will move swiftly within twenty-four hours.

Please advise on how you wish to proceed.

Sincerely,
Sam White
White & Day Lawyers

I rub my thumb over my bottom lip, my head swimming as I digest the words. This could happen. Within twenty-four hours, Leo could be with me, out of that neighborhood. But Cora...

The thought of taking him away from her doesn't sit right with me either. She loves him—I can't deny that. Maybe that's why she's been so damn stubborn, refusing my help. She's trying to protect him. In her own misguided way.

I grit my teeth, pushing the sympathy aside. It's her fault for not accepting help. Really, she's forced me into this. If only she would accept my money. I've tried. God knows I've tried. But Cora is stubborn. Too proud to take an honest gift, but not too proud to steal from my wallet.

I begin typing a reply to my lawyer, my fingers moving quickly over the keys.

Proceed with the filing.

I hesitate.

Dameon's voice cuts through my focus just as my finger hovers over Send. He strides into my office without so much as a knock.

"What the hell are you doing?"

I glance up, frowning as I sit straighter in my chair. "What are you talking about?"

"Lars just messaged me—said you're about to do something incredibly stupid."

I roll my eyes. "Didn't know you two were close."

"We're not," he snaps, crossing his arms, irritation rolling off him. "But she texts me whenever you're about to make a colossal mistake. And this"—he jerks his chin toward my computer—"this is about to be exactly that."

My phone screen lights up, Lars' message glaring at me.

I've called back-up. Don't do it, James.

Perfect. That's what I get for keeping her in the loop.

"I'm doing this for Leo, Dameon. You didn't see where he's living. That dump is no place for a kid. Cora can't provide for him, not like I can. And she won't take my money. What choice do I have?" My voice rises, the anger slipping out as I bang my fist on the desk. "He deserves better."

Dameon shakes his head, his face softening into something I'm not prepared for: pity. "Listen to yourself, James. You're talking about taking her kid. That's not providing for Leo. That's tearing him away from his mother."

"What would you have me do then?" I ask. I'm trying to hold it together, but everything is slipping.

He leans on my desk, looking me dead in the eye. "Talk to her. You used to talk to her. What happened?"

"There's nothing left to be said," I reply, my jaw tight.

Dameon straightens up, shaking his head slowly. "If you go down this path... you'll lose her forever."

I stare at him, refusing to let the words sink in. My fists clench, fingers digging into my palms. "I never had her in the first place."

Dameon's eyes soften. "Then don't make it worse."

Even now, as I stand on the brink of taking Leo away, I know what this will do to her. She'll be crushed. And I can't pretend that doesn't matter. I know what it feels like to lose someone, to have something precious ripped away. Would I be doing the same to her? But I can't risk Leo's future because of her feelings. That's not the priority here.

Dameon marches to the door, muttering words under his breath that I don't quite catch. But I don't need to. His warning was clear.

But he doesn't really get it. How could he? Cora was never mine to begin with. She was always Jonathon's. And Leo... Leo is all I have left of him.

I read my email again, my mouse hovering over the Send button. For a moment, I picture Leo—his big grin, his eyes bright when I handed him that milkshake. He deserves everything I can give him, and I've already promised I would protect him.

But taking him away from his mother? Would Jon have wanted that?

Jonathon never would've let his pride get in the way of doing what was right for his kid. He would've walked through fire to protect Leo. But... Jon wouldn't have wanted this. He wouldn't want me to rip apart the life Leo's built with Cora, no matter how flawed it is. He'd fight for his son, yes—but he'd fight for what's best for both of them. Am I doing that? Or am I just trying to control what I can't fix?

I rub my temples, the strain of the decision pressing down on me.

Jon's not here, but I am. I can give Leo the life Jon would have wanted for him. A better home, better opportunities.

I review my email once more and press Send.

CHAPTER THIRTY-EIGHT

Unfit. Unsafe. Prostitute. Debt. Addiction.

Those five damning words loop in my head, each one more brutal than the last. I barely make it to the bathroom before I'm on my knees, retching into the toilet. My body heaves, but it's my heart that's truly sick. Those words aren't just accusations. They're daggers, each one slicing deeper, hitting every vulnerable spot I've ever tried to hide.

How could he do this to me?

I cling to the edge of the toilet, gasping, shuddering as the words claw at me, refusing to let go. And the worst part is, I saw it coming. Somewhere deep down, I knew James would try to take Leo from me. But knowing doesn't soften the blow. It doesn't take away the sting of those ugly words.

Another heave comes, though there's nothing left. I slump to the floor, resting my cheek against the cold tiles, trying to steady the dizziness in my head. I'm a puppet whose strings have been severed; limp, lifeless. I thought I was stronger than this, but right now, I don't feel strong at all. I'm broken. Those words they're not just legal jargon—they're a cruel confirmation of every fear I've harbored since the day Leo was born.

You're a bad mother.

You'll never be good enough.

The whispers that have haunted me since I became a mother, the ones I've tried to bury, are now screaming in my head.

Tears sting my eyes, burning like acid.

I can't lose him. I can't lose Leo.

My worst nightmare is becoming a reality. Hot tears spill over, blurring my vision as grief leaves me breathless.

"Darling, James and the social worker are here to pick up Leo." Dad's voice cracks the silence. He pokes his head around the door and his face drops when he sees me sprawled on the floor. "Oh, sweetheart."

I hardly register him kneeling beside me, his hand warm on my back. "It'll be okay, you'll see. We'll fight this. And we'll win. Leo will be back in our arms in no time." His tone is full of the conviction that I can't find in myself. He's trying so hard to believe it. And for a second, just a second, I almost do too.

I nod. It's easier that way, easier to pretend. His hand tightens on my shoulder. "You need to pull yourself together. You can't let Leo see you like this."

I chew my bottom lip, forcing back the sob rising in my throat. He's right. I can't scare Leo. He can't see how close I am to falling apart. If he has to go, he needs to think that I'm okay with it.

Dad gives me a reassuring squeeze before leaving, allowing me the space to breathe, to gather myself.

Slowly I get to my feet, gripping the sink. My legs are made of jelly, weak, ready to collapse at the slightest touch.

I splash cold water on my face, hoping to wash away the despair, but the reflection staring back at me is bleak—red, blotchy skin, and puffy eyes. I drag a brush through my hair, swipe on some foundation, and dab eye drops into my swollen eyes. It's a feeble attempt at looking put-together, but it's all I have.

I draw in a shaky breath, forcing myself to stand tall.

Be strong for Leo.

You can do this.

With my shoulders drawn back, I walk into the living room. James shifts on his feet, running a hand through his hair, his eyes flicking to the stern-faced woman beside him. She stands to his left, clipboard in hand, watching with a cool detachment. The social worker's presence makes everything feel more real, more formal. My world is now under someone else's scrutiny.

My eyes meet James's and I see it: Guilt. Regret. His eyes flash with it before they harden, his expression shifting back to the cold mask he's been wearing lately. But seeing his regret doesn't soften the pain—it makes it worse. I bite down hard on my lip, tasting the metallic tang of blood. How dare he stand there and feel guilty about what he's about to take from me?

James steps closer, his hand reaching out like he's about to touch me, but then stops, glancing over his shoulder at the social worker, and pulls away at the last second.

I take a step back, arms wrapped tightly around myself, needing space. Needing air.

Don't, I mouth.

He flinches. "Cora—"

I shake my head, looking down.

"Momma! Look! Uncle James is here!" Leo's voice breaks through, his excitement pure and innocent. He's holding his little backpack, smiling up at me, completely unaware of the emotional war waging in the room.

Crouching down to Leo's level, I steady my voice even though every part of me is screaming inside. "You ready to go, baby?"

"Yup!" He bounces on his toes. "You wanna come too, Momma?"

I swallow hard, forcing a smile. "Not this time, pumpkin."

Leo wraps his arms around my neck, and I hold him tight, tighter than I should. I bury my face in his hair, closing my eyes as I breathe him in.

God, how do I let go?

I can't. He's my baby, no matter how old he gets.

My baby.

"Momma, you're squishing me!" Leo giggles, his laughter bright, and I desperately cling to it, to him.

I eventually loosen my grip, pressing a kiss to his cheek. "Go have fun, okay? I love you," I whisper, the words thick in my throat. My fingers tremble as I run them through his soft, dark hair, smoothing it down. The sob rises in my throat again, but I swallow it down, forcing myself to keep it together. I can't break in front of him. But every time I blink, the tears keep coming, and I have to clench my fists, dig my nails into my palms, to keep them from spilling over.

Leo flashes me a big grin and runs into the hallway. We all follow close behind, and as soon as Dad opens the front door, Leo bounds outside, his small backpack bouncing, carefree. The social worker gives me a curt nod, then follows him out, quickly falling into step beside him and starting up a conversation with a quiet question.

James stands in the doorway, his tall frame filling the space, but he hesitates. He turns back to me, and for a split second, the mask slips. Guilt flickers across his face again. He wants to say something—his mouth opens, then closes—but he doesn't. Instead, he dips his head slightly, his eyes holding mine before sliding away. He steps outside, his back rigid, leaving me here without my child, or any hope of seeing him again.

The door clicks shut, and the last fragile thread holding me together snaps. A sob rises out of nowhere, tearing through me with a force I didn't know I had. Instinctively, I slap my hand over my mouth, trying to muffle the sound as I drift back down the hallway in a daze, finding my way to the living room. I sink onto the couch, clutching the cushion as if it's the only thing keeping me from falling apart entirely. Dad rushes to my side, his reassuring voice a dull hum in the background, but I can't hear him over the roar of my own heartbreak. I can't focus on anything except the pain piercing my heart. It's too much, too sharp, and I can't stop it. I can't stop any of it.

I gasp for air, but my chest is tight, constricted, crushing me from the inside out.

Suddenly the front door bursts open and I hear the footsteps before I see him.

James.

He rushes over, crouching in front of me, his arms wrapping around me, pulling me into his chest.

"I'm sorry. I'm—fucking sorry, Cora." The words tumble out of him, desperate. I hardly hear them at first, too lost in my head.

"I... didn't—" He sucks in a ragged breath. "Cora, I swear... this isn't what I—I didn't want to hurt you like this." He swallows hard, like he's struggling to find the right words. "I thought I was... protecting him. I thought this was what was best for Leo, but—" His voice cracks. "I didn't mean... all this."

He keeps talking—about Leo, about Jonathon, about doing what was best. And for a moment, I almost believe him. Almost. But then the anger flares again, intense and burning. Sorry isn't enough. Sorry doesn't fix the mess he's made.

I don't know how long we stay like that—me sobbing into his chest, him holding me, apologizing over and over. His words wash over me, but they don't take away the hurt. They can't. Nothing can.

When I finally manage to catch my breath, the sobs fading into hiccups, I pull away. I don't look at James. I can't. I look for Leo. He's standing by the couch holding the social worker's hand, a confused, scared expression on his face. With a sob I lift him into my arms, bury my face in his shoulder and close my eyes, breathing him in. I need to feel his little body against mine.

I sense James hovering but I don't even acknowledge him. All I can do is hold on to Leo, my arms wrapped around him like a shield, rocking him gently as if that motion alone could somehow keep us both safe.

"I'm sorry, Cora," James whispers again, his voice rough. But I don't open my eyes.

"Ms. Rossi, Mr. Hayes has decided not to go ahead with the court order today, so Leo will stay in your care," the social worker says. I nod, still unable to lift my head.

I hear her heels clack across the floor and the soft shuffle of James's sneakers as he follows her down the hall. There's a hesitation in his step, and for a moment I think he might stay. But then the door clicks shut. He's gone.

And I'm still here, cradling Leo. He's the only thing keeping me together. My beautiful baby boy.

James held me like his arms could somehow piece together what he'd shattered. But no hug could fix this. No "sorry" could undo the damage, could erase the words he threw at me like knives—*unfit, unsafe, prostitute*. They still echo in my head, louder than his apology, louder than the sound of my own breaking heart.

He broke me.

And no amount of regret or whispered apologies could ever make it right again.

Chapter Thirty-Nine

James

Standing outside Cora's house at six in the morning with a vicious hangover and a massive bunch of flowers, I feel like a complete idiot. As if this ridiculous bouquet could somehow undo the biggest mistake of my life. The sound of Cora's heart-wrenching wail yesterday still echoes in my mind. It was like an animal being torn apart—piercing, visceral, and unforgettable.

I grip the flowers tighter and exhale a loud breath, pacing back and forth in front of her door. Walking away with Leo, taking her child—I thought I was doing the right thing. But the sound of her breaking—that harrowing sob—keeps replaying in my head. It eats at me, shredding my conscience with every step.

I was wrong.

Very wrong.

I caused the woman I love irreparable pain.

I downed half a bottle of scotch last night, hoping it would dull the guilt, but nothing worked. I tried to find the words that would make this right. But they're nowhere to be found.

And now, as I stand on her doorstep clutching these stupid flowers, a headache from the pits of hell throbbing in my temples, I'm still none the wiser.

I brush a hand over my T-shirt, attempting to smooth the creases, silently cursing myself for not showering and changing into my suit before showing up.

My knuckles rap the wood of her front door, harder than I intended. I suck in a breath, hold it and wait. After a few moments, I hear shuffling behind the door, but it doesn't open. I knock again, harder this time, but there's only silence. I slump down by the door. The flowers flop pathetically across my lap.

What was I thinking?

Of course she's not answering.

I sit and stare at the rusted fence, my head pounding with every passing second. The humid air does nothing to help the cold sweat dripping down my back.

At last, the door creaks open. Cora steps out, dressed for work. She slings her purse over her shoulder and moves past me without even acknowledging my existence.

"Cora, wait!" I scramble to my feet, abandoning the flowers on the doorstep as I rush after her. "Please, can we talk?"

She doesn't stop. Doesn't even turn. She just pulls her earphones from her bag and jams them in.

Desperation claws at me, and I lightly grasp her arm. "Cora, just—can you stop for a second?"

She jerks to a halt, yanking her earphones out. Her cold eyes pierce right through me. "What do you want, James?" she asks, her voice dangerously polite. "I'm going to be late for work."

"I can drive you." I point at my Range Rover parked at the curb. "We can talk on the way."

She shakes her head, a bitter laugh escaping her lips. "No, thanks. I'll take the train."

I glance around the street.

She walks to the station here? Alone? In this place?

"It's not safe for you to—"

"Stop, James," she snaps. "Just... stop. Don't pretend you care. You don't get to care."

I squeeze the back of my neck. "Cora, I didn't mean for any of this. I swear, I thought I was protecting him."

"Protecting him from *me*?" Her voice is low, cutting. "You don't get it, do you? You didn't just hurt me, James. You took everything." She stands there, arms crossed tightly across her chest, eyes glazed as she stares somewhere beyond me. She's shutting down, closing herself off. I step closer, tentatively reaching out, my fingers brushing her arm. Her body is warm and familiar, but she stiffens at the contact.

I lean in, my forehead nearly touching hers, whispering, "Please, Cora... I'm sorry."

Her lips press into a thin, unforgiving line. She doesn't pull away, but she doesn't lean toward me either. She's a statue, unmoving and cold.

I edge closer, hesitating just inches from her lips, silently pleading for a connection. When I finally close the distance, my kiss is soft, but filled with desperation—searching for something to hold on to. But she doesn't move. Her lips are still, frozen beneath mine, her body stiff as though she's turned to stone. I pull back slightly, hoping to spark a response, but her fists remain tightly clenched at her sides, her breath controlled, as if she's holding herself back. Our faces inches apart, I search her eyes. They're hard, glistening with unshed tears.

"It doesn't matter, James. It's over. You ruined us." Bitterness clings to every syllable.

"No," I choke out. "Please don't say that. We can fix this."

I bury my face in her neck, inhaling her familiar scent of vanilla and oranges, but it only deepens the ache in my chest. "I love you, Cora."

She steps back, slipping from my grasp like water through my fingers. When she looks at me, her eyes are drained of the light they once held. There's a finality in that glance.

"Too late."

She turns and walks away, her back straight, her shoulders stiff, adjusting the strap of her purse like she's shaking off the last pieces of me. When she puts her earphones back in, my heart shatters. She's slammed the door shut on everything we ever were or could have been.

I'm rooted to the spot, feet refusing to move. I want to chase her, to shout that I'm not giving up. But my hands hang useless at my sides, my chest hollow, my heart in pieces.

CHAPTER FORTY

James

It's Friday morning, and like every day for the past month, I'm back outside Cora's house. Same time, same place, same rejection. But today, I've come prepared. Today, I'm armed with takeaway coffee and raisin toast. I know she won't talk to me, but maybe I can get her to eat something.

Her back is rigid as she walks out the door, her purse slung over her shoulder, and I can see the exhaustion in the way she moves. She's thinner than she was when I first saw her at Eden, and I hate it. Her cheeks aren't as full, and there's a darkness under her eyes she didn't used to have.

But what hurts the most is the spark that's missing. The Cora I fell in love with was all fire—her wit sharp, her eyes bright. Now, the fire's gone, snuffed out by me, by my mistake. I'd give anything to see that spark again, even if it's directed at me in anger.

I take a controlled breath and step forward. "Morning," I say, holding out the coffee and toast. "I got you breakfast. Raisin toast."

She stops, her eyes narrowing as she glares at me. "Go away, James." She flicks her hair over her shoulder. "I don't like raisin toast."

I hold back a sigh. "Got it. So, raisin toast isn't your *go-to* breakfast every morning?" I ask, a smile pulling at my lips despite her arctic stare. "Coffee and raisin toast, buttered with a sprinkle of cinnamon." I raise the brown paper bag in between my fingers and swing it back and forth.

Her eyes widen briefly before narrowing back into that sharp glare. "Great. So now you're spying on me too," she shoots back.

"You're a creature of habit." I shrug. "Come on, it's warm and buttered, just the way you like it." I hold out the bag and coffee, hoping she'll take it. I know she hasn't been eating much this past month, and I don't want her going to work on an empty stomach anymore.

She glares, her lips drawn tight, her eyes like daggers. Then she snatches the toast from my hand. "Fine," she snaps, her voice like ice. "*Now* you can go away. But this doesn't change anything," she adds, her eyes flicking to mine for only a microsecond.

A small smile of victory creeps onto my face. She took it. It's small, almost nothing, but to me, it's everything. One tiny victory in this war I'm fighting to win her back. "You're welcome," I say, offering the coffee again.

She doesn't take it though, just strides toward the gate, her pace quick and determined. I hate that she doesn't even look at me most of the time. It's like I'm a ghost haunting the edges of her life, begging for scraps of her attention.

I fall into step beside her. "Let me take you to work," I offer, jutting my chin at my Range Rover parked just a few feet away. "It's faster than the train."

"No," she replies without even looking at me, pulling her earphones from her purse and shoving them in her ears.

I sigh, but I don't stop following her. We've had the same conversation all month. She picks up her pace like she's trying to lose me, and I stay a few steps behind, making sure she gets to the train station safely. Every time she walks alone through this neighborhood, it drives me insane. The cracked sidewalks and random drugged-out fuckers lurking feel like a trap waiting to spring. I can't stop imagining the worst—what if someone followed her? What if she screamed and I wasn't there to hear it? I wouldn't survive it.

When we reach the station, she doesn't spare me a glance as she heads for the platform. The crowd is already gathering and the loud screech of the brakes slices through the air as a train pulls in. Cora doesn't even look back at me as she weaves through the throng of commuters, her purse clutched tightly at her side. I stay back, watching as she boards the train, my heart filled with the tiniest bit of hope as the doors slide shut behind her. It's just a flicker, but it's there. She took the toast. After a month of silence, after endless mornings of cold stares, she *took* it. It wasn't much—probably an act born more of frustration than acceptance—but it was something. A crack in the wall she's built between us. Maybe tomorrow, she'll take the coffee, too. Maybe next time, she'll look me in the eye when she does.

Small steps. That's what I keep telling myself. If I can just keep showing up, keep proving that I'm not going anywhere, maybe one day those small steps will lead us back to where we were. Maybe she'll remember what we had before everything went wrong. Before I fucked it all up. For the first time in weeks, I feel like I've taken one small step forward. And I'll take it. I'll take whatever I can get.

At work, I could have called her into my office. I could have forced her to talk, to listen. But I haven't and I won't. Our personal shit has no place in the office. It'll only force her to quit to get away from me. I won't ruin her career or have her scrambling for money again. That's not love. I can't do that to her. She deserves better—even if she hates me.

But that doesn't mean I'm giving up.

Every morning, I'll continue to be here. I'll offer her breakfast, offer her a ride, offer her a sliver of the life she deserves, even if she won't take it yet. I'll wait. I'll wait as long as it takes for her heart to soften, for her walls to crack, for her to see that I'm not going anywhere.

Because I can't lose her. Not like this.

Not forever.

CHAPTER FORTY-ONE

Cora

The soft golden lights of Eden seem brighter tonight, almost intrusive. I kneel on stage, palms resting on my knees, fighting the urge to cover myself, to shield my body from the possessive gaze of potential clients. Even though I've been through this before, every look cuts through me tonight, picking apart my armor. It's my first night back at Le Jardin. Nerves hum beneath my skin, and although I'm not as scared as the first time—when I was on the verge of a panic attack—I'm still vulnerable. I doubt I'll ever be truly comfortable if it's not James I'm kneeling for.

I mentally shake my head. Now is not the time to be thinking about James. It will only lead me down a path I can't afford to go down. I force myself to shove the thoughts aside, focusing on the task at hand. I need to be present; I need to stay focused. This is just another night, another transaction.

Movement stirs around me, a subtle shift of the air, but I keep my eyes down, waiting to hear my fate. A voice. A choice.

Then I hear it.

"Stand."

His voice slides through the air, deep and unmistakable. My heart stumbles, equal parts anger and relief flood my body, crashing into one another like waves during a storm. Of course it's him. It had to be him.

I lift my eyes slowly. James stands before me, tall and commanding, his hands shoved into the pockets of his perfectly tailored suit.

Heat crawls up my neck.

I should turn him down. I should say no. But instead, I take his offered hand. My fingers curl around his, and without a word, I rise from my knees and follow him out of the lounge. Eden isn't the place for a scene, and I won't give him the satisfaction of seeing me fired.

As soon as we step into the private room and the door closes behind us, sealing us off from the world, I spin around, fury crackling through me.

"You've got some balls being here," I snap, crossing my arms tightly over my chest.

James doesn't flinch. His voice drops low. "I don't want to fight, Cora. I just need you to hear me out."

"You're crazy if you think I'm going to fuck you." I laugh bitterly, lifting my chin as I stare him down.

He takes a step closer, holding his hands up in surrender. "Cora, I'm not here for that. I'm here for *you*. To apologize."

I scoff, turning away from him, my jaw clenching.

Apologize? Now?

It's been three months since he tried to take my baby. Every morning, I see him on my way to work, and every morning, I ignore him. I shouldn't be surprised that he knew I'd be back working Le Jardin tonight.

I make my way to the bed, every muscle tight, like a wire stretched too thin. I'm not about to lose tonight's pay because of him. If nothing else, I'm going to get some damn sleep. I crawl under the covers, the sheets cool against my skin. I turn my back to him, let my body sink into the mattress.

"What are you doing?" he asks.

"What does it look like?" I pull the blanket up to my shoulder, my back still to him. "Go on, this is gonna be good. I'm listening."

For a moment, he doesn't move. Then I hear the rustle of fabric, the quiet clink of his belt being unbuckled. My breath catches for a second as I peek over my shoulder. He's undressing, but when he slides into the bed, he's still wearing his boxers. A tiny relief, though my guard doesn't drop.

Good. If he even thinks of coming near me with that monster cock of his...

He leaves a respectful stretch of space between us. I whack my pillow, fluffing it up before sinking into it again.

"I messed up," James starts. "I thought I was doing what was best for Leo... for Jonathon. I thought I was protecting him. That I was doing what Jon would have wanted."

The bed shifts as he mirrors my position, lying on his side, facing my back. I don't move, don't respond, but my heart pounds against my ribs.

"I know I hurt you, Cora. I hurt you in a way I can't take back. And I'm fucking sorry. I don't expect you to forgive me right now. But you need to know that I love you. I love you, and I'll be there for you. Every morning, until you're ready to let me back in. I'm not going anywhere."

I stare at the wall, biting the inside of my cheek, trying to keep my breathing steady. I want to stay angry, to keep that shield of bitterness between us. But his words—they're chipping away at the defenses I've tried so hard to keep up.

Rolling onto my back, I stare at the ceiling. My throat is tight, tears brimming behind my eyes. My mouth opens for all the words I want to throw at him—the things I should say, the hurt I should unleash. But my voice betrays me, trembling as I whisper, "You don't know how much you hurt me."

James shifts beside me, turning onto his back, our shoulders almost touching. The silence stretches, thick with everything we've left unsaid.

"I need time," I say softly, struggling to get the words out. "You hurt me in a way I can't just... forget."

His hand moves under the covers, searching for mine. Our fingers brush together, tentative, and for a moment, I hesitate. Every instinct screams at me to pull away, to hold on to my anger—it's safer. But then... I don't. I don't know why, but in that moment, I just... need something steady. And his hand is there. Our fingers entwined, and for the first time in what feels like forever, the tension eases. The silence between us feels lighter now, no longer suffocating.

"I get it," he says quietly. "I'll wait, Cora. For as long as it takes. I'll be here, waiting."

His words are soft but certain. And for once, I believe him. His hand tightens around mine under the covers, a quiet promise. We lie there, side by side. And finally, I allow myself to breathe.

We fall asleep like that, fingers entwined.

Nothing's fixed. We're not healed. But for tonight, maybe this fragile connection is all we need to survive the wreckage.

Chapter Forty-Two

Cora

Three Months Later

"See you tonight, Dad. Love you, Leo!" I call out, slamming the front door behind me. The cold morning air bites at my skin, and I instinctively rub my hands along my arms for warmth. I shrug into my jacket, but then freeze with my fingers on the zipper.

No James.

I stop at the gate, my hand gripping the cold metal, frowning as I scan the street. Empty. No familiar black SUV, no James leaning casually against it, waiting.

I bite the inside of my cheek.

Is he late? Or... did he give up?

For the past six months he's been as constant as the sunrise. Stationed outside my house, ready to offer me a ride and breakfast. Sometimes he would follow me to the station, other times he would join me on the train. I doubt he'd ever been on public transport before then. I had to press my lips together to stifle a laugh as he glanced around the train with his nose in the air. He always stood in case he dirtied his suit.

He can be such a princess.

We never talked, just walked in silence, but his presence had become... familiar. Comforting, in a way I never expected. It was the only time I got to see him. James has been keeping his distance at work, so I rarely catch a glimpse of him around the office or at Eden.

But today? There's no James.

I wait another minute, telling myself it doesn't matter. I should be relieved—he's finally leaving me be. But when it becomes clear he's not coming, a hollow sensation seeps into my heart. I shake my head, trying to push away the disappointment. It seems our expiration date on this dance is up.

It's better this way.

I shove my hands in my pockets and start walking, my footsteps slower than usual. My legs are heavier, and I hate that his absence has this effect on me. The empty space beside me feels more pronounced with every step.

Did he reach his limit?

Or did he wake up this morning and realize I wasn't worth the effort?

I reach the station, and for the first time in months, I'm alone.

When I arrive at the office, I'm in a pissy mood.

"Morning, Rossi!" Nathan booms, far too chipper for a Monday. "How was your weekend?" He's grinning from ear to ear, bouncing on the balls of his feet. The guy needs to lay off the caffeine. Stat.

I force a tight smile, tossing my purse into the desk drawer with a little more oomph than I intended.

"Meh." I shrug.

"Wow, someone's in a mood," he drawls. "Well, this'll brighten your day. Emergency town hall called for this morning."

"What? What's the emergency?" I ask, frowning. My thoughts immediately shift to work, relieved for the distraction.

"Beats me. If I knew, I wouldn't have to go," he deadpans.

"Whatever." I huff, rolling my eyes.

His grin widens, and I fight the urge to whack him with a file folder.

We stop for coffee on our way to the auditorium and I manage to convince Nathan to order decaffeinated, since he doesn't need more adrenaline running through his veins. We enter the crowded auditorium just in time to see James confidently stride onto the stage. I pause for a second, my heart flipping in that irritating way it always does when I see him.

So, he didn't sleep in after all.

I take my seat, forcing my eyes anywhere but on him, but I can't help stealing glances. My body betrays me every damn time. His baby blue shirt stretches over his chest, his sleeves are rolled up, showcasing those muscular forearms, and his hair is perfectly tousled.

Damn it.

But something about his stance is off today. He looks tense. Nervous, even. I take a sip of my coffee and sit up a little straighter, watching him closely.

"Good morning, everyone. Thanks for attending on such short notice." His voice is steady, but there's a stiffness in it that makes me uneasy. "I wanted to address some of the changes we've implemented in the company over the past year, particularly in regard to our work culture. I've seen significant improvements at all levels, and that's largely thanks to one person—Cora Rossi."

What?

The room seems to shrink as all eyes turn to me. My cheeks flush instantly, and I sink into my seat, suddenly too hot under the bright lights.

What the hell is he doing?

"Her leadership and commitment have been instrumental in improving morale and creating a more positive environment for everyone here."

The eyes of my colleagues are on me—some smiling, some murmuring—but all I can do is stare at James, my heart pounding.

"Most of what I've said could've been sent in an email." James clears his throat. "But the truth is... this town hall is personal for me." He pauses, taking an intentional breath, his fingers flexing on the edge of the podium. "I've learned that to be an effective leader, I need to demonstrate openness and vulnerability. So, I'm standing here today in front of you all, attempting to do just that. Because I've fallen in love... with someone in this room."

My stomach flips, and my coffee nearly slips from my grasp. The room collectively gasps, soft whispers rippling through the crowd.

Our eyes lock across the room, and in that moment, everything else fades. He looks at me like I'm the only person in the world. Like I'm his everything. He's laying his heart bare... in front of everyone.

"I fell in love with her," James continues, his voice thick with emotion. "And then I completely fucked it up. She hasn't spoken to me in months, and honestly, it's been the worst six months of my life."

I swallow hard, trying to push down the lump forming in my throat. My fingers tremble around my coffee cup.

Is this really happening?

I think of the mornings he showed up outside my door. How he didn't push, didn't force me to talk to him, but was just... there. Every single day. I told myself his presence didn't matter, that he was just trying to make up for what he did. But now, hearing him say that those months were as hard for him as they were for me—it changes things. It chips away at the armor I've built around my heart.

"I've realized I can't live without her. Her smile, her laugh, the way she puts me in my place with a single look…" He trails off, his lips twitching into a brief smile before it fades. "I don't deserve her forgiveness. I don't deserve anything from her, not after the way I hurt her. But if I don't say this now—if I don't tell her how much I love her, how much I need her—I'll regret it for the rest of my life."

The room is silent now, everyone watching, waiting. Tears burn at the corners of my eyes, but I blink them back. James just stands there, vulnerable and exposed in front of everyone. And it's something I never thought I'd see.

"If she can forgive me…" He falters, his voice cracking slightly. He steps back from the podium, runs a hand over his face and steps up again. "I'll be right here. Waiting. But if she can't… if I've lost her for good… then at least she knows. At least she knows how much I love her." His eyes find mine, and for a second, the room is too small, too quiet.

"That is all. You're all dismissed."

The auditorium starts buzzing with murmurs as the crowd starts to file out. But all I can focus on is James. Nathan gives my arm a reassuring squeeze as he passes, but I hardly feel it. My mind is spinning.

He loves me.

Part of me wants to run to him, to accept every word that just came out of his mouth. But the sting of betrayal lingers; the weight of what he did. Trust is fragile, and mine shattered the day he took Leo.

I squeeze my coffee cup, the cardboard crumpling under my fingers. If I go up there, it means lowering my guard. Letting him in. And what if he breaks my heart all over again? The fear pulls me in one direction, while the memory of his smile pulls me in another. The war between my heart and my head is raging.

I glance down at him. He's still standing there, waiting, his gaze locked on me. He looks different, though. There's no arrogance, no walls anymore, and my heart aches at the sight of him. He's the one that I want, but he's also the one who hurt me the most. And that's what makes this so damn hard.

When the room finally empties, I rise from my seat, my feet moving before my brain can catch up. But I can't stop. I can't walk away. Not now. Because there's one thing I know for sure: *I still love him.*

I reach him in the center of the stage, and for a moment, we just stand there, the silence thick between us.

"Well, that was ballsy," I finally say, my voice coming out lighter than I expected.

James cracks a small smile, his eyes searching mine. "Worth the risk, wouldn't you say?"

I arch a brow, crossing my arms. "Did you really mean what you said?"

"Which part?" he deadpans.

"You know which part!" I huff, swatting his arm lightly.

His face softens, his eyes warm. He steps closer, his hands reaching up to gently cradle my face. "I meant every word. I love you, Cora. I've never been more certain of anything in my life. I want you. I want Leo. I want us... if you'll give me that chance."

His thumb brushes softly against my cheek. "Can you ever forgive me?"

I pause, tapping my chin in mock contemplation, trying to keep the moment light, even though my heart is hammering. "Hmm... I'll think about it."

He laughs, a sound that warms me from the inside out, and before I can say anything else, his lips meet mine in a searing kiss that's more than just a promise. His hands hold me close, and I let myself believe that maybe this could work.

Maybe we can be whole again.

Chapter Forty-Three

Cora

One Year Later

The late afternoon sun streams through the sheer curtains, filling our bedroom with a golden glow, but it doesn't soften the intensity of James's gaze. His dark eyes lock onto mine, fierce and predatory, like a hunter waiting to strike.

There's power in the way he looks at me, a silent demand that I surrender completely. The air between us sizzles, and I feel it everywhere—beneath my skin, in my chest, in the way my pulse quickens. Goosebumps ripple across my bare skin, my body responding instinctively to his dominance, to the command simmering just beneath the surface of that look.

"Come here," he growls, deep and husky, sending a shiver down my spine. His gaze drags over my body, lingering on my swollen belly, then across to the ring on my finger, his lips twitching with a possessive grin. No matter how many times he sees me like this—bare and submissive—there's always that fire in his eyes, the hunger that never fades. He loves me like this, naked except for his ring, sometimes a collar. I belong to him in every way, and he never lets me forget it.

I take a slow step forward, the soft carpet sinking beneath my bare feet. The scent of him—mint, and that intoxicating cologne—surrounds around me as I approach. When I stop just inches away, he reaches out, his hand sliding around my throat, firm but not tight.

As his thumb strokes my pulse point, I feel not just the familiar thrill of submission, but the depth of everything we've been through. There was a time when I didn't think I could trust James this deeply again, when love felt too dangerous. But it's different now. He doesn't just control my body—he holds my heart and he keeps it safe.

He glances down at my belly, his expression softening for a moment.

"I think I've found my new kink," he murmurs. His eyes glitter with amusement, a twinkle that tells me exactly where his mind is heading.

I smirk, biting back a laugh. "Oh really?" I arch a brow. "If you think I'm going to stay barefoot and pregnant for years to come, you've got another thing coming, Hayes."

His grin widens, his eyes gleaming, but he doesn't bother with words. Instead, his grip on my throat tightens. The laughter fades as the tension between us swirls.

"Kneel," he commands.

The word sends a thrill through me. As I sink to my knees before him, the power shifts between us. I'm fully his in this moment, and it's a feeling I crave more than anything.

I can't help but smile at how far we've come. It's been a whirlwind ever since his public declaration at work. God, it feels like a lifetime ago. Dad, Leo, and I moved into his villa just a few months after, although I only agreed to stop his constant grumbling about my house and the neighborhood. He flat-out refused to sleep over.

Such a princess.

And six months later, James adopted Leo. One of the happiest moments of my life, and Leo's too. I can still picture that day—Leo's eyes lighting up as James scooped him into a hug; Leo calling him "Daddy" for the first time. That single moment made everything we'd been through worth it. James wasn't just my love anymore. He was Leo's too.

Saying goodbye to Eden was surprisingly easy. It was my choice, and I made it without hesitation. Not because James wanted me to, but because my desire for submission and everything that comes with it is tied to him, and him alone. I don't want to explore this new side of myself with anyone else. I only want him.

James tilts his head, narrowing his eyes slightly, and I'm pulled back to the moment. He crouches down, his thumb tracing my jawline, and the familiar rush of heat pools in my core. He looks down at my belly again, his eyes glinting with pride and possessive need. "You look fucking gorgeous like this," he murmurs, his hand sliding lower, resting on the curve of my stomach. "Pregnant with my child."

I roll my eyes playfully, but the warmth in his voice sends another flood of heat through me. "Don't get too used to it," I tease. "This is a limited-time offer."

He chuckles, his fingers returning to my throat just enough to make my breath hitch. "We'll see about that."

A soft smile dances on my lips as I remain on my knees before him. My body responds out of instinct, but it's more than that now. It's not just submission—it's trust. We've walked through fire, faced every doubt and fear, and yet here I am. Not because he commands it, but because I choose him.

Every time.

Every part of me knows this is where I belong—by his side, on my terms, in a love that's ours alone.

About the Author

Jade May is an international bestselling author of angst-filled, high-heat romances laced with kink—where the tension runs deep, the chemistry runs hot, and happily ever after is always guaranteed.

Jade is also an advocate for people with disabilities and those suffering from chronic illnesses. She has been featured in several major Australian media outlets speaking about the power of romance fiction to help people with disabilities awaken their sexuality and cope with chronic pain. Inspiring others to embrace their desires and live their best lives through her fiction is a dream come true for Jade.

Jade lives in sunny Sydney with her two favourite humans: her husband and son.

Connect with Jade

Sign up to Jade's newsletter for the latest news on releases, giveaways and previews of covers and exclusive book art!

www.authorjademay.com

@authorjademay